On a routine flight training assignment, Maj. Vincent Pirelli and a group of raw training recruits are ambushed by a RAM cruiser. Attempting to draw fire from his inexperienced charges, Vince's ship is put out of commission and tumbles helplessly in space.

Back at NEO headquarters, news of Major Pirelli's fate presents a major problem: If Vince has been captured by RAM, the safety of NEO's entire undercover intelligence operation could be compromised.

Meanwhile, there is still no word from Buck Rogers and Wilma Deering on their mysterious mission somewhere in deep space . . . .

ARRIVAL

THE MARTIAN WARS TRILOGY

THE INNER PLANETS TRILOGY

INVADERS OF CHARON

THE 25TH CENTURY

Invaders of Charon, Book Two

NOMADS OF THE SKY

William H. Keith, Jr.

TSR Inc.

NOMADS OF THE SKY

Random House and its affiliate companies have worldwide distribution rights in the book trade for English language products of TSR, Inc.

Distributed to the book and hobby trade in the United Kingdom by TSR Ltd.

Cover art by Doug Chaffee

Interior artwork by Mike Hernandez and Albert Deschesne

First Printing: October 1992
Printed in the United States of America
Library of Congress Catalog Card Number: 91-66491

9 8 7 6 5 4 3 2 1

ISBN: 1-56076-098-2

TSR, Inc.
P.O. Box 756
Lake Geneva, WI
53147
U.S.A.

TSR Ltd.
120 Church End
Cherry Hinton
Cambridge CB1 3LB
United Kingdom

To Nina

SOLAR SYSTEM

The Asteroid Belt

A scattered anarchy of tumbling planetoids and rough rock miners, where every sentient has the right to vote, and the majority rules among five hundred miniature worlds.

Mars

A terraformed paradise, Mars was reborn through the most sophisticated technology. Yet, the ruthless Martian corporate state of RAM spreads its evil tentacles throughout human space from this paradise.

Earth

A twisted wreckage despoiled by interplanetary looters, Earth is a declining civilization. Its people are divided and trapped in urban sprawls and mutant-infested reservations.

Luna

An iron-willed confederation of isolationist states, the highly advanced Lunars are the bankers of the Solar System, "peaceful" merchants willing to knock invading ships from the skies with mighty massdriver weapons.

Venus

A partially terraformed hellworld, where only the highest peaks can support human life. As the Uplanders build their great ceramic towers, the nomads of the vast, baloonlike Aerostates cruise the acidic skies. Far below, in the steaming swamps of the lowlands, reptilian humanoids struggle to make the world to their liking.

Mercury

Home to an underground civilization of miners, its surface is paved with huge solar collectors, massive mobile cities, and gaping strip mines. Far overhead, the mighty orbital palaces of the energy-rich Sun Kings spin in silent majesty.

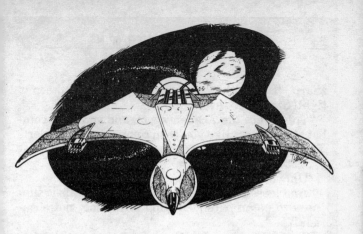

CHAPTER ONE

Space was a velvet blackness, made glorious by the unwinking diamond dust of stars. Half lit by the arc-light glare of a shrunken sun, fifteen shark-finned needles fell through emptiness. They seemed stationary, so vast was the backdrop against which they moved. In fact, they were moving very fast indeed, and the flight leader was less than pleased with the way several of his charges were keeping formation.

"Lance Leader to all Lancers." Strapped into the cramped cockpit of his F-66 Starfire, Maj. Vincent Pirelli watched the drift of computer-generated symbols on his tac display with growing concern. "Loosen it up, people. You look like a bunch of kay-dets on parade. Jamison! Ease off! Damn it, you're about to fly your nose right up Blakely's tail."

He caught a burst of laughter over his commo headset and a crude comment about Cadet Blakely.

"Can that chatter!" he snapped. "Jamison! Give me a negative delta-vee of ten feet per second before Blakely cuts in her jet and ruins your paint job."

"Y-Yessir!" Cadet Jamison's voice was tight and

sharp. "But at the Academy, they told us to keep it tight! Sir. Uh . . . over."

"This is not the Academy, son, and you're in combat. At least act like you're in combat and stay alert! You let your mind wander out here and you're dead . . . got that?"

"Uh, yessir."

"And loosen up. Spread out, all of you. This is supposed to be an extended wing formation, not a parade."

Vince remembered the boy's face when he'd reported for duty back at Trinity—painfully young, with a slide puppy's clinging eagerness to please. A kid, fresh from the Academy at Juno.

God, he thought. Where do they keep digging them up? . . .

His tac display showed Jamison's Starfire drifting clear of Blakely's ship, but it had somehow acquired a considerable side vector along the way. The kid was out of position and heading for trouble.

. . . and why do they keep sending them to me?

"Watch your vector, Jamison. You're skidding."

"Yessir. I've got it under control. I think. . . ."

Fourteen cadets, fresh from Juno Academy, recruited to the ranks of NEO and assigned to the Space Fighter School, specifically to his care and keeping. Theoretically, the training facility, tucked away within the subsurface warrens of the planetoid called Trinity, provided a refresher course for experienced pilots in space combat maneuvers, or SCM. It was a place where rocketjocks could hone their combat skills to a mono knife's edge, a place for the best to become better.

Unfortunately, experienced pilots were in painfully short supply, and NEO Command was assigning raw recruits fresh out of the Academy to Trinity to *learn* the skills of SCM, not just polish them.

As Vince learned afresh with each new crop of students, there was always an enormous gulf between *trained* and *experienced*.

Or was it possible to be too experienced? He was beginning to wonder.

Maj. Vincent Pirelli, of the New Earth Organization's Staff Command, thought of himself as a typical fighter jock. Tall and lean, with a spacer's rangy slouch, he could still count on his black hair and dark, rugged looks to score points with the female of the species. He had the veteran pilot's swagger, the independent-mindedness that most groundpounders swore was sheer arrogance.

But even Vince had to admit that the years were on the point of catching up with him. There was a touch of gray above his ears now, and his skin was beginning to acquire the leathery toughness that marked a man who'd spent too many years in space. Forty-two was old for a rocket fighter pilot . . . too old for him to think of himself as one of the fresh-faced kids, all sharp creases and enthusiasm, who took the point in NEO's ongoing guerrilla war against RAM, too young to admit that he might be losing the fighter jock's edge that was everything when it came to a ship-to-ship, man-to-man contest at fighter's range.

Losing his edge? Unthinkable. Angrily he pushed the thought from his mind. Checking his instruments, he noted the group's position by triangulating with three pulse navigation beacons. They'd come a long way from Trinity and they had a long way yet to go.

Time to start the exercise.

He glanced up through the transplex of his canopy, enjoying for a moment the sheer, desolate emptiness of surrounding space. Lancer Flight was plunging through the heart of the Asteroid Belt, but contrary to the images conjured by holovidic computer effects, the sky wasn't filled with mountain-sized rocks jostling one another for position. A solitary point of light off Vince's starboard bow was probably Davida, all but lost among far brighter stars. Another dead ahead, tagged by a winking diamond on his HUD, had been identified by his ship's computer as Ceres.

Those were the only asteroids visible to the naked eye at the moment. The Belt was enormous, one hundred thousand known asteroids scattered in multiple rings across a vast sweep of space beyond the orbit of Mars. Except for occasional gravitational clumpings, or the asteroids like Pallas that had moonlets of their own, that scattering was very thin and cold indeed.

No, the Belt was an empty place, more a state of mind than a spot you could point to on a chart.

It was a splendid place to hide.

He sighed. Time to begin earning his NEO nursemaid's pay. "Okay, boys and girls," he said over the wing's tactical channel, "listen up. The target for today's exercise is a real beauty. Any of you ever hear of the *Magnificus Triplanetary?*"

"Affirmative, sir," Cadet Blakely said. "Triplanetary Lines, Venus registry. An interplanetary spaceliner, Luxus Triplanetary class."

"Someone's been doing her homework," Vince approved. "That's right. A liner, eleven hundred feet long, three hundred passengers, fat as a Jovian bloat and twice as slow. We've had word that she's crossing our sector today, inbound, Jupiter-to-Mars. That liner, cadets, will be the object of this exercise. You are to adopt standard patrol formation, locate the *Magnificus*, and plot her track.

"For this run, your weapons will be disabled, with release locked through my console. You are not to approach the target closer than fifty miles. We wouldn't want to give her passengers or crew heart failure."

"How come we're hunting passenger liners, Major?" an anonymous voice asked. "I thought we were assigned to Trinity to learn dogfighting, not cowherding."

That had to be Sebastian Kent, the kid in the current crop of recruits with the biggest ego and the shortest fuse. He would make an excellent pilot someday . . . if he lived that long.

"Before you can dogfight with the enemy, Kent," Vince said, keeping his voice cold, "you have to find him. It's not as easy as it seems in a nice, warm, controlled simulator. Space is appallingly empty. Even a cow like the *Magnificus* can lose herself in all that nothing real easy. Okay. Configure for search sweep, full spectrum, passive mode. Begin formation dispersal on my mark. Three . . . two . . . one . . . mark!"

Attitude and control jets flared silently in space. Gently the wedge-shaped formation of rookie pilots began scattering across the darkness. Vince maintained position at the center of the flight, watching the drift rates and attitudes of his people on his tac display. Grudgingly satisfied with their performance, he engaged his own AGR-20 receiver and increased sensor gain to max. If an old hand like him couldn't find the *Maggie Tripe* before these rookies did, it was time to hang up his flight suit and work for a living.

Like submarines of old, spacecraft groped for one another in the emptiness by active mode—sending out radar pulses that were reflected back by the target—or passive mode—saying nothing but listening carefully for any of the host of signals broadcast by a living ship. Sound, of course, didn't travel through hard vacuum. But there were more subtle, more elusive energies that did—heat radiated from drives and life support, for example, or hard quanta liberated by a fusion drive's flare. Neutrinos from the fusion plant. Radio leakage from shipboard intercoms and computers, even low-frequency groans, called VLF, from the flexing of the hull itself.

Not that this exercise required anything so subtle. The *Maggie Tripe* was a commercial liner on a scheduled run, with no reason to cloak herself, and her IFF would be squawking at 288.8 on the dial. Vince simply hadn't informed his students of that fact. Privately he wondered how many of these kids would think about the liner's Identification, Friend or Foe system and run a freak search program through their scanners to find her.

He grinned. Sometimes the most difficult thing to think of was the obvious.

"Lance Leader, Lance Leader" sounded over his headset. "This is Lancer Four."

Kent again. "Go ahead, Four."

"Neuters at two-seven-niner, mark two-three. Looks pretty hot."

"Copy." Vince shifted his main display to neutrino trace. Yes . . . there it was, a faint reading for something big and hot and fusion powered, probably just above the plane of the Belt. The traces were barely registering. Kent had been sharp to pick it up.

Curious, Vince punched 288.8 into his radio scanner and listened for a moment. Nothing . . . nothing but the far-off hiss and crash of star-birth static.

Well, they might not be broadcasting IFF at the moment. *Maggie Tripe* might be worried about pirates in the area, or they could have just gotten sloppy. He punched in a search program, and additional data scrolled down his computer monitor. Thermal traces gave a probable size for the target—on the order of a thousand feet long—confirmed by VLF. Range . . . call it ten thousand miles. The target was decelerating at a constant one G, dropping sunward on the second leg of her Jupiter-to-Mars run.

It had to be the *Maggie*. Nothing else that big was out here.

"Lance Leader to all Lancers," he called. "We'll close in for a positive ID. Remember the rules of engagement. Maintain fifty miles to target minimum."

One by one the fourteen pilots of Lancer Flight acknowledged. "Right," he said. "Here we go. On my mark, engage thrusters for delta-vee plus four-point-two, zone two at three . . . two . . . one . . . *boost!*"

His gloved finger closed on the firing trigger of his Starfire's powerful main thruster. Thunder sounded from scant feet behind his head, filling the cockpit, transmitted through layers of shielding and the fighter's own hull. Star-hot plasma spewed white glory astern, and the heavy hand of high-G acceleration pressed him back against his seat. G-suit and seat together compensated somewhat for the weight of eight men sitting on his chest, but his vision blurred and movement became all but impossible. Peripheral vision showed pinprick flares to port and starboard as the other Lancers engaged their drives, and then tunnel vision closed down his sight, narrowing his view to the glowing lights and readouts of his instrument console and the dancing computer symbology of his Heads Up Display.

Port and ventral thrusters joined the thunder, easing the rapidly accelerating fighter into a vector change. The fighters would rise above the plane of the Belt a thousand miles spinward and astern of the lumbering passenger liner ahead.

There was something not quite right about the target.

Eyes narrowing, he checked the radio frequencies again. Lancer Flight wasn't squawking, but by now the liner's watch officers should have detected the plasma flares of the fifteen fighters, even picked up stray leakage from their tightly shielded radio transmissions.

There was still no IFF from the *Magnificus Triplanetary* ... no radioed challenge or warning to keep clear, nothing. They were plowing along on their original sunward heading, still at one G, apparently oblivious to the rest of the universe.

His engines cut off as the fighters reached the programmed delta-vee. Vince stabbed commands into the keyboard on his armrest, requesting a visual on the distant liner from the Starfire's high-gain electronic cameras.

He studied the minute, fuzzy image that appeared on his monitor. Nothing much to see yet ... a sliver against darkness.

"Lance Leader, this is Lancer Six." That was Rita Blakely. "There's something funny going on at the target."

He saw it, not on the visual display, but through the computer that monitored scanner data. There were new targets appearing now, spewing from the larger mass of the *Magnificus Triplanetary*.

"I've got a bad feeling about this," Cadet Gunther Helm announced.

"Fighters!" Cadet Willis added. "The thing's dropping *fighters!*"

"That's no freaking liner!" Kent shouted over the channel. "It's a damned RAM cruiser!"

Vince had already come to the same conclusion. A heavy cruiser with fighter escort—the fighters carried along in hull-mounted rider pods that let them operate far from any planetary base. A RAM trap ... and he and his fourteen rookies had just blundered full-jet into its jaws.

"Lancers, this is Leader! Break off! Break off!"

But the Starfires were hurtling toward the RAM cruiser at better than twelve miles per second.

Breaking off—avoiding the cruiser and its deadly brood—would be neither easy nor immediate.

The drive flares of the enemy fighters were visible now to his naked eyes, pinpoints of light spreading across his HUD as they boosted toward the oncoming Starfires. Their acceleration was fantastic. Vince punched away at his console keyboard, accessing the fighter's warbook. A 3-D wire-frame image hovered above his console projector as scrolling blocks of data flicked across a monitor.

Based on drive characteristics and acceleration, Vince's onboard computer had decided that the enemy fighters were Kraits, sleek, finned stilettos with stubby forward canards, superbly maneuverable in or out of atmosphere, the newest and hot-damn deadliest fighters in RAM's entire arsenal. NEO had a few Kraits, precious birds hoarded for special missions. The aging Starfires used for SFS training missions were seriously outmatched.

"Leader to all Lancers," Vince called over the tactical channel. "Your weapons are free! Good luck!"

The kids would need more than luck to survive this ambush. They needed a diversion. Vince rammed his throttle forward and felt the exhilarating slam of full acceleration, saw the pinpoints of light leap toward him as he rapidly closed the range. The RAM fighters were closer now. Much closer. Their pilots hadn't even bothered engaging their electronic stealth cloaks, so certain were they of the kill. . . .

And then he was among them.

The engagement was more slaughter than battle. The highly maneuverable Kraits flipped end-for-end and decelerated in bone-wrenching moves that must have brought their pilots to the point of blacking out, but then the sleek, agile fighters were on the Starfires' tails, weaving in for the kill.

"This is Lancer Two, Lancer Two!" Cadet Willis's

voice was on the verge of cracking as his ship drifted into view of Vince's starboard side. A Krait had dropped onto the kid's six, the slot dead astern of the larger, clumsier Starfire. "I've got one on my tail! I can't shake him! I can't shake him!"

Each Krait mounted a single Olympian Arms Mark XXI 25-mm gyrocannon in a ventral ball turret. As Willis threw his Starfire into a heavy roll to port, bringing his ship so close to Vince's starboard side that the NEO commander could read the kid's hull number, the Krait's turret swung left, tracked, then fired, sending a stream of high-velocity, high-explosive shells smashing through the Starfire's armor in a savage, silent *pop-pop-pop* of strobing white flashes. Willis's starboard wing peeled away, his fuselage splitting open from stern plates to cockpit, and then the Starfire exploded as the fusion bottle failed and the unchained fury of the drive erupted into open space, a storm of dazzling light and hard radiation.

The transplex of Vince's cockpit polarized to block the glare from the explosion. As it cleared, he had an instant's glimpse of the Krait angling past his bow. His mouth twisted into a harsh grin. Bad move, sand worm!

In a whiplash one-two-three of motion, Vince killed his main thruster, pegged the enemy fighter with a targeting lock on his HUD, and fired his attitude jets, pivoting the Starfire to bring his accelerator gun to bear. Crosshairs centered over the target as his ship slewed across its wake. He squeezed the trigger . . . again. . . .

The Starfire's only armament was a magnetic railgun running almost the entire thirty-foot length of the NEO fighter. Its projectiles were inert lumps of nickel-iron rather than explosive shells . . . but the weapon hurled them at nearly three miles a second.

A few grams of metal striking a space fighter's hull at such speeds makes a very nasty crater indeed.

He was rewarded by a flash of light. He'd hit something, though the Krait was already out of sight and he couldn't tell just how much damage he'd done.

Meanwhile, the dogfight had degenerated into a chaotic tangle of ships spread across a growing volume of space. A barrage of radio calls and fragments crackled from his headset:

"Jesus, I've got one on my tail! Get 'em off, get 'em—"

"Break right! Break right!"

"Hey, has anyone seen the major?"

"Watch out! Two Kraits at three-one-seven . . ."

"Mayday! Mayday! I've lost power! I've . . . ahhh—"

"Christ, did you see that? They nailed Sebastian!"

Vince's fist came down on his armrest. *Damn!* The kids had never had a chance to learn how to work together, to *fight* together. It was a nightmare. . . .

"Lancer Flight, this is Lance Leader." Somehow he kept the words cold and emotionless. "All units, disengage as best you can. Execute Sierra one-one. Repeat, Sierra one-one. RTB when clear."

RTB—Return To Base. Sierra one-one was the coded command for one of a number of contingency plans. It called for all vessels in the formation to scatter, then power down, drifting cold and seemingly lifeless until the enemy had passed them by.

A fighter was a tiny thing in all this emptiness, easily missed. It would be the only chance for escape any of his kids would have.

"I'm staying with you, Major!" Jamison's voice sounded shaky but determined.

"And me!" Blakely called.

"I'm in."

"God *damn* it!" Vince exploded. "All of you, clear out! You're no match for Kraits, and someone has to report what's happened to base. Do you read me?"

Somehow he anticipated a Krait's sweeping turn and angled his Starfire for a railgun shot that sheared off the enemy fighter's nose in a whirling flash of metal shards and bursting gas.

Reluctantly, ten of the cadets acknowledged. Had they lost four already?

The RAM cruiser lay dead ahead, anvil to the Krait fighters' hard-swung hammer. Vince's Starfire was still hurtling toward the ship at better than sixteen miles per second, fast enough that his ship's electronic cameras were having difficulty adjusting to the constantly changing range.

Bolts of light flared silently near his cockpit, and then his Starfire shuddered as his dorsal tail fin was shredded by a 25-mm gyrocannon shell.

Fortunately wings weren't needed in space, though he'd lost some of the ECM and commo electronics carried there. He shouted as he corrected the Starfire's momentary tumble, exultant. Four of the Kraits, at least, were on his tail now, ignoring the rest of Lancer Flight to pursue him. If only he could draw those Kraits away from his kids for a few precious moments, give them a chance to get clear and power down. . . .

The RAM cruiser loomed huge, filling his view forward. He could see clearly the enormous RAM logo along the vessel's flanks, sandblasted by micrometeorites, and her name emblazoned on her streamlined prow: "RMS *Amazonis*." She was a monster, almost as long as the passenger liner she'd been impersonating, painted a dark rust red and bristling with weapons. Most of those weapons were silent though, unable to fire for fear of hitting the Kraits closing on his six. Past her halfway point between Jupiter and Mars, she was moving tail first, her drives turned toward the distant sun, gleaming like a small nova.

Triggering his ventral jets, Vince twisted the control stick, angling the Starfire's massive main-drive venturi before ramming the throttle home and loosing the thunder of his drive briefly once more. In free-fall again, he had an instant's glimpse of the cruiser's endless length as he swept across its vast hull, of fairings and weapons turrets and the streamlined bulges of armor-sheathed nacelles, of the spiderweb struts mounting empty rider pods to her hull.

Then he was past, flashing across the deadly white void astern of the ship, where billion-gauss magnetic fields contained the ravening fusion blasts of *Amazonis*'s drives. With a delicate touch, he adjusted the Starfire's course. Too close to the fury of the cruiser's drives and the tiny fighter would flare and vanish like a moth in a flame. But the sheer, raw white radio noise of those engines, the flaring radiation, the dazzling light, were his only hopes for losing his Krait pursuers.

Almost he made it. . . .

One shark-fin wingtip dragged in a sea of magnetic flux. The Starfire whipped broadside as Vince battled the controls, slamming his head against the padded seat back. G-forces surged through his frame, threatening to pull him apart, and the battered fighter's hull shrieked metallic agony.

He opened the Starfire's throttle wide. His only chance now was to get well clear of the white-hell fury of the *Amazonis*'s drives. He saw the cruiser's stern flash past like an exploding star, lost from view almost at once, only to reappear, then vanish again . . . and again . . . and again. . . .

The heavens and the receding stern of the *Amazonis* swept past his line of sight approximately once each second. He was tumbling end-to-end, helplessly cartwheeling into blackness. For a moment, the violent motion threatened to empty his stomach. He

closed his eyes, concentrating on resolving the conflicting signals sent to his brain by the outraged balance sensors of his inner ears.

His seat was located well forward of the fighter's
center of spin. Centrifugal force shoved at him from
behind, creating the sensation of dangling facedown
against the straps of his harness. When he opened
his eyes once more, it was like hanging above a bottomless gulf, across which the stars were sweeping
like clouds of glowing insects.

Hands and fingers responded to training and long
experience, flipping switches, touching pressure-
sensitive console displays, dragging at stick and
throttle. His console was dead—stone cold dead,
without the faintest flicker of LED life or light to
give him hope.

He knew at once what had happened. The Starfire
had plunged deeper into the magnetic field around
the cruiser's drive flare than he'd planned, inducing
an electromagnetic surge that had fried every cir-
cuit, every board, every piece of electronics on the
ship. Hull shielding and his suit had protected him
from the burst of hard radiation that must have
plucked at him during his close encounter. His ship,
though, was dead.

And without radio, without life support, without
power, it wouldn't be long before Vince Pirelli was
dead as well.

CHAPTER TWO

The cold was starting to creep up his legs.

Vince had been able to hook emergency batteries into the jury-rigged repairs he'd cobbled together on his life-support system, purchasing a few extra hours of life. But already their trickle of power was dwindling. He was broadcasting a distress call, but the energy in that signal was a scant handful of watts. He had no hope at all that anyone would hear him, not this far out in the emptiness of the Belt.

Somehow he'd learned to shut out the dizzying sweep of stars that continued to rush across the heavens beyond the transplex of his canopy. Centrifugal force's imitation of gravity continued to tug him forward in his seat, and the straps of his harness bit uncomfortably through the padding of his flight suit.

The air was getting stuffy. He hoped that was his imagination. His life-support system ought to be good for some hours of breathable atmosphere yet. The cold was most certainly *not* his imagination, however. Each breath fogged his helmet visor with puffs of white vapor, and he was having trouble feeling his feet now.

How much longer did he have?

Maybe his first assessment had been right. He was getting old, too old to be booting single-seat space fighters around the solar system. His reactions were slow; he tended to *think* about what he had to do, rather than reacting with a rocketjock's lightning blend of anticipation and instinct.

According to Jovanna Trask, he was entering "his difficult years." Maybe that was why NEO Command had insisted on giving him barely housebroken puppies with delusions of grandeur.

"His difficult years." The thought of Jovanna and her impish grin as she'd said that made him smile.

Vince still considered himself to be primarily a fighter jock, though he wore several hats now in the NEO hierarchy. He'd been a combat fighter pilot since the beginning, and for several years now he'd been a senior instructor on the staff at NEO's Training Command, teaching younger men and women the intricacies of SCM.

For the past couple of months, he'd added a third job description to the list, serving as leader of a team of NEO operatives based out here in the Belt.

They were a diverse lot: Galen, the diminutive, sleek-furred Tinker who preferred medicine to engineering, unlike most of his gene-engineered brothers; Rolf, a long-legged Martian Runner who preferred guns to his own species' primitive crossbows; Sandra, a human Belter who looked too young and too pretty to know as much about ship engineering as she did; and, of course, Jovanna Trask.

Good old Jovanna. He'd known her for better than twenty years—ever since the Wydlin affair, in fact, when she'd been recruited into NEO as a computer tech. She was probably the one woman in the system he'd never approached with the fighter jock's usual predatory arrogance.

It suddenly struck Vince as strange that he'd never made a play for Jovanna. When he'd first met her, she'd been easy to overlook—painfully plain, with mouse-brown hair and an almost gratingly hesitant and apologetic manner that suggested she was lots more comfortable with computers than with people. Vince had lost touch with her for twenty years then, and when he'd run into her again in the course of a mission, he'd been startled by the change. A more flattering hair style, a judicious use of makeup, an exercise-hardened body, and most important of all, a new maturity and self-confidence had transformed her.

Vince still wasn't certain how to relate to this new Jovanna Trask. The simplest solution had been to think of her as just another member of his team and not as a potential conquest. Hell, he didn't even think about Sandra that way, and she was a nova knockout without even trying. Getting intimate with the troops was a surefire recipe for disaster. Besides, Vince was damned if he was going to tie himself down to a one-woman relationship now. . . .

Or was he really longing for just that sort of stability, that sense of belonging? . . .

Damn. Sealed into the cockpit of a wrecked, single-seat fighter, adrift helplessly a hundred thousand miles from anywhere, was most decidedly not the time to brood about a lifestyle that was increasingly unsatisfying. He was shivering now as the warmth leached from the cockpit, and his fingers were beginning to turn numb even beneath the insulation of his flight gloves. How much longer would he have to worry about lifestyle, anyway?

Not a hell of a lot longer, he guessed.

Vince watched the wheeling stars. I must be getting old, he thought. Why else did they send the rest of the team to Mars and leave me here?

Their last mission had been to Thebe, one of Jupiter's outer moons, where they'd rescued a captured NEO agent. Part of the booty from that scrape had been reference to a RAM project, something called Operation Far Star. Galen, Rolf, Sandra, and Jovanna had all been covertly dispatched to Mars to investigate, while he had been left . . . here, training wet-behind-the-ears kids in the art of not getting themselves killed in space combat.

He felt a rush of self-pity. For twenty-one years he'd played out his part in NEO's fight for freedom behind the scenes. Damn it, why had NEO's Intelligence unit sent the others but held him back? Colonel Hamilton, his immediate superior in NEO's Training Command, had explained that they needed his skills as an instructor now more than ever. But Beowulf, the team's control in NEO Intelligence, could have reversed that order easily enough. Jovanna was only a couple of years younger than he was, so the idea that he was getting too old for this sort of thing didn't hold air.

Or did it? Jovanna was a computer jock *par excellence*, and he could easily imagine how valuable she would be in a covert penetration of RAM's computer assets at Mars. What was he good for? Instruction . . . and screwing up badly enough to leave him tumbling helplessly in a wrecked ship.

Vince slammed his fist against his thigh. That sort of thinking would get him exactly nowhere. Checking the chronometer built into the smart circuitry of his suit, he was startled to see how much time had passed. With luck, Lancer Flight—what was left of it, anyway—would have made it back to Trinity. He hoped they'd made it. Again he wondered if someone might come looking for him, then angrily dismissed the thought. It was far more likely that boats from the *Amazonis* would find him, and *that* thought made him shiver even more.

I'm freezing to death, he thought.

It was ironic, really. NEO's penultimate hero was the man sometimes called the Relic from the Past, Anthony "Buck" Rogers. Born and raised almost five hundred years ago in what had then been called the United States of America, Rogers had secured a place for himself in the history vids by carrying out a one-man suicide mission against an orbital space fortress called Masterlink. That mission had ended the last attempt by the old Russian empire to subjugate Earth, had in fact set the scene for man's peaceful expansion into the solar system during the next century.

Against all odds, Rogers's attack had turned out not to be suicidal after all. During his last, desperate run on Masterlink in his F-37 Wraith, a primitive piece of hardware by twenty-fifth century standards, Rogers's control systems had been destroyed and his ship was sent hurtling into deep space. Coolant leaks and a primitive emergency life-support unit had somehow combined to freeze Rogers's body, keeping him alive in suspended animation for almost five long centuries.

How many times had Vince lectured junior pilots on what had happened to the famous Buck Rogers? About how the twentieth-century pilot had survived, reawakened in the year 2456, about how he'd gone on to become the living, breathing symbol of NEO's resistance to the RAM overlords of Earth?

RAM—the letters were an acronym for the Russian-American Mercantile Combine, though that name was no longer used—was the Mars-based corporate entity that politically and militarily dominated the Inner System. Once the underdog fighting for independence from Earth, it now ruled the shattered and toxin-ridden homeworld of man with an iron fist. Only NEO outwardly challenged that rule, but it did so from hidden bases such as Trinity or its secret headquarters at Salvation III, using outnumbered, obsolete ships that were no match for the RAM giant.

Perhaps the only thing NEO had going for it in this war of hit and run, of strike and counterstrike, was the heroism, the dedication, the sheer, odds-beating daring of its individual warriors.

And luck, of course. Like the luck that had preserved Buck Rogers.

Unfortunately, Vince thought, what had happened to Rogers wasn't about to happen to him. Modern science still didn't understand the chain of fortunate accidents that had let Rogers's body freeze without rupturing his cells. No, when they found Vince Pirelli—*if* they found him—he would be well preserved in an icy shroud, but definitely dead.

Strangely, though, he didn't feel cold any longer. The numbness in his legs and arms seemed to have faded, almost as though his cockpit heater was working again. He tried to focus on his control board, looking for the light indicating positive function on the life-support heater.

No light ... no light ... funny. He was sure he could feel the heater running. Maybe the fault was in his control panel indicators, not the Starfire's systems.

Now that he thought about it, he was actually feeling rather warm.

And *sleepy* ...

O O O O O

Jovanna Trask lay on her back on the padded couch of the tubecar, enjoying the illusion of gravity even if it was only a tenth of a G, a quarter of what she was accustomed to. There were no windows; there was nothing outside to see but hurtling rock walls and magnetic accelerator rings. However, a large screen at the front of the compartment she shared with forty other passengers showed the time of arrival at their next stop—three minutes and twelve seconds—and the time to midpoint turnaround—twenty-two seconds.

The transit vehicle was accelerating smoothly along one of the tunnels that riddled Phobos, connecting the various civilian and RAM military facilities with one another through miles of solid rock. If she closed her eyes and concentrated on the solid feeling of the couch pressing against her back and legs, she could almost imagine that she was back home.

Jovanna had always hated low-G worldlets like Phobos. Born and raised on Mars, she was used to wide open, nonclaustrophobic spaces and cloudless skies, to the tideless, purple-blue majesty of the Boreal Sea, and, most especially, to gravity . . . to a *decent* .38 G that kept a girl's feet firmly on the ground.

For nearly all of her twenty-one years of working for the New Earth Organization, she'd been stationed on her home world, helping NEO keep track of RAM's activities, but several weeks earlier, she'd been pulled from her assignment within the bureaucratic warrens of RAM's vast Coprates offices and reassigned to the special NEO intelligence team operating in the Asteroid Belt. Then, just as suddenly, she'd been ordered back to Mars and reinserted into the RAM network.

But instead of getting an assignment on the planet's surface, she'd found herself transferred to RAM-Phobos Prime, an enormous military complex on Mars's inner moon, with orders to penetrate RAM's computer network and discover all she could about

Operation Far Star.

So far her investigations had turned up nothing.

The tubecar's countdown to midpoint reached zero. Acceleration ceased, and for a moment, Jovanna braced herself against the queasy, free-fall feeling of microgravity. Her seat, in unison with every other seat in the car, swiveled smoothly to face the rear of the compartment, where a second screen read two minutes and forty-five seconds, the time remaining until they reached their destination. The seat nudged her in the back as the car began decelerating, restoring the sensation of weight, of up and down.

After all these years, Jovanna still had ambivalent feelings about intelligence work. Her particular specialty was systems programming; she was *very* good with computers. More than once she'd hacked her way into RAM's secret files through the secret passages and trapdoors of the system-wide cybermatrix.

Too often, though, intelligence work demanded personal interaction, going one-on-one with flesh and blood. More often than not, that flesh and blood was wary, armed, and vicious, but it wasn't the physical danger that bothered her. Jovanna simply didn't relate well to people, even to the people who were on her side. The computer cybermatrix was much less messy, less confusing.

Less painful.

She called to mind once again the personal message that had printed itself that morning on her workstation screen in RAM-Phobos Prime: *Meet me for a drink at eighteen. Your folks back on the farm want to know if your boy friend is giving you much trouble.—G.*

"G," of course, was Galen, the NEO team member who'd been assigned to Phobos with her. His innocuous, if somewhat clumsily worded message, had shocked and worried her more than she cared to admit, even to herself.

Meet me for a drink at eighteen sounded straightforward enough, but "eighteen" wasn't eighteen hundred, a time, but a code referring to a particular rendezvous, a sleazy carousel dive called the Fundown. By counting six words from *meet* to *eighteen*, she got the key to the rest of the message: "farm . . . boy . . . trouble." "Farm boy" was Vince's code name, and "trouble" was self-explanatory.

And finally, the number six itself was a warning that she was about to receive new orders.

Damn! What kind of trouble was Vince in now?

Jovanna still wasn't sure she trusted her own feelings about Vince Pirelli. When she'd first met him, she'd been fascinated by the young, handsome, and dashing rocketjock who, by mistaking her for a NEO agent, had accidentally swept her into the shadow world of intelligence. That early fascination had given way to frustration, then anger when he'd repeatedly failed to recognize her value during the Wydlin Affair. They'd ended at last as . . . friends? Possibly. As teammates, certainly. There was nothing like a firefight to create bonds of trust and respect between two people, whatever else they felt about each other.

Part of the problem was that Vince Pirelli was a natural-born hero, the sort of man NEO depended on in its unequal struggle against RAM—outgoing, dynamic, confident. . . .

The stuff of personal interaction, traits that Jovanna was convinced she would never acquire.

The tubecar slowed to a stop and the doors hissed open. Jovanna unhooked her seat harness and followed the other passengers into the kaleidoscopic swirl of Phobosport.

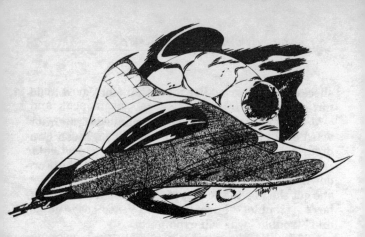

CHAPTER THREE

The noise and the confusion assaulted Jovanna's senses as she pulled herself away from the tubecar platform. She had emerged in a vast cavern that had been transformed by surreal architecture and holographic displays and crowds of people into a three-dimensional metropolis buried within the heart of Phobos.

The Mars-Pavonis Space Elevator had been constructed two centuries before, the engineering miracle of the spacefaring age that had transformed Phobosport into the busiest space terminal in the solar system. Phobos, Mars's inner moon, a potato-shaped chunk of rock barely sixteen miles wide through its long axis, had been boosted by precisely applied thermonuclear nudges into a new orbit almost twice as far from Mars as before. Repositioned in an aerostationary orbit some 10,200 miles above the Martian surface, Phobos now circled Mars in exact step with the planet's rotation, fixed unmoving in the sky directly above an extinct volcano on the Martian equator called Pavonis Mons. Next, a tether of super-strong diacarballoy had been lowered to the

surface and anchored in bedrock. Cars now rode
magnetic tubes from moon to mountain peak and
back again, the cheapest and most efficient way yet
discovered of reaching space from a planetary surface. Deimos—Mars's smaller, outer moon—had been
repositioned and accelerated to serve as a counter-
balance to Phobos, connected to the inner moon by
another diacarballoy tether, its mass maintaining
the tension necessary to keep the Space Elevator in
position.

Inevitably then, Phobos had become a docking
complex of enormous wealth and prestige, the principal spaceport for an entire world, a linchpin of
RAM's incredible wealth and power . . .

. . . and one of the best-defended sites in the solar
system.

Jovanna saw heavily armed RAM guards everywhere, anonymous in their dark visors and combat
armor. She was ignored as she made her way clear of
the tubecar platform. The ID card attached to her
gray bodysuit identified her as a civilian computer
technician assigned to the military base, and that
alone granted her nearly complete security from random searches or questioning.

She wormed her way into the thickest part of the
mob thronging the Grand Gallery, enjoying the additional protection afforded by the crowd. Jovanna had
long ago learned the value of urban camouflage, the
knack of being nondescript, one plain face among
thousands.

Since Phobos was attached to the Space Elevator, it
couldn't be spun like other small, inhabited planetoids to produce artificial gravity. Phobos's surface
gravity was a scant six ten-thousandths of a G,
which meant that it took several seconds of staring
at an object released in midair to be sure it was actually falling, and Jovanna weighed a bit more than

one ounce. The Grand Gallery was crisscrossed by a 3-D spiderweb of hand lines, along which thousands of new arrivals—up from Mars to board ships bound for other worlds, or just debarked from liners secured at Phobosport's docking bays—moved like hurrying lines of ants. Jovanna found a moving dragline running out across the cavern in the direction she wanted to go, grabbed a handhold, and let it whisk her into the gulf.

At first she kept her eyes tightly closed. Draglines were the most common means of transport inside microgravity habitats, especially in large, open chambers like the gallery, but she hated the stomach-twisting disorientation. After a moment, though, she opened her eyes but kept them fixed on the cavern wall ahead.

Every surface of the Grand Gallery was crowded with shops, arcades, pleasure domes, thumper booths, merchants' stalls, and the huge rotating wheels of spin-grav habitats, all masked by the dazzling colors and shifting animation of holographic signs and facade illusions. Jovanna's destination was one of the rotating habitats, a squat, pastel-swirled cylinder sixty feet across, turning steadily on its axis beneath flashing neon holography outlining the cartoon image of a nude girl and the name "Fundown." As far as she could tell as she released the drag and caught hold of a stationary safety railing mounted outside the slowly turning entranceway, it was identical to a hundred other spacemen's bars and dives shouldering one another in the press and glitter of Phobos's Grand Gallery.

She entered Fundown at the hub, traversing a darkened tunnel lined with luminous erotic murals that rotated around her as she pulled herself hand-over-hand along a pull line. Climbing into a transplex cubicle at the end, she braced herself as it dropped from the hub to the carousel floor, and the sensation of gravity rose from almost nonexistent to a healthy four-tenths of a G, Mars normal.

The Fundown was a typical carousel bar, its rotation providing an out-is-down spin gravity. "Up" was in the direction of the wheel's hub; the floor ran all the way around the rim, and Jovanna could look past the central hub and see patrons seated upside down on the other side of the bar. The air was thick with smoke from various recreational weeds and trembling to the heartbeat throb of novajag music pulsing from the walls and curving floor. The only light came from the waitresses, who wore holographic images of living flame, and from the frosty light spotlighting a nude dancer cavorting in the microgravity next to the carousel's hub, twenty feet over her head.

Jovanna had to stand by the elevator for a moment, blinking until her eyes adjusted to the uncertain light and visual disorientation. Only a handful of the tables were occupied, most by scruffy Belter types, miners or freighter crewmen probably, big, rough-looking humans sporting wildly individualistic patterns of dress, hairstyle, and body ornamentation. A few of the bar's patrons were gennies, genetically engineered creatures bred for specific tasks too dangerous, difficult, or demeaning for humans. There were hundreds of different gennie species, but few shared the human preferences of environmental comfort and recreation. In the dim light of the Fundown, she recognized only three different types—several gray-furred Tinkers, a couple of hulking Workers, and one reptilian-looking Slither. After watching their movements for a moment, Jovanna decided that the Fundown's waitresses and the dancer were probably gennies as well, pleasure gennies pulling double duty tending tables out front and serving as entertainment in the bar's dingy back rooms.

Finally Jovanna spotted the party she was looking for sitting head-down at a table high up on the opposite side of the floor. She felt the human Belters' eyes on her as she made her way along the up-curved floor to where Galen was waiting for her.

A massive hand snaked out from one of the tables as she passed, groping after her. "Hey, sweet bottom," its owner rasped. "Lookin' fer comp'ny?"

Jovanna almost flinched as she looked down into the man's scarred face and yellowed teeth, but she maintained her composure, outwardly at least. "I've got a date," she said, loudly enough to be heard above the insistent throb of the music, "with something more highly evolved." She walked away to a chorus of guffaws, whistles, and catcalls from the other Belters at the table.

Jovanna hated places like this and had never been able to understand the people who frequented them. The need some felt to fry their brains with drugs or alcohol struck her as irrational, a kind of lust for self-destruction that should have been bred out of the human species centuries ago by the relentless logic of Darwin. People came to this kind of place for entertainment? The so-called music, loud, primitive, and insistent, gave her a headache. Her own tastes ran to the mathematical perfection of Bach.

Still, the high-decibel novajag was partial insurance, at least, against hidden listening devices or a RAM agent with an audiosnooper. A determined eavesdropper could use computer enhancement to filter out any background noise, even jag, but at least their meeting would be secure from casual listeners.

Nearly everyone in the Fundown, she decided ruefully, was probably deaf by now anyway.

Galen gave a wry smile and raised a glass of something transparent in salute as she approached. Propped up on his chair by a canvas pack, his boots dangling a foot above the floor, Galen was a gennie of the species known as a Tinker. Less than three feet tall, with long, slender fingers that reminded Jovanna of spiders' legs, he had a muzzle and an inhumanly long reach that revealed his simian ancestry. His close-set eyes and the keen and curious intelligence behind them, however, were quite human.

RAM had originally created Tinkers to work as engineers in the cramped ducts, tunnels, and conduits of space stations and colonies. Their intelligence had surprised their inventors, however, and many had shown an independence of mind that let them break out of the niche for which they'd been designed. Galen, for example, was a medic, and a good one. He himself insisted that he was still nothing but an engineer, one who liked to tinker with human bodies instead of fusion plants and life-support systems.

Though Galen had been introduced to NEO by the notorious pirate Black Barney, it was hard to feel uncomfortable in his presence. He was covered with soft, downy gray fur that shaded to silver around his naked face and hands, and Jovanna had to resist an impulse to pet him.

"Thank you for coming," Galen said. His words were oddly shaped by his lipless gibbon's mouth. The brown, human eyes flicked left and right, as though searching for eavesdroppers.

"Your message said Vince was in trouble."

"He is." The Tinker hesitated, as though wondering how to put unpleasant thoughts into hard words. "Jovanna . . . Vince may be dead."

"*Dead!* . . ." The word bit, cold and steel-hard. Her worry over the cryptic "farm boy trouble" message crystalized like ice beneath her breastbone.

"*May be,*" Galen insisted. "Headquarters isn't

sure, and they want us to find out. And . . . this may
give us a line on Far Star."

She steeled herself. "Okay, tell me. What did they
say?"

It was ironic. Jovanna's covert assignment had her
working in RAM-Phobos Prime's communications
center, with access to a comnet that spanned the inhabited solar system, but precisely because coded
messages coming into or leaving the center would
have attracted attention, her only contact with NEO
was through Galen. The Tinker's cover as an engineer at Phobos's civilian spaceport gave him access
to the surface, where he'd hidden a tight-beam mi-
croburst transmitter and receiver. Once each Martian day, when Phobos was properly aligned with
Trinity, he transmitted the team's report in a coded
millisecond burst and recorded incoming traffic.
There was a time lag of over seven minutes with
Mars and the Trinity asteroid in their current rela-
tive positions, making true conversation impossible,
but the arrangement served well enough to keep
them in touch with NEO.

Vince, Galen told Jovanna, had run into a RAM
Chryse-class cruiser while leading a group of students in an exercise. Five ships had been lost, including Vince's. Ten had made it back to Trinity, but only
because Pirelli had thrown himself at the enemy
ship in a diversionary action. Recorders aboard the
surviving NEO Starfires had spotted his ship tumbling clear of the cruiser's drive flare, but the students had been unable to get a line on his new vector.
In order to accurately track his new course, they
would have had to go active on their radars, and that
would have given away their positions.

"Are you saying they're not even going to *try* to
search for him?" Fear drove her anger, made it explosive. "Damn it, his Starfire's batteries could run his

life support for days! He could still be alive!"

Galen spread small, slim-fingered hands. "How could they search so much emptiness? With the velocity his ship had after the encounter, he could be anywhere within a volume of millions of cubic miles, a mere speck in the void. The search would require years, not days."

Their conversation was interrupted as a waitress approached their table, wearing a flickering, holographic image of cool flames, now concealing, now revealing with her movements. As Jovanna had suspected, she was a pleasure gennie, though there was nothing to advertise the fact beyond a certain blankness about her eyes and the mindless way she chewed on some rubbery material in her mouth. High intelligence was not a usual characteristic of pleasure gennies. "Whatcha have?" she asked.

Galen was already nursing a glass of distilled water. Not wishing to appear conspicuous, Jovanna asked for orange juice, then settled for water when it turned out that that was the only nonalcoholic drink available. The price was outrageous, but Jovanna scarcely noticed.

Galen took a sip from his glass. "The students picked up the name of that RAM cruiser. It was the *Amazonis*."

"The *Amazonis*?" Jovanna shook her head, puzzled. "She's docked at RAM-Phobos Prime. Has been for three weeks."

"Have you seen her?"

"Well, no. But she's on the list of capital ships in port."

"Apparently RAM's been playing a shell game with their heavy cruisers," Galen replied. "The ship Vince's flight encountered was supposed to be a civilian liner, the *Magnificus Triplanetary*."

"I know the name. She's supposed to dock early tomorrow."

"RAM's using her schedule for cover. As near as NEO Intelligence can tell, the *Maggie Tripe*'s still at Jupiter. The *Amazonis* was following *Maggie*'s flight plan. She'll dock at RAM-Phobos Prime at zero-five-thirty tomorrow."

Jovanna's eyes widened. "And headquarters thinks that Vince was picked up by the *Amazonis*?"

The Tinker shrugged his thin shoulders expressively. "They don't know. It's only a possibility, and a thin one at that. If they were curious about running into NEO fighters that far from any known base, they might have tried to collect prisoners for interrogation."

Jovanna fought to hold back the rush of fear that rose at Galen's words. The thought that Vince was dead was bad enough. The possibility that he was a prisoner of RAM filled her with a sick, twisting horror. Her fingers strayed to her personal uplink, a hand-sized curve of plastic strapped above her left wrist. She knew too well what RAM's interrogators were capable of.

She swallowed part of her anguish. "I still don't get it. Why the cloak-and-dagger games, scrambling a passenger liner's flight plan with a cruiser's?"

"That's part of what headquarters wants us to find out." He dropped his voice. "It might have something to do with Far Star."

"They want to read *Amazonis*'s computers," she guessed.

Galen nodded. "They want you to use RW. If anything can penetrate *Amazonis*'s computers, it can."

"RW is not an it," Jovanna said through clenched teeth.

"As you wish. In any case, if Vince is being held aboard that ship, there'll be a record of it somewhere. And headquarters thinks there might be something on Far Star there as well."

That made sense. They'd discovered a reference to the enigmatic Far Star during their raid on Thebe in the Jovian system. For some reason, soon after, RAM had dispatched a heavy cruiser to Jupiter and back . . . and tried to keep the trip secret.

There had to be a link.

"There's more," Galen continued.

"Yes?"

This time the Tinker leaned forward across the table, his voice now so low she could scarcely catch the words. "NEO is going to raid Phobos."

"*What?*"

"Shh!" The Tinker's eyes darted nervously back and forth. "Not so loud!"

"Sorry." Jovanna sat for a moment, stunned. She had no military mind, but she knew enough to realize the implications were staggering. "How do they expect to pull *that* off?" she whispered. "And why? Phobos is a damned fortress!"

"As to why," Galen said with an injured air, "headquarters did not see fit to inform me. As to how, I know only that they will be using our . . . ah . . . newest allies."

"The Rogues' Guild."

"One of their people is supposed to meet us here today."

"Here?"

"You know a better place?"

She glanced up at the scruffy, less-than-reputable occupants of the nearest tables. "I guess not."

"His name's Kaiten, and he . . . Uh-oh—"

A hand closed on her shoulder from behind, making her jump. "Listen, sweetums," a gravelly voice said in her ear, "you really oughta be more choosy about the comp'ny ya keep."

It was the yellow-toothed man who'd grabbed her

earlier. He stood behind her now, leering as he caressed her with pressure enough to keep her pinned
against the seat of her chair.

Galen hopped off his chair, one furry hand dropping to a pouch on the utility harness he wore, but
Jovanna saw him hesitate at the same moment she
sensed movement on either side of her. Someone gig-
gled, a high-pitched, unpleasant sound. Yellow Tooth
had at least two friends backing him up, and she
could tell by the look in Galen's eyes that they were
armed.

"Hey, let's keep this friendly, Tink," Yellow Tooth
said. "You shoot me and this girlie here could really
get messed up. Know what I mean? And you're *not*
gonna get a second shot."

"I'm . . . not armed," Galen said. Jovanna wondered if he was telling the truth and decided that he
must be. Tinkers could be quite skillful with weapons but weren't known for their combat prowess.

Carefully she set her glass down on the table. "Let
go," she said, her voice icy.

"No way, sweets," Yellow Tooth murmured in her
ear. "You insulted me in front of my friends, y'know?
I think you oughta come tell us how sorry you are."

This, she realized, could become ugly fast.

"Let's burn 'em, Sid," another voice said.

"Nah," Yellow Tooth—Sid—replied. "Not yet. I
came here to have me a good time, and I think I just
found it." Something went *snick* alongside Jovanna's
ear, and she felt a tingle of heat. Turning her head,
she looked into the emerald gleam of a mono knife,
held inches from the side of her face.

The mono knife's blade was a single crystal of arti-
ficially grown diamond, the crystalline lattice drawn
and bonded into an edge one molecule thick, as deadly as monofilament wire. A low-wattage laser illuminated the crystal blade from within, casting an eerie

green glow from handle to point and radiating enough heat to give her a nasty burn if it touched her skin.

Instinctively Jovanna jerked her face back, but Sid shifted his grip with lightning speed from her shoulder to her hair, giving it a painful twist and holding her head rigidly still. The blade weaved hypnotically back and forth, nearly brushing her cheek.

"Hey, you guys!" a woman's voice called. Jovanna could just see one of the gennie waitresses out of the corner of her eye. "No fighting in here, or I'll hafta call the constabs! Take it outside!"

"Whaddaya say, Sid?" The giggle grated at her nerves again. "Ya wanna take it outside?"

"Nah. We ain't fightin'," Sid said. "I jes' didn't care for this girlie's smart-mouthin' me earlier—that thing she said about 'evolved.' It wasn't polite-like." When the gennie hesitated, he snarled a curse. "Go on! Beat it, G-toy! This don't concern you!"

"Let's sit down and discuss this like—" Jovanna began.

His hand twisted her hair tighter, cutting her off. "Y'know," he continued as if she hadn't spoken, "I think maybe you was comparin' me to your fuzzy tinkle friend here, and that makes me feel bad."

The blade weaved closer, nearly touching her eye. . . .

CHAPTER FOUR

Jovanna tried to pull free, but the man's grip tightened, making her gasp with pain.

"Look, put the knife away—" Galen began.

"Shaddup, tinkle! I don't like you. And I don't think my girlfriend here likes you either. Why don't you just skim off before I decide to carve my initials in your face?"

Galen took a step past the table, but one of the gunmen reached out and gave the Tinker a hard shove, sending him sprawling on the floor.

"Whaddaya see in garbage like this, honey?" Sid asked.

"Maybe she likes tinkles better than real men," one of the gunmen said.

"Yeah," the other man said, giggling. "Maybe she don't know what she's—"

"Release her!" The new voice boomed through the Fundown bar, a guttural bass that overpowered even the throb of the music. Sid let go of Jovanna's hair and she spun away, dropping into a combat crouch, ready for anything.

Or so she thought. Across the room, a towering figure was striding down the slope of the floor, monstrous, a giant caricature of a man, with brow ridges like rock ledges on a cliff, a bald skull gnarled by a wrinkled crest of bone, and fangs that seemed to have worn grooves into the sides of the muscular, armor-plated jaw.

There were startled exclamations from the other patrons in the bar, and overhead the dancer flickered with static, then vanished. Until that moment, Jovanna hadn't realized that the girl was a holographic projection.

The newcomer was definitely not a projection. Long, ropelike muscles bunched and knotted in its arm and shoulder as it swung one massive fist. A crash sounded, and a table in its way shattered in splinters of whirling plastic. The figure stepped over the wreckage as the Belters who'd been sitting there scrambled for cover.

"My God," Jovanna said, her eyes wide. "It's a *Terrine! . . .*"

She'd never seen a Terrine without combat armor. This one wore only a jerkin and a kind of steel and leather harness, with boots that reached its knees. The face was vaguely catlike, flat, with slitted pupils in glittering, yellow eyes and pointed ears folded flat against the sides of its head. Terrines were combat gennies, bioengineered from a witches' brew of human, cat, and shark genes for only one purpose: *killing*. The way this one was moving left no doubt that he was coming after Sid and his friends.

The giggling thug squeaked panic and swung his laser pistol up, thumbing off the safety.

Behind them, something went *ping*, and a slender rod telescoped from Galen's hand, flicking across the laser pistol's barrel and knocking it aside. At the same instant, the movement galvanized the Terrine into action. Muscles writhed, and the creature seemed to blur.

"Look here!" Sid yelled. "We ain't got no gripe with—*urk!*"

Faster than sight, the Terrine merged with the gunmen. Limbs thrashed, and someone screamed. A single laser burst scored the floor with a flare of light and the hiss of frying insulation. The giggling thug shrieked all the way across the room, until he collided back-first and upside down with a wall. Sid was sprawled across a nearby tabletop, the handle of his mono knife protruding awkwardly from between his eyes, the blade emerging from the back of his skull to nail it to the tabletop. The third man whimpered and collapsed where he stood, blood trickling from the corner of his mouth as he dropped to his knees, the side of his head oddly misshapen, then toppled onto his face with a dull thud.

The entire fight had lasted less than a second. Jovanna hadn't been able to more than twitch between the first rush and the final blow. Only Galen had been quick enough to participate, by jogging the gunman's hand with the silvery rod that he was now collapsing into a thumb-sized capsule and replacing in a harness pouch.

"Grabber," the Tinker explained as Jovanna stared at him. "A little thing I tinkered up for snagging things in zero-G. Knew it would come in handy someday." He gestured as the Terrine approached, towering over them, seven feet tall. Even in the bar's Mars-normal spin-gravity, he must have weighed a hundred and twenty pounds. "And here's our new friend."

Jovanna saw blood on one of the bony spurs projecting from the creature's elbows and felt suddenly ill. "Oh, no!" she groaned. "Don't tell me *you're—*"

"Jovanna," Galen said happily, "permit me to introduce Kaiten."

"Not sure," the monster rumbled, its voice like deep bass thunder, "that I am pleased to meet *you*."

"That's okay," Jovanna said weakly. She groped for a chair and let herself sink into it. "No offense, but the feeling is mutual."

"Still," the Terrine boomed, "we must talk. We should also leave before stabbers arrive."

Stabbers—the local constabs. Kaiten was right. The Fundown's owners had no doubt sounded an alarm, and even an obvious case of self-defense would tie them up longer than they could afford with questions and official inquiries—RAM inquiries. And Jovanna didn't want to jeopardize her security position at RAM-Phobos Prime's comm center. No doubt the pirate preferred to keep his entanglements with the law to a minimum as well.

"Okay. Where do you want to go?"

The Terrine glanced about the carousel bar, then locked its hard yellow eyes on hers. "Where we not be seen. We go."

"Yeah, right. We go." With growing misgivings, Jovanna followed the big combat gennie to the bar's elevator, closely followed by Galen.

It was remarkable, she thought, how quickly the place had emptied out.

At a tubecar terminal a block from the Fundown, Kaiten punched a destination request into a public board, and the words "STICKNEY BASE" appeared on an overhead display. Moments later, a tubecar floated silently out of a tunnel opening and drifted to a stop in front of them, hovering on invisible cushions of magnetic flux. Doors hissed open and they all climbed aboard. Three Worker gennies and a couple of Martians started to follow them aboard, but Kaiten stood in the accessway and rumbled down at them like an awakening volcano. The other would-be passengers decided to wait for another car, which left

Jovanna and Galen alone in this one with the Terrine.

"STICKNEY BASE" appeared on a bulkhead monitor as they strapped themselves into adjacent couches, and an unseen robot controller set the vehicle into smooth, silent motion. The time remaining to their destination, Jovanna saw was 5:30.

Jovanna looked at the huge figure who squatted in one of the cabin's padded seats, so large he had to stoop forward slightly so that his head cleared the low ceiling. She'd never even been this close to a Terrine before, and, like most humans, she had a deep-seated dread of the things.

He seemed less human than most other gennies she'd encountered . . . less human than Galen, for example, who came across as a short, fuzzy man with arms and fingers too long for his body. Kaiten, on the other hand, was monstrous. There was no hair anywhere on his body, and his torso and parts of his limbs were plated with calluses that looked like bone armor. Up close, the rest of his skin had a gritty texture, like sandpaper. That would be the shark genes, she decided, wondering what other dark and nasty snippets of DNA in the thing's makeup had been taken from sharks. Beyond Kaiten's basic symmetry, there seemed to be very little that was human, except possibly for the obvious intelligence glimpsed through cat-slitted eyes.

"Why do you stare?" Kaiten rumbled, his yellow gaze hard on Jovanna.

"I've never, ah, socialized with a Terrine before," she said, startled. "I thought you all served RAM."

"Negative," he replied, gravel on steel. Fascinated, she watched one horny hand clench into a rock-hard fist as it rested on his knee, tendons bulging beneath sandpaper skin.

Terrines were RAM's front-line warriors in their

war to keep Earth subjugated. They'd been designed
to fight on Earth; the name *Terrine* was a reflection
of that. They were supremely adaptable, though, and
they were found wherever humans were, generally
in RAM security and military forces. Inhumanly
strong, inhumanly fast, inhumanly vicious in combat, they were pictured by RAM propaganda as perfect soldiers, unafraid, unquestioning, and
unwaveringly loyal to those in command over them.

Kaiten's denial jarred her. He was the exact opposite of the Terrine stereotype she'd always accepted
without question.

Galen seemed to sense what she was thinking.
"Kaiten is an Imperial Terrine," he said, then added
the scientific name. "*Miles fabricatus imperitorius.*
Not all of them are brainless monsters, you know.
You might think of Kaiten as—well, as a noncommis-
sioned officer. A sergeant. Human officers give him
orders. He keeps his platoon of ordinary Terrines in
line."

"*Gave* me orders," Kaiten grumbled. "Once. No
more. No more . . . ever." The fist clenched again, and
Jovanna could imagine that he was crushing some
remembered enemy in his tremendous grip.

A renegade Terrine. Jovanna hadn't realized that
there were such things.

"What kind of name is 'Kaiten'?" she wanted to
know.

"RAM serial number K10-783645," the Terrine replied. His ears, like conical sections of thin leather,
folded flat beside his skull, and a sigh like the rumble of a volcano sounded from his chest. He gestured
at the monitor, which now read 3:55. "Time passes.
Do not waste it with useless questions. You," he said,
turning his baleful gaze on Galen. "What have you
told her?"

"I'd just come to the part about the raid," Galen

said. "Operation Skytower."

Jovanna shook her head in disbelief. "You guys can't be planning on attacking Phobos! It's crazy!"

"Black Barney prefers the unexpected," Galen pointed out.

Jovanna's eyes widened. "Black Barney!" She turned to stare at Kaiten. "Are you one of *his* . . . people?"

"Not precisely," Kaiten rumbled. "I'm with Captain Stark."

Jovanna frowned. She thought she recognized the name, a minor Belter pirate known for his sheer, bloodthirsty viciousness. "Then how does Barney fit into this?"

"He . . . recruited us," Kaiten said. "For reasons of his own."

"The word is," Galen added, "that Barney promised Stark one million credits, plus salvage."

Jovanna suppressed a shudder. "Salvage" in that context meant loot. Stark and Black Barney! Damn. Why in all the hells of space? . . .

NEO was sharply divided over whether or not using pirates in paramilitary operations against RAM was a good idea. Some said NEO needed all the help it could get, no matter what the source. Others insisted that NEO was engaged in a war of liberty against tyranny, of good against evil, and enlisting the aid of murdering freebooters who were only interested in loot would, in the long run, only hurt Earth's fight for freedom.

Usually Jovanna sided with those who opposed recruiting pirates, if only because using them added fuel to RAM's propaganda campaign that claimed that NEO itself was a pirate organization. Black Barney was different. More than once during previous NEO operations, she'd suggested using him.

But that was because he was Black Barney—not

human at all, but a gennie, an organic hybrid manufactured twenty-one years before by the Wydlin Corporation. Black Barney was outwardly human, but
faster, stronger, and deadlier than any man . . . and
he detested RAM with a vehemence that matched
his superhuman strength. Jovanna had been involved in his creation, and the battle that had liberated Barney and his clone brothers from their RAM
masters had been her baptism of fire with NEO.

But she'd made some mistakes . . . most especially
that of thinking of the Barneys as *things* rather than
as living, feeling beings. That bit of insensitivity in
particular had left a legacy of mistrust between *the*
Barney—Black Barney—and Jovanna.

Working with Black Barney would have been bad
enough. He, at least, had something invested in the
fight against RAM, even if it was just raw hatred.
But Stark was pure human, the very image of the
bloody, murdering cutthroat of the spaceways, while
Kaiten was a RAM-designed terror weapon. Using
them could be deadly.

"NEO Command has worked out a plan," Galen
continued, speaking quickly as though he'd heard
Jovanna's misgivings and wanted to cut them off.
"Operation Skytower. We are going to raid Phobos,
and you and I, Jovanna, are central to the whole operation."

Jovanna was still shaken by the knowledge that
NEO was working with Stark. "This I've got to
hear," she said sourly.

The tubecar completed the trip to Stickney Base,
where Kaiten again discouraged other passengers
from getting on. Galen reprogrammed the board for
a trip to Outpole, clear on the other side of Phobos.

That gave him plenty of time to fill Jovanna in,
while Kaiten silently watched.

O O O O O

This, Vince thought through the chill, bleary fog that surrounded him, was not his day. He'd been dreaming—he thought it had been a dream, anyway—of warmth. And a party . . . someplace warm, with a huge, blazing fire in a fireplace. There'd been a girl in the dream, a blonde . . . what was her name? He'd known her, he was sure, but he couldn't remember now.

"Vince," she had been telling him, her lips next to his ear as she snuggled closer, "you're freezing to death. Silly, don't you remember that people always feel warm when they're freezing to death?"

He remembered her laughing . . . and how he'd laughed with her.

Damn . . . what was her name? One of his girlfriends from Trinity. Rhonda? No. Not Deb, either. That dazzler up in Intelligence? No. He hadn't gotten to first base with that one yet, though not for lack of trying. Jovanna?

Jovanna wasn't a blonde, except when she made herself up for a covert operation. Besides, he thought of the introvert computer expert as a friend, not as recreation.

Jovanna. . . .

Blinking through the fog, he could make out the interior of his Starfire's cockpit, illuminated by the wan light of a distant, shrunken sun hanging unmoving off his starboard side. Elsewhere, stars—stars by the millions—dusted across the inky sky beyond his canopy, unmoving, astonishing in their numbers and sheer, cold beauty.

More astonishing was the fact that he still lived. How much time had passed? He didn't know. His console was stone cold dead, his wrist chronometer inaccessible beneath the sleeve of his pressure suit.

Sheets of ice had formed over his instrument console and in patches on the inside of his canopy, made faintly visible by the refracted haze of sunlight filtering through them. Why hadn't he frozen to death by now? There was no sensation in his legs or arms at all. Why was he still alive, dreaming of girls and parties and fires?

There was no answer, save that ship and suit and hard vacuum outside must have provided him with unexpected insulation. And the sun provided some heat, even three astronomical units distant.

Vince hadn't thought it would take him this long to die.

His brow furrowed, wrestling with the thought. What made him think time had passed? He could remember—barely—an endless parade of dreams, phantasms . . . had he been delirious? Maybe so. It felt like a long time had passed, many hours, certainly. Possibly days.

With an effort of will, he tried to move his left arm. It was suddenly important to know what time it was, *very* important, a matter of life and death.

His arm wouldn't respond. He could feel nothing beyond a vague area of discomfort in his shoulder and upper arm. His failure made him almost frantic; he had to pull his arm free, roll up his sleeve, look at his wrist chrono. . . .

Pain exploded in his shoulder. Chips of ice flaked away from his space suit and danced, glistening, in the sunlight, bouncing from one side of the cockpit to the other in zero-G. A silvery something drifted in front of his helmet, blocking his vision. What? . . .

It was his arm, still empty of feeling. His movements had set it adrift, and it hung now in front of his face, as weightless as the dancing chips of ice.

Vince tried to think . . . *think.* A nagging feeling of danger—no, of *difference*—tried to worm its way up through the depths of his shock and cold and exhaustion-fogged mind. Something was very wrong, something having to do with gravity.

That was it! Realization triggered a burst of adrenaline, burning through the stupor that still clung to his thoughts like thick, cold mud. The last time he'd been aware of his surroundings, his Starfire had been spinning end-over-end. Centrifugal force had mimicked gravity. He'd been hanging face-down from his seat harness.

Now he was weightless, adrift in zero-G. Fogged his brain might be, but one thing he *did* know. His Starfire had not stopped its spin by itself, not without power.

That thought made him feel colder than the sub-zero chill already gripping the Starfire's cockpit. That RAM cruiser could have tracked his outbound fall, then vectored a recovery team after him.

RAM!

He tried to move again but could do little more than thrash against the inertia of unfelt arms and legs. If they'd come close enough to grapple with the Starfire and stop its spin, he should be able to see them. If he could only *move.* . . .

The sound, a deep metallic *clunk* vibrating through the Starfire's hull, echoed faintly in the cockpit's frosty air. The chill deepened. That sound had come from forward, as though something had just attached itself to his hull.

Something moved outside, a shadow against the stars. Terror, a black, primeval gibbering, rose in the back of his mind. His breathing quickened, each panicky exhalation misting the lower half of his helmet visor, each indrawn breath clearing it again. He squinted, straining to see. There was something alive, alive and moving, making its way slowly along the Starfire's needle prow, crawling over the hull toward his canopy.

Then the thing moved into the sunlight, and he saw it clearly for the first time. A face peered in at him from the darkness outside his cockpit, an emotionless, inhuman face etched in silver and jet black, lacking ears or nose or anything more than an almost invisible slit of a mouth. The eyes were huge, unwinking eggs, at one instant as silver-bright as pools of mercury, the next as black as space itself.

Dimly Vince became aware of other details, of a blunt, hairless head, of a humanoid torso and arms softened by insulating layers beneath a skin that shifted capriciously in color, like the eyes, between silver and black. It wore no clothing beyond some kind of harness. The quicksilver body gave no hint whether the thing was male or female, or indeed whether such concepts even applied to it.

But it was inquisitive. One hand came up, a curiously human hand splayed against the transplex of his canopy, as though seeking a way to get at the man trapped inside.

Terror welled up from the depths of Vince's mind. Thrashing, screaming, he struggled to free himself. The exertion proved too much for his already badly weakened frame, and in a few seconds, the cold darkness reclaimed him.

But he no longer dreamed of pretty girls or fires. Instead, he watched helplessly as blank-faced, silver-black beings gathered over him like flies, watching him, reaching for him. . . .

CHAPTER FIVE

That night, Jovanna stood alone in her quarters, her feet in Velcro slippers that kept her lightly anchored to the carpet, and touched the personal uplink on her sleeve. Her fear and unhappiness were almost palpable.

The unpleasant surprises had arrowed in almost too quickly for comprehension. First the news that Vince was dead or, worse, a RAM prisoner. Then the discovery that NEO had recruited Black Barney for this operation ... and through him the pirate scum of Captain Stark.

Finally she'd learned that she would be sending RW back into RAM cyberspace once more. And that, she thought with fists clenched and tears forming tiny, glittering spheres that hung before her eyes in Phobos's microgravity, was the most painful news of all.

The news about Vince was bad enough. It wasn't that the two of them had any kind of special relationship, beyond their partnership on the team. But somehow, now that she was alone, she couldn't hold back her tears. Whatever else he might or might not be in her life, he was a friend. If he wasn't dead, he was a prisoner of RAM, and she knew precisely what RAM was capable of.

But now, to find out whether or not he was a prisoner aboard that incoming cruiser, she was going to have to risk RW, a friend who had already faced the horror of RAM captivity and torture.

Once, an eternity ago, RW had been Rachel Wydlin, Jovanna's dearest friend. A young and vivacious woman, Rachel had tried to take on RAM's monolith of terror and injustice alone and lost. She'd been mind-wiped, her thoughts, her memories, her very soul leeched away by RAM's interrogators and her body left an all-but-empty husk. By some sick twist of fate it had been Jovanna, then a programmer working for Rachel's father, who had been chosen to download what was left of her friend's identity into a computer before the flesh-and-blood body that housed it died.

The process had given Rachel life of a sort, even a kind of immortality, though not an entirely satisfactory one. The rape of her mind had caused horrible damage; the digital personality known as "RW" had no memory of herself as Rachel Wydlin, no memory of her father or of her friend, Jovanna. She was a creature of the cybermatrix, that abstract universe representing the combined memories, directories, and programs of every interconnected computer network in the solar system.

She was also, emphatically, still Jovanna's friend. It hurt when others like Galen referred to RW as *it*, as something less than human, as a *tool*. . . .

Jovanna looked about her rather Spartan quarters, her gaze coming to rest at last on the curved wall monitor and console that dominated the room. There was no putting it off. Her orders, her part in Operation Skytower, were explicit.

With a savage determination, Jovanna keyed an access code into the uplink device on her arm, using its input panel to interface with the terminal in her room. There was a flicker in the air next to the console, and Jovanna found herself looking at a much younger version of herself.

"Hi, Jo!" the image said with a cheerful smile. "What's up? As if I didn't know!"

As a self-sustaining program dwelling within the cybermatrix, RW could display a three-dimensional image representing herself anywhere within the range of a computer console equipped with holographic projection lenses . . . and she could tailor that image into any form desired. Twenty-one years before, RW had stopped projecting herself as Rachel because the unconscious traits and expressions and bits of self that had survived in her downloaded personality had distressed those who had known the original Rachel.

RW's choice of Jovanna as the archetype of her public image had been disconcerting at first, making Jovanna wonder how much of herself she'd somehow put into the program that had called her friend back from death. RW's holographic appearance matched her own as it had been all those years ago—hair too short for her rather square face; waist thicker than it was now, giving RW a chunky look; hazel-green eyes that still looked innocent and perhaps a century younger than Jovanna felt at that moment.

"Hello, RW," Jovanna said. She never thought of her friend as Rachel any longer. In twenty-one years—an eternity to an entity whose thoughts moved at the speed of light through the cybermatrix—RW had grown and changed in astonishing ways, developing the speed and power and sheer intellect possible only to entities defined by patterns of electrons within C-space. "We've got a problem."

"So I gathered," RW replied. "I tapped the orders when they came through and decoded them."

Jovanna's jaw dropped. "How did you manage that? Galen's receiver isn't hooked into the matrix!"

RW grinned. "Oh, there are ways. Don't worry, your network's still secure. I'm sorry about Vince. He was a good man. A good friend."

"Don't talk about him as if he's dead!" Jovanna was surprised by the sharpness, the anger of her own words.

RW seemed oblivious to Jovanna's outburst. "The odds against Major Pirelli's survival are on the order of tens of thousands to one, and that one chance was to be rescued by the *Amazonis*. I don't need to remind you of what that would mean."

"No," Jovanna said, her fists clenching until her nails bit flesh. "No, you don't."

"I imagine that Vince himself would count himself lucky to die of anoxia, or explosive decompression, or hypothermia, or—"

"Damn it, I get the picture!" Jovanna struggled for control. Somehow the passing years had stripped the digital personality of more and more of what had once made her human, but that surely wasn't her fault. It helped sometimes to think of RW not as a human friend, but as a sophisticated AI program, a *thing*, despite the pain.

Which, of course, was an attitude Jovanna herself hated.

She took a deep breath. "RW, the problem is we don't know. And if you read our orders, you know there's a lot more to it than just Vince."

"Things are certainly getting interesting," RW said, still cheerful. "However, I should warn you that it may be difficult to search *Amazonis*'s main memory without triggering an alarm."

"I know. There won't be much free space in the ship's memory, and there are sure to be security programs running. Do you think you can pull it off?"

"Hey, this is your old friend RW you're talking to, Jo, remember? I've been haunting the Phobos nodes for weeks now, and they don't even know I'm here!"

Jovanna wished she could feel as confident. "They'll know you're there if you trip some kind of an alarm, RW. I don't care how good you are, the security is going to be damned tight."

"Still shouldn't be a problem, Jo. Even if they spot me, there're *lots* of places to hide in C-space. If things get too tight, I can always transmit myself to Trinity or Earth or someplace else where I'll be safe. Don't *worry!*"

But Jovanna was worried. There was so much about Operation Skytower that could go wrong, so much that still didn't make sense.

Her part of things, as Galen had explained it earlier that evening during their aimless tubecar transits of Phobos's interior, was straightforward enough. NEO Command wanted to know if Vince had been picked up by the *Amazonis*. If he had, NEO had to know, because Vince knew a lot—like the location of NEO's fighter training center at Trinity—that could hurt the organization badly if RAM questioned him. Jovanna was under no illusions about *any* man's chances of holding out for long against RAM's interrogators.

Just as important, in NEO Command's view, was the completion of their original mission. The team had been searching for weeks now, with Sandra and Rolf on Mars and Galen and Jovanna on Phobos, but there still was no clue to where data on RAM's mysterious Project Far Star might be stored.

Whatever Far Star was, it had something to do with Jupiter, since that was where they'd stumbled across the name in the first place. The *Amazonis* had just returned from the Jovian system cloaked in secrecy. It stood to reason that if information on Far Star was anyplace, it should be locked away in *Amazonis*'s computer files. Their only chance to find out what Far Star was all about might well be to probe the RAM cruiser's computer storage.

So her part of the plan was to send RW into the cybermatrix, there to await *Amazonis*'s approach to RAM-Phobos Prime early tomorrow. If things followed normal procedure, *Amazonis* would interface her computer with Phobos Approach Control for final docking. At that moment, RW would feed as much of herself into *Amazonis*'s computer as she could, search for any information on prisoners held aboard, copy any data on Far Star, and depart. Simple.

And dangerous. It was true that the digital personality had spent the last few weeks quietly sneaking through the RAM-Phobos cybermatrix nodes and remained undetected, but breaking into a ship's computer would be a lot harder. The difference was like that between a person trying to slip undetected into a city and the same person trying to sneak into a well-guarded house.

Jovanna knew enough about the cybermatrix to know that this really was an area where she was going to have to defer to the digital personality's skill and knowledge. Still, RW's confidence didn't make her feel any better.

Galen, meanwhile, would maintain contact with the NEO base at Trinity, using a radio hidden on Phobos's surface. Once Jovanna and RW had completed their part of the job, he would send a message to that effect, and then, at NEO's command, broadcast a prearranged code word: "Dagger." A small passenger liner berthed at Phobosport would be waiting to take Galen and Jovanna to safety.

Operation Dagger, meanwhile, would commence after they left, a raid on Phobos involving pirates and a team of NEO commandos.

That was the part that really had Jovanna concerned.

"I'm still worried," she admitted to RW. "Why use pirates at all? NEO has enough trouble with its public image without *them*."

"A thorough perusal of all data available at this time suggests that we do not have access to all pertinent facts."

Jovanna blinked. At times, RW's tone and mannerisms were those of a young, human woman, cheerful, optimistic, and irreverent. At others, the DP slipped into the precise and coldly logical guise of a computer program, often with a jarring abruptness.

"In other words," RW added, "they're not telling us everything."

"I . . . hadn't thought of that."

"What we don't know we can't tell RAM if we are captured and interrogated."

A flicker ran through RW's holographic image at that, and Jovanna wondered if the DP was reacting somehow to the thought. How much did RW remember on some unconscious level of Rachel Wydlin's interrogation at the hands of RAM?

"I calculate a ninety-seven percent or higher probability that NEO is planning some additional operation in conjunction with the pirate raid, something that they have chosen not to reveal to us."

"What do you think it could be?"

"Data insufficient. However, there are numerous possibilities. I estimate a twenty-seven percent possibility of an assassination attempt against one or more RAM officials, including, conceivably, Simund Holzerhein himself. Other possible motives include the capture or destruction of naval vessels docked at RAM-Phobos Prime, the temporary destruction of the Phobos computer network, or the use of Skytower as a diversionary tactic for a raid against RAM assets elsewhere in circum-Mars space."

"Well, I'm sure NEO Command knows what it's doing, RW." Her own words sounded flat and hollow to her.

"And anyway," RW added, dropping back into her cheerful mode, "we won't be here to see it. I'll get what we need from the *Amazonis* tomorrow, then we're out of here. Kaiten and his friends won't hit Phobos until we're aboard the *Komarov* and long gone."

Jovanna nodded. The *Vladimir Komarov* was the independent commercial liner scheduled to dock the following day at Phobosport. Galen had already acquired tickets. Tomorrow afternoon, Phobos time, they would board the *Komarov* separately under false IDs, and by tomorrow night, they would be on their way back to the Belt.

It couldn't be too soon to suit Jovanna.

"I'd better slip back into the matrix," RW said, interrupting her thoughts. "I've got to get some things ready, including positioning our little surprise. I'll wait until I get the word from you to proceed." Her form started to shimmer.

"RW—"

The image solidified again. "Yes?"

"Please be careful."

"Jovanna, I should think my knowledge of C-space considerably exceeds even yours." But RW's smile softened the words. "Besides, you have me backed up on disk somewhere, don't you?"

Jovanna nodded. "Of course." Unlike most humans, digital personalities enjoyed the certainty of immortality, of resurrection, even though individual copies of themselves could be destroyed.

RW twinkled. "Then I'll be back no matter what happens to me!" Then she was gone.

I wonder if we really did Rachel a favor when I downloaded her twenty years ago? Jovanna thought. Sometimes it's as though there's nothing human left at all.

Unsteadily Jovanna made her way to the small bar unit built into one wall of her room and punched in a number. Seconds later, a squeeze bulb, still frosty from refrigeration, popped into the dispenser slot.

She took a sip. Orange juice . . . something the Earth-born Vince had taught her to enjoy. Born and raised on Mars, she'd never known the tart, sweet liquid until he'd introduced it to her years before.

Worry churned inside her as she swallowed, worry for Vince, for RW . . . and for herself. The moral implications of recruiting Black Barney and Captain Stark were disturbing.

"God," she thought. "I can't wait to board the *Komarov* and get out of here."

It was going to be a long night.

O   O   O   O   O

Capt. Joachin Stark swam through the debris-cluttered corridor, pausing once to place one booted foot on a body drifting in midair. Bracing against a handhold on one laser-scorched bulkhead, he gave the corpse a shove, sending it spinning aside. The movement set a galaxy of crimson globules dancing and jittering in the air, some of which splattered against his combat armor as he drifted through them. Smoke hung in dirty clots in the air, and his helmet phones were filled with the urgent chatter of his crew reporting section after section of their target secure.

Stark grinned wolfishly behind the transplex visor of his helmet. Easy pickings. The passenger liner was an old converted transport, completely lacking defenses. When *Dread Reprisal* had matched its course and drawn alongside lock to lock, its captain had elected to surrender without a shot being fired. A hundred of Stark's men had swarmed aboard. When some of the members of the liner's crew had resisted, the killing had begun.

He pushed past another corpse and entered the liner's main passenger lounge. A half-dozen of his men were holding the prisoners there, stripping them of valuables. One space-suited pirate was struggling weightlessly with a young woman as Stark entered, while the others laughed and shouted encouragement.

"You!" Stark bellowed, the volume on his suit's external speakers turned up full. "Get your slimy gauntlets off her!"

The pirate nearly put himself into an awkward, zero-G spin trying to back off from the girl he'd been pawing. "Y-Yessir, Captain Stark, sir!"

"That goes for the rest of you gicks! These girls are valuable property—as of now. I don't want 'em damaged, I don't want 'em *touched* till we have a chance to put 'em on the block! Hear me?"

"Yessir!" several men barked in chorus.

He spared a glance at the captives. One man and seven women, they looked terrified but seemed otherwise unhurt.

A fair haul. There hadn't been much on this rust-bucket of a liner worth snatching, but the prisoners should help him make expenses for the next couple of months. The man and one of the women were RAM executives, according to the ID records they'd been carrying, and their bosses might be persuaded to pay ransom. The rest were the prettiest women aboard, the ship's purser and four of the passengers. There were plenty of places in the Belt or out at the Jovian Trojans where such cargoes brought good prices.

As for the other nineteen of the liner's passengers and crew, they'd already been herded into the aft air lock, their fears quieted by repeated assurances that they were simply being put someplace safe for the time being. Well, hard vacuum was always a safe place to keep cargo you didn't need anymore. A touch of a button and they'd be blasted into space, a problem easily disposed of.

Now all that remained was to tell off a prize crew and have them set course for a suitable port. Davida, maybe . . . or Ardala's Pleasure Planetoid.

"Captain Stark!" A voice over his suit radio interrupted his thoughts. It was Malik, *Reprisal*'s communications officer. "We have incoming radio traffic. Sir . . . it's, it's *him*."

Stark scowled. He knew well enough who *him* must be. "Pipe it across to the viewscreen down here in the lounge," he said. Gesturing at the prisoners, he added, "Vreech, get 'em out of here. Stow 'em aft."

As the pirates shepherded the straggling, sobbing captives out of the lounge, Stark floated toward the viewscreen. A green light winked, indicating that Malik had patched the call through to the captured liner.

He touched a key on the console. A face—a hard, square face that might have been chiseled from duralloy instead of flesh—materialized on the screen, five times larger than life. "Stark!" The voice, a rumbling bass, needed no amplification. "What in the black hell of Jove's core do you think you're doing? I gave you your orders! You're supposed to be on your way to Mars!"

"We *are* on our way, Barney," Stark said, smoothly, he thought. He managed a smile. "Actually, we picked up this transport en route and thought we'd add her to our collection. Didn't take us out of our way at all."

For several seconds, the face of Black Barney glowered at him, unmoving. "Think?" the pirate leader bellowed suddenly. "*Think?* Who gave you orders to *think?* You know how critical the timing is on this operation, and you jeopardized it all for some fun and games! Didn't you get Kaiten's message?"

"I got it." To tell the truth, Stark hadn't been that impressed by his second-in-command's report. He didn't have half the confidence in Barney's plan that Kaiten did, and he had none of the Terrine's hatred of RAM. He thought about his two executive hostages. Hell, RAM could be as good a customer as anyone else in the solar system.

"I don't understand you, Stark," Barney growled. "This Phobos operation is going to make us rich, Kaiten and the NEO people are already in place, and you sit there on your tail playing with scrap iron and trinkets!"

Stark glowered as Barney continued to chew him out. The time lag, he guessed, was about five seconds, which meant that Barney and the *Free Enterprise* were nearly half a million miles away. How the hell had he been able to spot *Reprisal*'s attack on the liner?

"Listen, Barney," Stark said when the glowering face on the screen paused for breath. "You might be Mister Big in the Guild, but you don't dictate to us like we was your crew. We're our own bosses, and all you can do is advise, right?"

Defiantly he waited out the seconds for his words to make the trip and for Barney's reply to return.

When Barney spoke again his words were surprisingly soft. "You're right, Captain Stark. Of course you are. I wouldn't dream of interfering with the exe-

cution of your business." Suddenly that steel-hard
face darkened like an acid-storm cloud over the Venusian lowlands, the veins on the neck standing out
like stress strut mountings on the *Reprisal's* main
drive. "But if you gumping slimers miss rendezvous
on this one, I'll see to it that no one in the Belt or the
Trojans or anywhere in the whole gumping system
ever does business with you again! I'll pass the word
that you're blackballed and hand your ship to Kaiten
on a platter! Get me?"

Carefully Stark swallowed his pride. "I get you,
sir."

The reply came five seconds later. "Good. Now, I
advise you to drop what you're doing and shape orbit
for Mars. I want to see your drive flares in ten minutes, or I cut you out of the deal. Now, move!"

"Yes, sir." He ground his teeth together. "We're on
our way."

The transmission was already cut, switched off
from Barney's end. Damn, damn, *damn!* Black Barney was getting entirely too impressed with himself,
that was dead certain. Someone was going to have to
trim that big loud gennie down to size, and soon.

But after Mars. Barney had been right about one
thing. This contract he'd put together at Mars promised to make all of them rich, and Stark wanted a
piece of it. He opened his suit's comm channel and
began transmitting orders to his crew.

They would have to leave the prize, of course.
There was no time to organize a crew or reprogram
the nav computer. They'd smash the radio and leave
her adrift; a purser and six passengers wouldn't be
able to get her into port, and the *Reprisal* ought to be
able to snag them again after this mysterious contract of Barney's was complete. Stark wasn't about
to let any profit slip through his fingers, no matter
how much the Mars operation netted them!

A satchel of jewelry, personal computers, credit disks, and smart clothing taken from the prisoners floated in the lounge. He grabbed it and headed for the main lock.

O O O O O

Long minutes later, in one of the liner's cargo lockers, the captives huddled together as a deep-throated clang reverberated through the ship. The purser reassured the others that the sound had been that of the magnetic grapples being released. The pirate had just cast off. More minutes passed in silence as they waited for the acceleration that meant the pirates had put a prize crew aboard and were changing course, or for the first explosions when the raider began blasting the evidence out of existence.

But the silence continued, the minutes dragging out into hours. It took some time with a screwdriver, but the ship's purser was able at last to pry open an access panel and short out the door's locking circuits. The others stayed behind as she slipped out into the silent, body-strewn passageways.

The pirates were gone, at least for now. All radios and emergency beacons aboard had been smashed, and the controls were disabled. They'd been left a derelict ship, probably so that the pirates could calculate their drift later and retrieve them.

The purser bit back a savage and uncharacteristic obscenity. She was the only member of the liner's crew left alive, the only one who knew that the ship was secretly owned by NEO. They were supposed to dock at Phobos tomorrow, where they were to take part in a secret NEO operation.

But the *Vladimir Komarov* wasn't going to make that rendezvous, and with no radio and no controls there wasn't a damned thing she could do about it.

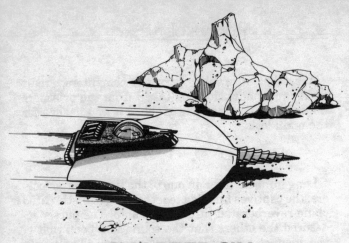

CHAPTER SIX

Consciousness had been a touch-and-go proposition for Vince for some time, with vague memories of mingled dreams and delirium and waking experiences that were as confused as nightmares. He seemed to remember some kind of face, horribly blank and insectlike, peering at him through the Starfire's transplex canopy. . . .

Memory—and awareness—returned with the force of a heavy cruiser at full thrust. That had been no dream, even if he was still having trouble making sense of what he'd seen.

He opened his eyes, then shut them tightly again against the radiance that bathed him from glow panels overhead. Overhead? That wasn't quite right. He was aware of the bottomless, endless-fall feeling of zero gravity, so concepts like "up," "down," and "overhead" had no meaning. Still, what he was looking at appeared to be a thickly padded ceiling inset with bright white glow panels. Looking around, he saw the walls, also padded and looking much like the interior of a free-fall hospital room.

The contraption he was in added to the resemblance. It was a capsule, a stainless steel pod anchored to the deck that left only his head free. Vince had seen photos from the late Middle Ages of the iron lungs once used to treat victims of polio and other diseases, and this was similar, like a modern automed unit but bulkier and more primitive.

He couldn't feel his body.

"Ah!" a man's voice said from somewhere beyond his line of sight. "*Nos pasien'd mistera es dispert. Inten me?*"

Vince tried to turn his head to see the speaker, but his movement was restricted by the pod. Instead, a man swam into view, weightless, interposing himself between Vince's head and the lighting panels. He wore rather severe-looking gray coveralls and a bushy black mustache that made his pale skin seem almost white.

"I'm sorry," Vince said, blinking. "I can't understand you. Anybody here speak System Anglic?"

"I do," a woman's voice said from somewhere. "He said, 'Our mystery patient is awake,' and asked if you understood. How do you feel?"

She spoke with a soft accent that Vince could not place. "Uh . . . pretty good . . . I think. I, uh, can't feel much of anything below my neck."

The woman drifted into Vince's line of sight, catching herself on a handhold mounted atop the pod. Seeing humans was reassuring. For a moment, Vince had wondered if his rescuers were the alien-looking creatures he'd seen earlier.

Pushing the chill of that memory aside, he studied the woman. She was dark-eyed and pretty, with skin even paler than the man's, as white as ivory. Her black hair was quite short, and she wore a sleeveless bright green garment that was too bulky to show off what Vince was certain was a lovely figure. Her smile was professionally reassuring. "Electronic anesthesia," she explained. "You were in pretty bad shape when they brought you in. Severe frostbite . . . hypothermia. You almost lost your fingers and toes."

Fear stirred within him. Frozen fingers were no problem at all for a well-equipped medical facility like the one on Trinity, but the level of medical technology varied widely across the solar system. But she had said "almost." Maybe . . .

"Don't worry," the woman said, reacting to what she must have seen in his eyes. "All your parts are still there. You've been in the rejuv pod for ten hours. If you feel a bit weak, that's normal. Full healing—getting your muscle tone back—will take some time, but I'd guess that we can take you out of the pod anytime now."

The man whispered something to her, his voice too low to hear, and then he touched some controls hidden from Vince by the curve of the pod. Vince heard a click and felt a kind of electric thrill, almost a tickle, starting at the base of his skull and spreading outward from there. Arms . . . fingers . . . legs . . . feet. Once again he could *feel* them. The medical technology in this place might be primitive by Inner System standards, but it worked.

"We've cut the anesthesia. Any pain?" she asked.

"No. I can feel my hands and feet again."

"Good. Hungry?"

Tentatively his tongue explored the inside of his mouth. "Very thirsty." And, now that she mentioned it . . . "Yeah, and hungry, too."

"We'll see about getting you something to eat. And your clothes. We'll have you out of there in no time."

She spoke again, this time addressing the man with the mustache in a blur of words that seemed to lie just beyond Vince's understanding. The language sounded like Spanish, but distorted, as though it had changed with time and distance.

The man grunted something that might have been an affirmative and propelled himself across the room, out of Vince's line of sight.

"What's that language you're speaking?" he asked.

"Espen," the woman replied, turning back to face him. "I'm afraid only a few of us speak System Anglic, but I will serve as your interpreter for . . . for as long as you need one."

"Uh, where am I, anyway?" Vince asked. He'd never heard of Espen, though the word sounded as if it might be related to *Español*—Spanish. The microgravity suggested he was in an asteroid, probably a pretty small one, or aboard a large ship in free-fall. "Who are you people? The last I remember . . ." He stopped, and shuddered. His last memory had been of that *face*.

"That was Dr. Gomis," she said. "Head of our city medical services. I am Senita Varga. We were wondering much the same about you. There was no identification aboard your ship or in your pressure suit."

"Yeah, but who found me? I remember these black and silver humanoids, with big eyes—"

She laughed. "You must mean our Vacs. They grappled your spacecraft and towed it in."

"Vacs?"

"Vacumorphs. You know them as Spacers."

Of course. Among all gene-engineered species, Spacers were perhaps the strangest, the most alien in metabolism and thought from their human creators. Designed to exist in total vacuum, they were cyborgs, intricate blendings of life and machine. Their silvery outer skin was actually a layer of metal alloys a few molecules thick, usually highly reflective but designed to turn to energy-drinking black at will. Most of the Spacers' energy came directly from sunlight absorbed through their skin.

"Spacers," Vince said, relieved. "I should have known. I kind of lost it for a minute out there. . . ."

"Understandable," the woman said. "You were in bad shape by the time they got you here. I doubt that you were thinking straight."

"Yeah." He looked around, as much as he was able to. "So, where is 'here'?"

She pursed her lips, regarding him with a mixture of open curiosity and wry humor. "I'd say it's your turn to supply us with some information," she said. "Your pressure suit had a tag reading 'Pirelli, V.,' for instance. Your name?"

"That's right. You can call me Vince."

"Okay, Vince. Where are you from?"

He hesitated before answering. There were thousands of human communities in the Belt, colonies and outposts and cities and worldlet communities popularly lumped together under the term Belter Anarchy, but that name suggested a measure of unity that simply did not exist. Many Belter worlds were openly allied with RAM; others were themselves RAM military or commercial outposts. Others supported NEO or were, like Trinity, secret NEO bases. Some dealt openly with both sides, especially the pirate dens like Metis and Nysa, while the majority wanted only to be left alone.

Best to be cautious until he knew more, he thought.

"Uh . . . your name is what?" he asked, sidestepping the question. "Senita?"

"Actually, that is my bonding status."

"Oh. And that is? . . ."

"Unbonded."

"That's nice. What's your name? I mean your full name. I'd like to be able to call you something other than 'Unbonded Varga.' "

She arched one eyebrow. "My proper name would

take you a while to memorize. All of us have short names, though. Mine is Katarine."

"Katarine. That will do nicely." He tried his most winning smile, but it was difficult to employ it to best effect while he was immobile inside the steel capsule.

"You still haven't answered my question, Vince. Where are you from?"

"Uh . . . the Belt," he said, truthfully enough, if incompletely. Then he added a lie. "From Davida."

Davida was a large asteroid circling the outer fringes of the Belt. Its independence from system political intrigue was well known. A number of prominent mercenaries had their headquarters there . . . and Freeport, the principal city, was an important crossroads for much of the pirated merchandise in the Belt. Davida had the reputation for dealing openly with both sides in the RAM-NEO struggle.

It was also in the same general Belt sector as Trinity—not close, but not impossibly distant, either. He was probably safe in claiming Davida as his place of origin no matter which side these people were on.

"I see," she said. "We've traded with them in the past, I think. A mercenary, then? Or a pirate?"

"Mercenary," he decided. "It was pirates who jumped me."

He couldn't tell whether Katarine believed him or not, but at least she didn't challenge his lies. She seemed to be working at the unseen control panel.

"All of your bodily functions appear to be normal," she said after several seconds.

"Are you a doctor?"

"No, though I've had some medical training. Actually, I am a receiver. I've been chosen for you."

Vince had no idea what a receiver might be in that context. Something like a professional greeter?

He heard a hissing sound, and a sensation of pres-

sure rippled over his body. Then one side of the rejuv
pod split open, sliding back on hinges like a massive
coffin lid. Cool air bathed his bare skin, and he was
free.

Vince lay still as Katarine examined his body with
a clinical directness that embarrassed him. Though
dress and customs varied tremendously from world
to world and from culture to culture, most Earth humans retained an age-old nudity taboo, at least in
the presence of strangers. He salvaged his pride by
thinking of her as a doctor even if she wasn't. He concentrated on a featureless spot on the blank white
ceiling, gently testing the limits of his weakness.

Dr. Gomis and another man appeared while he was
still trying to maneuver himself into a sitting position, entering the room through a curious circular
door set in one wall. The new man, a big guy with a
military look about him despite his nondescript coveralls, handed Vince a plastic drinking bulb that
contained a thick, hot liquid. The taste was unpleasantly sour, but he found himself gulping the stuff
down as the sensation of warmth spread through his
body, leaving him comfortably full.

Curious, he hung the empty bulb in the air and
watched it for a moment. The experiment convinced
him that there was gravity, but very, very little, a
few thousandths of a G, perhaps. That suggested
that he was in an asteroid.

He was still painfully weak. In anything like a decent planetary gravity field, he knew, he wouldn't
have been able to stand up. He was also, he realized,
clean . . . cleaner than he should have been after days
in a space suit. Someone must have bathed and
shaved him before he'd been awakened in his pod.

Clothing was provided in a sealed plastic bag, a
one-piece garment like those worn by Katarine and
the men except that it had neither sleeves nor long

legs and was colored bright orange. The texture was unusual, soft and very light. When he asked about it, Katarine told him that all clothing here was a gift of Arbel, which told him exactly nothing.

With some help, he wrestled himself into the garment and fastened the Velcro seals. There were no shoes. Neither Katarine nor the men wore shoes, he noticed, and all three seemed to be remarkably dexterous with their feet, snagging holds with their toes as often as with their fingers, and once Dr. Gomis retrieved a stylus from the air with his right foot.

Fed and dressed, he felt considerably better, both physically and psychologically. He told them so.

"Excellent," Katarine said. "I'm told they're waiting for you in the Grand Audience Hall."

" 'They'? Who's 'they'?"

Katarine exchanged glances with the two men, who remained mute and impassive. He wondered if they really didn't understand System Anglic. Just how remote was this place, anyway?

" 'They,' " Katarine said carefully, "are the council and His Excellency the Efay. The rulers of this city."

An audience? The way she said it made Vince think that there was more to it than diplomatic courtesy. He looked down at his bare legs and arms uncertainly. He certainly didn't want to meet important people dressed like *this*.

"You will be presented to them," Katarine continued, "and also you will face the *pelepovida*."

"Whoa," he said. The way she'd said that worried him. "Hang on. What's this '*pelepovo*' thing?"

"It is our way," Katarine said slowly.

"I don't understand."

She spread her hands. "Our custom. You must understand, Vince, that we have so little contact with outsiders that it is necessary to clothe our meetings with them in a certain amount of formal ceremony."

"Yeah, but I don't know what—"

"Everything will be fine," she said. "You are quite strong. An *excellent* prospect."

He didn't *feel* strong. And what was that remark about his being 'an excellent prospect'?

Ever since he'd awakened he'd been aware of subtle differences in the local culture, differences hinted at by the language, by the out-of-date technology, even by Katarine's mention of her long and difficult name. He had the strong impression that these people were members of a culture distinct from those of Earth, Mars, or the majority of the Belt.

The fact that Katarine spoke flawless Anglic meant nothing. If Vince had learned anything in his years of voyaging among the worlds of the solar system, it was that even subtle differences between cultures could cause major misunderstandings.

"This . . . *pelevo*—"

"*Pelepovida*."

"Yeah. It's some kind of test?"

"Exactly! You're very quick."

Vince nodded. He was imagining some sort of symbolic ritual, an exercise of skill or strength to demonstrate that he was worthy to talk to the city's rulers. It all sounded rather primitive, but he'd heard of cultures, especially among the more isolated of the Belter worlds, that clung to such I'm-as-good-as-you-are shows. This, he thought, must be one of those worlds.

"Maybe you'd better tell me a bit more," he said. "You know, I still don't have the faintest idea where I am. Which asteroid is this, anyway?"

Katarine laughed. "A natural enough mistake," she said. She turned to the men and translated his question.

They laughed, and Vince frowned. Okay. So this wasn't an asteroid. A ship, then, but it would have to be a fairly large one, a liner like the *Magnificus Tri-*

planetary, say.

No, that still didn't make sense. The Spanish-sounding language these people shared, the symbolic ritual . . . all of that suggested an entire culture, not a shipload of passengers traveling from one world to another.

Katarine took his hand with a directness that seemed out of place with a stranger . . . another indication of the differing social customs and mores here. "Come, Vince Pirelli. Come and see our world!"

Reluctantly he let her guide him from the room and into a padded corridor outside. There were guards there, he saw, lanky, helmeted men in red and white coveralls who carried wicked-looking pole-arms that combined the sharpest parts of spears, axes, and sabers. Guards . . . for him?

Apparently so. Dr. Gomis remained behind, but the bearded man snapped an order, and the two soldiers followed.

This didn't seem to be the time to question his own status, however, and whatever it looked like to him, the soldiers could as easily be an honor escort as guards. Vince doubted that was the case, however.

He bumped along beside the woman, his arms and legs still clumsy and a bit weak. Katarine did most of the work, hauling him along almost effortlessly in the microgravity as the bearded man and the soldiers brought up the rear. The corridor passed several circular doorways resembling hatches on a ship, took a sharp turn, and opened . . .

. . . onto wonder.

Vince caught his breath. He was staring into an enormous enclosed space. Like a sports amphitheater on Earth or Mars, two bowls pressed rim to rim, the structure was a flattened sphere over half a mile across. Most of its walls were transparent, giving an uninterrupted view out into the velvet blackness of deep space, but the design had a haphazard look to it, with beams, struts, and panels of metal or colored plastic interspersed almost at random with transplex in a patchwork of clear and opaque materials. The sphere appeared to be embedded within a tangled webwork of what looked like leafless branches, slender twistings visible through the transparent sections. Outside, other structures rested among the branches, not easily identifiable from this angle, but evidence of an enormous complex of habitats and free-fall engineering.

His attention was drawn at once, however, to the dark-colored mass that dominated the center of the open room like a single, huge pillar, a gigantic column that reminded Vince of nothing so much as the trunk of an enormous tree.

On all of Earth, only the long-extinct California redwood could have approached that growth for sheer mass and girth. Only a tiny fraction of its entire length was enclosed within the flattened sphere of the amphitheater. At least a hundred feet thick, it grew right through the center of the structure, like the axle of a wheel, connected to the flattened sphere's equator by slender spokes.

His mind struggled for comparisons, searching for familiarity in the midst of strangeness. Take two very large trees. Join them together, roots to roots, and enclose the joining in a half-mile-wide bubble, itself surrounded by a webwork of interlaced roots holding the structure in place. Then set the whole structure spinning, very slowly, in space.

That, Vince thought, best described what he was seeing. The trees were turning—he could just make out the slow drift of the stars in the background—which explained the microgravity. Here, at the hub, the rotation created an almost nonexistent microgravity; out at either end of those towering trunks, miles in length, the spin gravity would be substantial, as much, he estimated, as half a G.

With an effort, Vince dragged his attention back within the confines of the sphere, which he now realized was a small city filled with people, hundreds of them, drifting or swimming in micro-G. Those nearest to where he and Katarine and the soldiers had emerged from the wall of the dome were watching him with frank and open curiosity, and Vince found himself staring back. Most, he saw, were humans, though a few of the small, slender, silver-coated gennies called Spacers were present as well. It was unusual, he knew, for Spacers to live with humans, so different were their needs and their minds. He wondered if these were just visiting the city, or if they had some closer, more permanent, tie.

Clothing within the city ran the gamut from outrageously colored jumpsuits to complete undress. Most wore simple, practical designs with no loose ends, nothing to snag or tangle in micro-G. The air within the sphere was almost tropically warm and moist, and many had dispensed with clothing entirely. As Vince had already discovered, their modesty taboos were different from his own.

"The Core Sphere," Katarine said, indicating the vast enclosed space with evident pride. "Once two gene-engineered trees embraced a carbonaceous asteroid here, incorporating it as raw material for very rapid growth. Eventually the two met and were made to grow together, end to end. The sphere is braced by the root network outside."

"That dome looks . . . fragile."

"It's two layers of transplex with a clear liquid sealer between them. If there's a breach, air hardens the liquid and plugs the hole. Occasionally we replace sections with other materials. That's why the mix of transparent and opaque. So, what do you think of our city?"

"It's . . . impressive," he managed to reply.

"Everyone has turned out to see you," she said. "We have very little contact with . . . others. Our city is called Ciudestreya. In Anglic, that would be 'the City of the Stars.'"

He looked at her, realization dawning. He thought he knew now who these people were. "And you? What do you call yourselves?"

"*Vagos*," she said. "Travelers. But most in the Inner System call us Nomads."

"Nomads." His earlier weakness threatened to reclaim him, and he tightened his grip on a handhold at the side of the passageway. *Nomads*. He knew the name, if only through rumor.

"Really, Vince," Katarine said, coming closer. "We are not the monsters you Inner Worlders always seem to think we are. . . ."

But Vince wasn't so sure. He couldn't help drawing back from her a little. He felt . . . *contaminated*, just by her presence, and he was uncomfortably aware of the two . . . no, three guards floating behind him in the passageway only a few feet away.

He thought about escape but dismissed the idea almost at once. Which way would he go? He didn't have the faintest idea which way the city's docking facilities might be. With his fighter destroyed, he'd have to find a ship and steal it.

The bearded man said something to Katarine, a burst of rapid, liquid words. He gestured impatiently toward the tree.

"He says that we must hurry," Katarine said. "They are waiting to meet you. To judge."

She took his hand again, and Vince felt his skin crawl unpleasantly at her touch. His mind raced. If half of what he'd heard about the Nomads was true, he was in very serious trouble indeed.

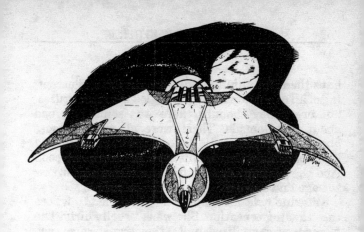

CHAPTER SEVEN

Vince clung to the opening in one dome wall overlooking the vast interior of the core and tried to come to grips with his own jumbled thoughts and preconceptions. He could see that he was going to have to do some rethinking about attitudes, about prejudices that he'd never even known he possessed.

The Nomad clans were usually considered part of the Belter Anarchy, but that was an oversimplification. No one knew how many Nomad cities there were in all, but there were at least eight or ten major deep-space communities that regularly passed through the Inner System, and others that remained forever in the frozen wastes far beyond the Belt. They owed allegiance to none but themselves, tight-knit, clannish, and suspicious of outsiders. The stories told about them throughout the Inner System painted them as unscrupulous, even piratical, with moral and sexual standards quite different from those of other people.

Vince had heard his share of unsavory stories about the Nomads. Belters, he thought, were perhaps the most uninhibitedly democratic and accepting of all of the hundreds of mingled human cultures, but even they thought there was something odd about the Nomads. There were all those rumors about incest and genetic deficiencies, of mutants and kidnappings in order to invigorate the genetic pool. And the stories about what they did with their raw sewage and dead bodies. . . .

Katarine held his hand and Vince tried to ignore the crawling sensation. She wasn't really dirty. The Nomads were civilized, and if they transformed sewage into food and water and air, wasn't that the same thing that had been happening on Earth for hundreds of millions of years?

Well, wasn't it? Forcibly confronting his own cultural bias wasn't pleasant. Hell, he hadn't even thought about Nomads for years, and then only in the context of an obscene joke or two he'd heard in bars.

If he was going to get along with these people, he would have to lose those prejudices, and damned fast. He still didn't know what this *pelepovida* ritual was all about. If he said or did the wrong thing, he might never get out of this place.

Katarine seemed to think his hesitation was because of the gulf they now had to cross. "There's nothing to it," she said. "Just jump with me, and do what I do."

"Jump? Where?"

She pointed, indicating the trunk of the central pillar a quarter of a mile away.

"My God," he said, his eyes widening. "Is that thing really alive?"

She nodded. "Of course. We call her Arbel. I suppose the name means 'tree' in Anglic, but she is far more than that . . . to us."

Vince heard the respect in her voice, a sense of almost religious awe. He recognized the Spanish origins of the name Arbel, though the Spanish *Drbol* had a rounder sound and was accented on the first syllable instead of the second. It was clearly a *name*, not mere identification.

And . . . had Katarine called that thing "she?"

He felt her tense her legs, and then she leaped, hard, dragging him into space at her side.

They sailed through the air, and the swarm of people gathered in front of them parted as if by unspoken command. For a moment, Vince felt a clutch of vertigo. He steadied himself by concentrating on the enormous pillar growing ahead, orienting himself to it.

As his eyes followed its shape, it struck him that the brown-gray pillar did indeed look as if two trees had grown together, their roots and trunks merging while their crowns stretched miles away in opposite directions. Looking through the dome transparencies, he could just make out the masses of foliage trailing at each end, black, cottony masses distinguishable from the black of space only by the occasional flash of a reflection from the distant sun.

Obviously the Tree was a genetically engineered organism. Ever since the twentieth century, men had dreamed of creating a life-form such as this, a bioengineered organism that could take root in the ice and carbonaceous compounds of a comet nucleus or asteroid, harness sunlight for energy, and create a viable habitat for man. With terraforming on a planetary scale common, the idea of orbiting gennied sequoias had been forgotten.

Someone had realized the dream, though. The reality, the enormity of the organism, was staggering. It took him several moments as he sailed through space at Katarine's side before he noticed other aspects of the architecture of cradle and core and the massive, anchoring beam of that titanic Tree.

It *was* a city; there was no other word for so complex an engineering feat. Like the building materials of the core dome, it had a haphazard look about it, as though it had been built over a period of many years from odd bits and pieces bought, scavenged, or stolen from a dozen worlds and attached at various points to the trunk of the Tree and to each other. He saw a number of cylindrical "bottles," self-contained space habitats manufactured in Hygeia and a few other Belt manufacturing centers. These were linked together in clusters outside the dome, interconnected by a spaghetti tangle of pressurized tubeways, access tunnels, and even the occasional torpedo shape of a scavenged spacecraft. Vince saw the blunt, finned outline of a large freighter of some kind. At first he thought the ship was docked with the Tree, but the longer he looked, the more he realized that the tubeways and support struts had so encompassed the ship that it was now a permanent part of the city.

More and more of his view was blocked by the mass of the tree that loomed ahead like a vast, rugged wall. Dozens of Ciudestreya's inhabitants watched, staring with expressions ranging from gawking curiosity to dark suspicion, as he and Katarine fell toward the Tree.

Then they were at the trunk. Katarine hit first with a boneless slump, grabbing for the shaggy texture of the bark, which stopped her forward momentum without sending her rebounding back into the open air. Vince landed an instant after she did but far less gracefully. Their three escorts followed, arresting their flight with practiced ease. Though Vince had trained long and hard in zero-G, it was clear that the inhabitants of Ciudestreya were far better adapted to microgravity than he.

"Welcome to Arbel," Katarine said, smiling. She twisted in midair and began pulling herself across the trunk.

He followed, somewhat more cautiously. The matted, thick-tufted bark was easy to cling to. Movement was a simple matter of pulling along hand-over-hand. Katarine led him toward an opening in the Tree, one of several dozen entrances he could see. Each was an irregular gap at least six feet across and appeared to mark the incomplete joining of two ancestral trees. From the number of people continually entering or leaving these openings, they appeared to be part of an extensive transport system tunneling through the wood in all directions. Elsewhere, Vince saw windows cut into the side of the Tree, rectangular openings covered over by transplex or glass.

"You *live* inside this thing?" he asked Katarine. The image the tunnels called to mind was of beetles or other small, burrowing creatures. The analogy was appropriate, he realized, when he considered the size of a human compared to the monstrous growth. Just that part of the Tree enclosed within the crystalline sphere of the core was larger than most buildings he'd seen, a kind of organic counterpart to the arcologies of Earth.

"The bark in this part of the Tree is over thirty feet thick," Katarine explained. "It has to be, to conserve heat and withstand the vacuum of space. We've hollowed out enormous chambers and tunnels beneath the surface. It's all part of Arbel's bounty."

"Yeah, right."

She dove headfirst into the opening and he followed. Within the tunnel, the smell of the Tree was overwhelming, mingling pine and the scent of fresh sawdust remembered from his childhood on a farm in the American Midwest. The tunnel twisted through the bark, illuminated along the way by glow panels embedded in the wood, as though they somehow drew power from the substance of the Tree itself. Traffic along the passageway went both ways, with frequent branchings and cross corridors turning the system into a vast and labyrinthine maze. Small, illuminated signs with cryptic jumbles of letters and numerals appeared to provide the inhabitants with some sort of guidance, but after three turnings, Vince was hopelessly lost.

They arrived at last at a vast chamber carved from the solid wood, a place that Vince guessed must be the Grand Audience Hall. More red-and-white-uniformed guards floated on either side of the door, their feet hooked to restraints on the wall, the archaic-looking blade weapons gleaming in their hands. Attached to their belts were coils, like bull-whips, but not made of leather.

Perhaps a hundred people floated within the chamber with more arriving every moment, their conversation a low-voiced murmur that filled the place like the odor of fresh wood. Again Vince saw a diversity of fashion and adornment running from nudity to elaborate decadence.

One side of the room was dominated by what looked like a throne, raised behind a dozen seats and a long table of polished mahogany. Seats being unnecessary in microgravity, it was clear that throne, chairs, and table all were there more for the aura of power they projected than for comfort.

Light flooded the chamber from a many-faceted hemisphere fastened to what Vince decided was the room's ceiling. The ceiling, the opaque walls, and the floor of the cavernous room were *growing*, though it took a moment for Vince to comprehend what he was looking at. Through some piece of gene-splicing trickery, the walls had been induced to grow branch-es, providing hand-and footholds ranging from the size of his finger to as long and as thick as his arm.

There were leaves on the branches, each a polyhedral strip of something resembling obsidian, but flexible and soft, a glassy plastic-feeling substance so black that it seemed to drink every bit of light that fell upon it.

Katarine noticed his examination of one of the leaves. "On Earth, leaves convert sunlight to sugar," she said, anchoring her bare feet on a convenient branch. "The genetic engineers who designed Arbel found a way to turn sunlight—*any* radiant energy, actually—directly into electricity. Arbel provides us with all our energy needs . . . as well as food, water, oxygen—"

"Water?"

"As a waste product. We give Arbel organic matter, which it converts into its own substance. What's left over we tap for our own use. Food, water, clothing, chemicals for various industrial processes." She gestured. "These very walls give off oxygen and nitrogen in the appropriate quantities. Arbel even provides us with warmth. Its core radiates heat at a constant—"

"Right, right," Vince interrupted, fighting an impulse to gag. Remembering the stories he'd heard about Nomads, he suddenly decided that he really didn't want to hear how their city's ecology worked. A spacefaring community as small as this one couldn't afford to waste any organic resources. The city dwellers own waste products, the bodies of their dead, all would have to be recycled.

Vince was used to the idea of recycled wastes from the environmental systems of spacecraft and asteroid colonies, but those were machines. Having a gigantic plant transform sewage into food, water, and the air he was breathing seemed unclean . . . even though a similar cycle had served every living creature on Earth for hundreds of millions of years.

On an open planet, it was possible to ignore where, say, an apple really came from. Here, it was impossible. He thought about that sour-tasting liquid now resting uneasily in his stomach and stifled another retching gag.

"Are you well?" Katarine wanted to know.

"I'm . . . fine. Fine. Give me a moment."

"The Efay is coming!"

"The who?"

"You will tell your story to him. He will question you. Then comes the test of the *pelepovida.*"

"Listen, I still feel pretty weak," he said.

"You will have to do your best," she said, her dark eyes staring hard into his. "I am sorry that you couldn't be more fully prepared, but Ciudestreya faces a dangerous threat. Your status here must be settled quickly, before more outsiders come."

"My . . . status?" Why didn't he like the way that sounded?

She sighed. "Either you will be accepted as one of us—" She looked away without finishing the sentence. There was a stir at the far end of the chamber, where men and women in gaudily colored jumpsuits were emerging from hatchways set behind the raised throne. Men, most of them elderly, took their places behind the table. Someone was speaking loudly in the Ciudestreyan language.

"Yeah? I'll be accepted or what?"

"Or you will feed Arbel," she declared simply.

"Feed . . . ." He stopped, swallowing hard.

"It is time, Vince. Be honest before the Efay. Answer his questions directly and be strong in your challenge!"

"Now, wait just a damn minute!" His shout turned a number of heads nearby, and he could hear the murmur rising, harsh with disapproval. "I'm not going to challenge anyone!"

"*Sieno*, Vince. You have no choice. It is our way."

"Well, it's not mine!" Hands closed on his upper arms from behind him. He struggled in the grasp of the two soldiers who had followed them across from the medunit, but their grip was like iron. "I didn't ask for this!"

"But you are *here*, Vince. And it is our ways that must govern." She raised one slender hand, as though in benediction. "May Arbel prosper you!"

With military precision, his captors launched themselves from the wall before he could respond, dragging Vince between them. Sailing across the audience hall, they landed on the surface Vince had decided to call the floor, snagging branches with their bare feet to arrest their flight immediately in front of the long table.

From between the guards, Vince looked past the elderly men behind the table and into the eyes of the Efay himself. He was a small man, bald and obscenely fat. He wore nothing but a kind of diaper over his loins, and the seatbelt that secured him to his throne was nearly lost in rolls of blubber.

At his feet, the twelve older men stared back at Vince with unnerving silence. They wore baggy, dark brown garments like formal robes. These, Vince decided, must be the members of the council Katarine had mentioned. All of them, councillors and Efay, regarded Vince with all the enthusiasm of scientists examining a new and somewhat repellent species of parasitic worm.

Vince couldn't guess what the protocol for greeting the Efay was. Besides, his position appeared to have shifted in the past few minutes from rescued spacefarer to prisoner. He floated between the two soldiers, anchored still by their grip on his arms.

The Efay stirred on his throne. "*Ulah*," he said.

The voice was gratingly unpleasant, high-pitched and nasal. *"Binveda a Ciudestreya."*

"His Supreme Excellency the Efay greets you and welcomes you to our city," Katarine's voice said at his back. He hadn't realized that she had followed him across the room. So she was to be his translator. Good. He'd wondered how he was going to manage in this one-sided conversation.

"Pelemeyor!" The Efay grinned, a malevolent grimace. *"Espro kay t morisbin, Forano. Gusto n bin mort!"*

There was a burst of laughter and applause from the audience, though the soldiers and the councillors remained impassive.

"His . . . his Supreme Excellency says that he hopes you die well," Katarine translated. Her voice sounded subdued now, almost broken. "He . . . he says he likes a good death."

"Well," Vince said, finding his voice, "I'll see if I can oblige him."

He still didn't know what it meant, but the word *pelepovida* had suddenly assumed a rather more sinister feel than it had possessed before.

CHAPTER EIGHT

There was a sharp Espen command from one of the councillors, and the crowd in the Grand Audience Hall parted, leaving Vince alone with Katarine and the two soldiers. "I don't understand," Vince said, pitching his voice so only Katarine could hear. "What's wrong?"

The woman was visibly shaken. "I had hoped . . ."

"Blast it, pull yourself together, Katarine! I'm the one on trial here, not you."

"It's . . . you're not on trial, Vince. It's more than that. I'd hoped you would face the *pelemenor*, the Little Challenge. The Efay was supposed to question you, maybe ask you to engage in a test of strength with his champion. It's what we use in most of our contacts with outsiders. But it looks as if he's already decided on the Great Challenge, the *pelemeyor*."

He scowled. "You're talking about a fight to the death, right?"

"*Pelepovida*," Katarine said. "You must understand that we do not think of it as a fight to the death. It is a fight for *life*."

"I'm not entirely sure I see the distinction. Okay, I

fight someone. If I win, I get to live. Is that it?"

"You live . . . and you win me. If you lose, you feed Arbel, and I belong to the winner."

He looked at her sharply. "What kind of barbaric—"

"Vince, please!" She looked frightened. His voice had gotten louder. His guards and several of the councillors were staring at the two of them with undisguised displeasure. "It is our way!"

One of the councillors snapped something in Espen. Across the hall, a figure detached itself from the wall and drifted toward them as the crowd exploded with shouts and fresh applause. "Him?" Vince asked. "Are you saying I have to fight *him?*"

The newcomer was enormous, nearly seven feet tall. He wore a bright orange torso suit like Vince's. The NEO man doubted that the giant was pure human; his exposed arms and legs were so shaggy with matted body hair that he looked almost simian. His low forehead and sunken eyes reinforced the impression. There were Worker genes in his ancestry, Vince decided, though most Worker gennies were only four or five feet tall. This guy was a monster.

"That is Dobo," Katarine said in a small voice. "It is he who challenges you in the *pelemeyor.*"

Dobo landed twenty feet away, grasping the branches with almost prehensile toes. He looked at Vince and grinned with yellow teeth too large for his face. One of the councillors rose from his seat and began making a speech, his voice cracking and wavering as he addressed the assembled crowd.

"What's he saying?" Vince wanted to know.

"Just formalities," Katarine told him. She sounded subdued.

Maintaining his foothold in the branches to keep the sudden movement from sending him drifting into the air, Vince whirled, reached out, and grabbed Katarine by her arms. He pulled her closer, staring hard into her dark eyes. "Listen, lady," he said, his voice hard and threatening, "you've been jerking me around ever since I woke up. Don't give me any more of this 'it's our way' garbage. You tell me this second what I need to know, or I'll pull your grand exalted Efay off his chair and give him a little *pelepovida* of my own!"

"You'd be cut down before you went three feet," Katarine said, her voice dull. She nodded toward the two guards, who were closing in on him once again. "Vince, I'm so very sorry." She sighed, and she dropped her head. "We don't . . . we don't all believe that this is the way to do things. Just because our ancestors—"

"Look, don't be sorry," he said, releasing her and lowering his voice. "Just tell me what I need to know. What is this fight supposed to be about?"

"It is the way our ancestors proved their worthiness to breed. And we needed a way to weed out the unfit from among our guests."

" 'Guests?' You mean prisoners."

"If you wish. We call them *convidas*. It means guests, people who live with us. It's not . . . an unpleasant life. We treat them well."

"Yeah . . . if they live. They don't get to leave afterward, do they?"

She shook her head. "My grandmother was taken from a miner's ship fifty years ago," she said. "My father was a merchant trading with Ciudestreya. Most of the people in this city have at least one outsider in their lineage."

Vince was beginning to understand how the Nomads had gotten their sinister reputation. Ciudestreya had a long orbit, one lasting many years. Each time the city passed through the Inner System, a few merchants or Belters must show up missing.

Why? To recharge the city's gene pool?

A few yards away, the Neanderthal character Katarine had called Dobo was mugging for the audience, flexing his muscles and baring his teeth.

"That guy's been working out," Vince observed. Those muscles could only have come from training in significant gravity. "Out at the end of this big, spinning stick, right?"

"That's right," Katarine said. "We have settlements at one end, connected with the city by tubes beneath Arbel's bark. There's a military base for training, nurseries for our children. Our schools are there." She grimaced, and Vince knew she'd been there and didn't like it. "We call it Heavydown."

"I can see why. It must be a shock to have to visit a decent gravity field." Zero-G was not by itself fatal, but too long in microgravity and a person would never be able to visit a high-G world like Earth.

"Many of us never go back after childhood," she explained. "It's not as though we're ever going to have to visit a planet's surface." She shuddered visibly. "All that flat, horrible openness . . . ."

Vince looked at Dobo and wished he knew just how much of a G-load they pulled at Heavydown. Knowing might improve his chances with his opponent.

A ringing clash, like a gong, shivered the air, and the murmur from the audience died away. It grew unnaturally quiet in the hall, and Vince knew that the main event was about to get under way.

Eight young women, each clad in little more than a brightly colored scrap of paper-cloth and carrying a long bundle in her arms, pushed off from openings in the throne wall and floated gracefully toward the floor. Four approached Dobo, while the rest came toward Vince, chanting in unintelligible, singsong words, clustering in the air around him and unwrapping the packages they carried.

It was like some medieval ceremony, the knight receiving his weapons and armor from his men-at-arms. One woman placed a helmet on Vince's head. It was a fanciful design, carved from wood in the shape of a dragon's head and exposing his face through its gaping mouth. Two others began strapping wooden protective braces to his forearms.

Katarine continued to float nearby, impassive. "Look," he said, "suppose I just refuse to go through with this? I don't *have* to fight anyone."

Katarine looked away. "Then you will . . . feed Arbel. Vince, you *must* fight. At least this way you have a chance!"

His attendants began strapping ornately carved greaves to his shins. "You say that if I win this, I win you. What do *you* think about all this? Do you care what happens to me? Or is this just a job?"

"It's hardly 'just a job,' Vince. Believe me, I care. I was *chosen* for you. But you must win me first."

Somewhere a drum was thumping, a heavy, measured pulse beat. "What happens to you if I lose? Or don't fight?"

"Then you will have failed in your challenge. You will die. And I will be bonded to Dobo."

"Bonded to—" Turning his head, Vince looked across the hall and saw a bevy of young females just drawing back from Dobo. The Nomad caught his stare and returned it with a toothy grin.

Reluctantly Vince took a weapon one of his ladies-in-waiting held before him. Identical to the polearms he'd seen already, it was fashioned from tooled steel and quite massive. On Earth, he estimated, it would have weighed ten or twelve pounds. In micro-G, it weighed nothing, but it still required an effort to move it. A little shorter than his five-feet-nine-inch height, it had a dense, rounded grip at one end and a wicked collection of machine-honed blades, points, hooks, and spikes on the other. One lance point swept back and under into a long, razor-edged slashing hook like a halberd from the Middle Ages.

Properly handled, he guessed, the weapon could be used in a number of ways. The spear points could thrust and stab, the long, edged blade could slash like a saber or an axe, and the back hook could grab an opponent's leg, arm, or weapon. The massive haft could be used as a club, and the entire weapon could block, parry, and thrust like a quarterstaff.

How long, he wondered, did someone have to practice with these things to become proficient with them?

One of the women snugged a metal-studded belt tight around his waist. Another clipped a coiled length of something like flexible rope to a hook in the belt. The thing was too light to be a whip, he decided, but it had a handle on one end and a weighted ball the size of his fist on the other. What was he supposed to use that for, tying his opponent up? Choking him?

The women withdrew, and Katarine drifted close, facing him. She touched the bladed weapon. "This is an *ohalans*," Katarine told him. She touched the rope on his belt. "And this is an *azoten*. They are your weapons and your means of movement in the arena."

He moved the polearm back and forth, testing its inertia. "I don't suppose these things come with an instruction manual, huh?"

She shrugged. "You won't have much time to practice with them, if that's what you mean."

"Yeah, but suppose I commit a foul or something? I don't know what the rules of this game are."

He could see the fear in her eyes. Maybe she really did care what happened to him. "Vince, there are no rules in the *pelepovida*. You must kill or cripple Dobo any way you can. In a match like this, it's usually the most innovative fighter who wins."

"Usually? You people do this often?"

"It is our life, Vince. It is what we are. . . ."

The gong tolled again. Katarine touched Vince's hand and managed a smile. "I must go. You will have a few minutes to practice. You might keep an eye on Dobo while you try out your weapons. He's very good. You might get some ideas watching him."

"How often has he done this?"

"I'm not sure," she said. "Six or seven times, at least."

"Six or—" Vince shook his head in disbelief. "And he's won all of them? Damn it, Katarine! This isn't fair!"

"You should have had more time to prepare, I know." She leaned closer, whispering urgently. "Remember, though, that you are stronger than he is. He is bigger, and he has trained at Heavydown. But you have grown up with gravity. Your muscles and your bones are stronger. That will give you an advantage!" Impulsively she moved closer, pressing her lips against his.

Then she was gone.

His guards had departed as well. He was alone now on the floor, facing Dobo.

An advantage, Katarine had said. Perhaps . . . but strength was only a small part of it. He'd been raised in a one-G environment, and he'd worked out every day in the centrifuge on Trinity. But he was still feeling as weak as a kitten after his ordeal.

Worse, he couldn't hope to match Dobo in micro-G combat. Vince had already noticed how clumsy his movements were compared to Katarine's. Dobo was certain to be a hell of a lot more skillful than Vince in this environment.

As he watched, Dobo went through a series of slashing maneuvers with his *ohalans*. Katarine had been right when she said they were means of movement as well as weapons. A hard thrust with the *oha-*

lans pushed Dobo's body in the opposite direction;
jerking it back stopped his drift. Newton's third law,
Vince thought wryly. Every action has an equal and
opposite reaction. But what did one do with the whip,
the . . . what had Katarine called it? The *azoten*.

For several minutes, Vince practiced on his own.
He knew that he'd never match Dobo's skill, especially with unfamiliar weapons. His only chance
would be an all-out, berserker's rush. Catch his opponent by surprise, batter down his defenses with
sheer strength, and hope for a crippling blow early
on. It was a fighter pilot's strategy. Fancy maneuvers, he'd often told his students, were fine, so long
as the other guy gave you the opportunity to use
them. Nine times out of ten, the best move was the
fast, direct one: Get on the bad guy's tail and score
the kill. Firepower counted for a lot more than finesse.

The gong sounded a third time. Vince heard a far-
off creaking sound, and slowly the clear space before
the throne split down the middle. The floor was dropping away, opening into another chamber.

As his half of the floor dropped beneath him, Dobo
gave a little push with one bare foot off the edge, pro-
pelling himself gently into the opening chamber.
Vince could feel a warm, wet rush of air into that area, as though the room were trying to draw him in.
He took a last look around, met Katarine's worried
eyes watching him from the wall at his back, then
pushed off after Dobo.

A dull red glow illuminated this lower room, which
was perhaps half as large as the audience hall. The
back wall was open, split by a twelve-foot seam in the
blackened wood. The glow was coming from inside
the seam. The current of air was rushing into that
alien gullet, feeding unseen flames.

Vince understood. The central pith of Arbel must

involve something akin to an enormous fermentation vat, but much hotter, much more efficient than the processes that liberated alcohol or made bread rise. The heat it yielded was enough to warm the human habitats, a kind of natural, organic furnace that took whatever the Nomads fed into it, giving off heat and the gases they breathed in return.

Vertigo plucked at his senses as he fell, the unfamiliar surroundings teasing his notions of up and down.

Worse was the odor. The smells here, warm and wet, were overpowering, the mingled stenches of raw sewage, rotting garbage, ammonia, and charred meat. Vince's stomach contracted sharply, and for a moment, he thought he was going to be sick.

The thought of disgracing himself that way before all those people steadied him, however. Arbitrarily he assigned up and down references: the surface with the gaping pit was "down." Opposite it, toward the audience hall with its watching Nomads clinging to the walls and ceiling like flies, was "up." The four walls were covered with slender branches, hand and footholds for the coming match.

As though drawn by the breeze, Dobo drifted toward the pit. His feet hit the floor a few feet from the opening, then anchored him on an arm-sized branch. Vince landed a moment later on the other side, and they faced one another across the crevasse. The eerie glow reminded Vince of a holovid he'd seen once of Io, the volcanic Jovian moon, and of a canyon there shaped by a river of molten sulfur.

He gripped his *ohalans* tightly in both hands. Fast and hard, he told himself. Hit him fast and hard, before he knows what—

The gong sounded a final time, and Dobo vaulted the open pit, his grimace stage-lit by the ruddy, coal-bright glow. "*Moray!*" the Nomad warrior screamed.

And then Vince was fighting for his life.

CHAPTER NINE

Dobo lashed out with his *ohalans*, the curved saber blade slicing toward Vince's head. The Earthman brought his own weapon up, and there was a ringing shock of steel striking steel. Vince ducked as Dobo sailed over his head.

The crowd roared as the Ciudestreyan landed, gripped a branch with his bare feet, and struck another slashing sideways blow. With a pilot's reflexes, Vince tucked his knees against his chest and vaulted over his *ohalans*, using the weapon's mass to shove himself clear of the attack.

The air sang as Dobo clove the air inches from Vince's body. The Earthman held his tuck, hurtling past Dobo's head, thrusting out and down with the handle of his weapon and connecting solidly with the Nomad's helmet. There was a solid *thunk* of steel on wood. Dobo spun aside, hit the floor, and bounced. Vince grabbed a branch on one wall and swung himself around, ready for another strike. Dobo stopped his motion with a deft reach-and-snag with one of the barbed hooks on the head of his pike, shook his head as though clearing it, then turned a hideous, leering scowl toward Vince.

The Earthman panted for breath. That first encounter had lasted perhaps two seconds. He'd nearly been killed twice, and he'd managed to annoy Dobo once. He'd lost any chance of surprise or a first strike, and now the Neanderthal was mad.

So far, things weren't going well at all.

Dobo screamed again, then leaped toward Vince, his *ohalans* held out rigidly in front of him, blades gleaming. Vince pushed off hard with his feet, timing his effort so that Dobo sailed headfirst through the air where Vince had been an instant before. He lunged with his pike, only to find the thrust blocked as Dobo twisted in midair and parried with his shaft. Vince's blow sent the Ciudestreyan sailing harmlessly into a wall.

The Nomad spun and lunged, the movement lightning fast, striking Vince's left leg hard. There was a crack, and Vince's leg protector sailed away in two uneven pieces still connected by the straps, the wood neatly split by the blade.

Vince hit a wall, gasping as one of the branches stabbed his side. He gathered his feet beneath him but held his position, waiting to see what Dobo would do next. The crowd's roar swelled, echoing and reechoing from the walls of the two connected rooms.

The big Nomad sailed toward him, but slowly, his eyes glittering in the glowing-coal light. Damn it, he was *asking* for an attack, holding his halberd low in front of his body, leaving his chest and head invitingly open to a thrust.

Okay, buddy, Vince thought fiercely. What's on your mind? His heavy pike held rigid before him, the spearhead to his body's spear, he pushed off as hard as he could, aiming not at Dobo's head, but just beyond it, at the point where he estimated the Nomad's chest would be by the time his path intersected Dobo's.

The instant Vince's feet left the wall, Dobo lashed up and out with his *ohalans*. The movement checked his forward momentum, and Vince sailed past the Nomad.

But Vince had been expecting something of the sort. Dobo's approach had been too calculating, too obvious. Vince pulled into a tuck as he flew past, and Dobo's pike lunge missed by inches. The Nomad recovered, however, and snapped his *ohalans* back, snagging Vince's right ankle in one sharp-edged hook.

Biting pain seared Vince's foot. Dobo yanked hard, and Vince went into a spin, tumbling helplessly across the yawning pit, unable to stop until he hit the opposite wall. Scrabbling among the branches, he clung to the wall, chest heaving. A constellation of scarlet droplets sailed toward the pit, caught in the airstream. Blood . . . *his* blood. Dobo's hook had slashed his right foot just beneath the edge of his protector. It was painful, but he wasn't seriously hurt.

Yet.

He glanced up into the Grand Audience Hall, which from his vantage point looked like a solid mass of screaming people suspended above him. Fists waved in time with shrilled chants.

Opposite him, Dobo shifted his *ohalans* to his left hand and reached for the coiled length of rope with his right, freeing it with an easy flick of his wrist. With a hiss and a snap, the *azoten* uncoiled through the air, the metal ball on the end passing over Vince's bare left shin. The nylon rope that followed, three yards long, caught, then whipped tightly around his ankle.

Dobo yanked hard, and Vince thought the monster had just dislocated his leg. Vince fell helplessly toward the Nomad, who was swinging the spear points of his *ohalans* into line in a wicked greeting.

Thinking fast, Vince twisted and slashed with his saber blade, slicing through the soft rope. That freed him from Dobo's pull, but he was still dropping toward the Nomad at several feet per second. He brought his *ohalans* down to block. Dobo stabbed upward, striking sparks from the Earthman's steel. Vince twisted aside, struck, was parried, struck again. For several seconds, the two men hovered almost face-to-face just above the wall, thrusting and slashing and parrying so quickly that the air rang with their blows.

A slash narrowly missed Dobo's skull, cutting the helmet's jaw protector and gashing the Nomad's cheek. The crowd went wild as blood flashed scarlet in the air between the men. Ignoring the blow, Dobo pivoted and delivered a slash of his own. It glanced off Vince's *ohalans* with a clang and sliced into the underside of his left arm, inside the protection of the wooden forearm protector.

He felt the cut, but strangely there was little pain, just a cold shock and a sharp sting, as though someone had hit him with a chunk of ice. There was a lot of blood, though. Marble-sized spheres of scarlet slid from his skin and danced through the air.

Before Vince could recover, Dobo twisted his pike sharply, locking one of its hooks into the head of the Earthman's *ohalans*. With savage force, the Nomad jerked his halberd sideways, breaking Vince's weakened grip and sending his weapon spinning away.

Disarmed, he knew he didn't have a chance, but he did have a second or so while the Nomad recovered from the force of his blow. Still dropping toward Dobo, Vince curled his feet beneath him, then kicked explosively, catching the Ciudestreyan full in the chest with both feet, catapulting himself through the air after his *ohalans*. Blood pinwheeled from his arm in a spray of droplets. If he kept bleeding like that he would be getting lightheaded soon . . . and then he'd soon be too weak to fight. So far he'd been struggling as hard as he could just to stay alive.

He had to find a way to end this fight fast.

His kick-off from Dobo's chest had been hastily aimed at best. He hit the opposite wall a long way from the point where his *ohalans* had struck, and after the weapon had already rebounded and was spinning back across the center of the room. Dobo watched for a second, then kicked off from the wall, gliding across the chamber, intercepting Vince's weapon with a deft hook-and-yank of his own, then landed on the floor next to the mouth, two *ohalans* in his hands now instead of one.

Wildly Vince clung to a branch and searched for something else he could use as a weapon. His *azoten* was still coiled at his side, but he was as likely to tangle himself in the thing as his opponent. He looked up toward the crowd. There'd be no escape *that* way. Feet wrapped around a branch, Dobo reared upright above the mouth, an *ohalans* in each hand. As the crowd screamed and cheered, the Nomad put on a show, shaking the weapons and thrusting them at imaginary enemies.

Katarine's words came back to Vince with renewed force: *In a match like this, it's usually the fighter with the most innovative approach who wins.* Okay, so what could he do that was unexpected? With only his *azoten* left, his opponent would be expecting him to use that. What was he supposed to do instead—attack that giant bare-handed?

That gave him an idea.

As Dobo watched with glittering, victory-bright eyes, Vince reached down and unhooked the *azoten* from his belt. Gauging the distance between himself and his opponent carefully, he grasped the whip a foot behind the steel ball at the tip and began spinning it, letting the rest of the whip uncoil gently from his left hand. At the same time, he tensed his legs. . . .

The ball sang in the air, a circular blur of motion. With a snap, he released it, sending the ball sailing across the chamber, the length of the *azoten* uncoiling behind it like a comet's tail.

As hard as he could, Vince pushed off from the wall an instant later, following the flying whip. Dobo, juggling a massive *ohalans* in each hand, was caught off guard. He hesitated before dropping his left-hand pike, then lost another quarter-second trying to get the other into position . . .

. . . and then the steel ball struck his arm, and three yards of nylon rope came sailing after it, draping itself across his face and chest in a free-fall tangle. The blow couldn't have hurt Dobo, but for a critical second, he was encumbered by the snaking coils of the whip.

Vince hurtled into Dobo's belly, his head down. Dobo folded like a rag doll as the helmet's crest rammed into him, then the Ciudestreyan collided with the wall in a thrashing of arms, legs, and branches.

But Dobo didn't lose his pike, not quite. As Vince grabbed a branch and tried to turn, the Nomad managed a one-handed lunge, severing the branch with a neat *snick*, and the Earthman tumbled backward over the gaping, red-hot pit.

Vince could feel a gentle suction drawing him toward that maw, could feel and smell the foul, humid heat rising from the thing like the fetid breath of some immense carnivore.

Dobo snagged Vince's foot again with the hook. Thrashing in midair, Vince started drifting toward the pit. Bending double, he reached past Dobo's blades and grabbed the *ohalans*'s shaft. The movement brought him face-to-face with Dobo, and for a moment, they struggled silently. Then Vince ducked his head and yanked the shaft hard toward his belly, using the leverage to ram his helmet into Dobo's face with a crunch audible to the watchers in the gallery above.

The Nomad grunted. Vince lunged again. *Crack!* Stunned, Dobo let the *ohalans* slip from nerveless fingers and drift toward Vince's feet, blood dribbling in small, glittering pellets from the huge warrior's lip and nose and the gash in his cheek. Senseless, Dobo was drifting toward the open furnace. Heat and stench assaulted Vince in a sickening wave.

At the last moment, Dobo recovered enough to realize what was happening and let out a single, soul-curdling shriek.

The scream galvanized Vince into action. Tossing aside the *ohalans*, he reached down and grabbed the Nomad by the collar of his tunic, hauling him back from that foul, sullen-burning light, out of the deadly maw.

The crowd was screaming and shouting, a thunder that rang through the chamber in a deafening peal upon peal. Above him, the Efay had risen and was holding one pale hand up in a wordless demand for silence. Slowly the tumult subsided.

The Efay shouted something in Espen, clearly a command. A moment later, another voice translated, a man's voice this time. "His Excellency the Efay of Ciudestreya commands that you complete the Great Cycle. The loser must feed Arbel. The winner may claim his prize."

Breathing hard, Vince swept his eyes across the watching throng, then fixed his gaze on the city's leader. "No!" he shouted back.

There was a stir in the crowd. Evidently the word "no" was common to both Anglic and Espen. He felt lightheaded. The savage exertion and loss of blood both were taking their toll.

"No!" he called again, louder this time. "This damned custom of yours has gone on long enough! I'm putting a stop to it right now!"

Two Ciudestreyan soldiers dropped into the chamber on either side of him. Too exhausted now to resist, he let them take his arms. Gently they propelled him out of that noisome combat chamber and back into the Grand Audience Hall.

The air seemed unbelievably cleaner in the upper room. He gulped down deep, shuddering breaths as Nomads clustered around him, gawking at him, some daring to reach out and touch him. Two of the girls who had prepared him for the fight—he thought they were the same ones, anyway—appeared at his side. One held his bleeding arm still while the other covered the wound with stuff that looked like wet shavings of wood, then wrapped it in gauze. The shavings were astringent, stinging him, but the bleeding stopped almost at once. As they finished, he saw a pair of soldiers rising from the lower chamber, a dazed and blank-looking Dobo supported between them. With a creak and rumble of hidden machinery, the floor of the audience hall swung back into place, shutting off the stench and hot-breathed horror of the arena below.

Crowd noises rumbled and murmured around him, an ugly sound. He wondered if they felt cheated because neither combatant had been devoured by that snake-tongued horror below.

Then a swirl of motion parted the crowd, and Vince found himself floating alone again, facing the stern-faced councillors and the fat ruler perched on the throne behind them. One of the councillors spoke in grave tones, as though pronouncing sentence.

A tall man in a green coverall hovered nearby,

translating.

"His Excellency the Conseo Veya declares that you have answered the challenge and have emerged victorious from the *pelemeyor*. You are worthy to remain now with us, a living part of Arbel and our city, sharing our food, water, air, and life."

A drum thumped several measured beats. The aged councillor spoke again.

"This, His Excellency says, is a great honor," the translator continued. "But this honor carries with it great responsibility. You are part of our community now, subject to our laws, our customs, our tradition. By allowing Dobo to live, by pulling him from Arbel's very mouth, you have already defied that custom.

"Normally the penalty for such an act would be that you yourself feed Arbel in his place. We on the council, with the gracious permission of His Grand Excellency the Altefay Waldez, have decided that you acted in ignorance and may be forgiven . . . this time.

"But be warned that life is a continuing struggle for existence, imparting no mercy. If you defy our customs again, you will feed Arbel, as would any of us found guilty of such a transgression."

Vince felt a presence at his shoulder. Turning, he saw Katarine floating beside him. She didn't look up at him but kept her eyes fixed on the branch-covered floor at his feet.

The aged councillor continued. "This woman has been chosen for you," the man in green translated. "By the law of challenge and the fight for life, the Conseos of the city declares the woman bonded to your hand and rule. Her life is yours, as your life is Arbel's."

There was an awkward silence, and Vince realized that something was expected of him. Several of the councillors leaned their heads together, speaking in low murmurs among themselves.

"Touch my head," Katarine whispered at his side, her voice urgent, insistent.

"Why?"

"Touch me! If you don't, another will be chosen for you."

He laid his hand on her head. The councillors seemed to relax, and several nodded happily.

"Go now," the translator said. "Fulfill the custom of our fathers."

Someone cheered, and then the crowd was roaring with what Vince hoped was approval. With a shock, Vince realized that he had either just gotten married or acquired a slave. He wasn't certain which . . . and neither possibility was at all attractive. All he could do, he decided, was play along until he could talk to Katarine in private.

He hoped that the customs of these people allowed newlyweds to spend some time together alone.

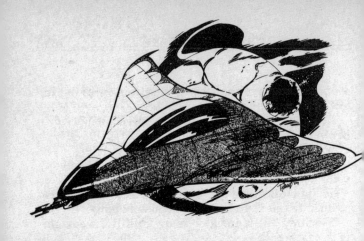

CHAPTER TEN

The wedding procession—Vince decided that was as good a name for it as any—took them through corridors that wormed their way beneath the bark of the Tree, ending at last in a small cube-shaped room with a window looking out across the geometric clutter of the city. Since the room was inside Arbel itself, he couldn't see the dizzying reach of the Tree stretching above the city, but the pine-sawdust smell and the dark-colored twists and coils of branches looping from every wall were constant reminders of its presence.

Just as the two guards stationed outside the locked door were reminders that his own status here was still less than certain.

For now, though, Vince was grateful for privacy and a chance to get cleaned up, eat, and rest. A cubical in one corner housed a shower bag, allowing him to wash the blood and sweat from his aching body. A fresh jumper made him feel somewhat more human.

He had some trouble with dinner. In his mind, he could still smell the stench issuing from the core of the Tree, and the food—crisp, flat things like potato chips that Katarine called "manna"did nothing to ease his queasiness about where the stuff came from.

It was a rather unromantic dinner. Vince was still fighting his own anti-Nomad feelings, trying to view the universe from their point of view and finding that he had prejudices he'd never even known about. Stubbornly he questioned Katarine about her city and about her culture. He had to find out what made the Nomads tick if he was ever going to have a chance of getting out of here.

Vince felt sick that he was participating in what amounted to slavery. Ciudestreyan women weren't owned in the sense that they were bought and sold, but the men here were the undisputed masters. Instead of husbands and wives among the Nomads, there were "protectors" and "bonded companions." Unbonded girls were the wards of their male relatives. A man who wanted a particular woman could win her by challenging her protector. Katarine would be bonded to Vince, she told him, only so long as he was victorious against other challengers.

The challenge dominated every aspect of life within the tightly closed community. Rulers gained power, laws were changed, even court cases were decided by combat in the arena. Citizens—meaning men, of course—could challenge city councillors or the Efay himself for their titles and positions, a kind of democracy by might.

Except that things were slanted in favor of those in power. A fat weakling like the Altefay could hardly hope to emerge victorious from the arena, even in the symbolic confrontation of the *pelemenor*, but he could afford a champion like Dobo.

Women couldn't enter the arena at all. The very idea, Vince learned, was unthinkable for any well-bred girl. Discouraged from even visiting Heavy-down or engaging in combat-oriented training or sport, mired by tradition in the notion that women were weak, helpless, and needed a strong male protector, they could never hope to challenge the system that kept them second-class citizens.

Tradition was a key word in Ciudestreyan life, a word that shaped the law, kept the ruling clique in power, and rationalized what amounted to slavery for a third of the city's population.

To Vince, the entire culture seemed twisted, diseased. He still didn't understand how *foranos*, the Espen word for "outsiders," came into the equation. His own situation was an immediate case in point. Rescued from deep space, healed by Ciudestreyan doctors, he'd been assigned a "receiver" by the council while he was still unconscious and awoke to find himself already a part of the Nomad city's cultural drama, with no say in the matter at all.

Well, after all, Katarine insisted, Ciudestreya had lavished valuable care and resources on his rescue and on his healing. It was only right that he pay for his life *with* his life, by becoming a productive member of Ciudestreyan society.

Vince was glad they'd rescued and healed him, but he questioned their right to kidnap him and make him part of some kind of city genetics program.

"God, why do you *do* it?" he demanded. He and Katarine floated a few feet apart, next to the rectangular transparency that looked out into the star-strewn velvet of deep space.

"Why do we do what?"

"Kidnap people! Make them fight! Damn it, it's . . . it's barbaric!"

She wouldn't meet his eyes. "There are reasons."

"What reasons? How can you justify it?"

"Look at it scientifically," she said. "Ciudestreya is a tiny community. It has an orbital period of almost thirty years, and that isolates us from everyone else, even the other Nomad cities."

Vince nodded. That much, at least, was obvious. The laws of orbital mechanics dictated that an object with a highly elliptical orbit moved very slowly along that part of its path far from the sun, while its perihelion would be fast and brief. With a thirty-year orbit, Ciudestreya must graze the orbit of Uranus, spending most of its long "year" far beyond the orbit of Saturn. The sheer emptiness of space beyond the Asteroid Belt meant that the Nomad city's nearest neighbors—the few other deep-space cities, the handful of settlements among Saturn's moons—would always be very far away.

"We have a population of fewer than four hundred here," Katarine continued. "That means we have a small gene pool. And very few chances to bring in fresh . . . blood from outside."

Vince remembered the stories he'd heard of Nomads capturing ships and people as their cities passed through the Inner System. Usually those stories hinted that the victims were used as breeding stock, all part of the sinister aura their cities had acquired over the years and the basis for most anti-Nomad prejudice.

He could understand their problem. After a couple of centuries, everyone in so small a population must be related in some degree to almost everyone else. Inbreeding would be a real problem, concentrating some nasty, unwanted genetic traits.

The ritual of *pelepovida* must have had its beginnings in the early days of the city, possibly as a means of weeding out the unfit. With more men than women in the early colony, the ritual of challenge and combat ensured that only the strongest fighters would pass their genes on to the next generation.

But damn it, this was the twenty-fifth century! There had to be a better way!

Wonderingly he looked down at his fingers, healed by their rejuv pod. Ciudestreya had the medical technology to meet that kind of genetic challenge! This culture was such a strange, incongruous mix of modern technology and outdated ideas, as incongruous as polearms and trial by combat in a spacefaring city.

"So you get fresh blood by kidnapping people."

"What else can we do?" She sounded bitter.

"Come on! You could trade for what you need! Any good genetics lab in the Inner System would have all the frozen genetic material you could possibly—"

"Gah!" She looked as though he'd struck her. "That's *disgusting!*" She wrinkled her nose, her face expressing what Vince felt when he contemplated the fact that their dinner was another "gift of Arbel."

Okay, he thought. The Nomads had some taboo against artificial insemination. Or possibly it was the use of frozen genetic material from faceless donors, or the idea of tinkering with the natural processes of life. Whatever the reason, Katarine thought he'd suggested something filthy and perverted.

The differences between her worldview and his, he realized, were enormous. "Sorry," he said. "But try to see my side of it. Kidnapping, ritual combat . . . ."

Katarine looked puzzled. "I don't see your problem. We do what we *have* to do. We only take a few, people who won't be missed. Our survival as a people outweighs the convenience of the individual. I would think that was obvious!"

He shook his head, helpless. Their cultures might never find a common meeting ground. She thought raids for breeding stock were part of the natural order; he believed trial by combat belonged in the Dark Ages. For him, genetic prosthesis, in vitro fertilization, and sperm banks were accepted parts of modern medical technology; for her, aspects of that technology were unnatural, repellant.

"I see what you're saying," she continued. "Of course it would be better if we could get outsiders to stay voluntarily. But outsiders don't understand us. They don't even try." She popped another chip in her mouth and chewed thoughtfully. "Besides, our way has worked well for two centuries."

"Shooting an unpleasant neighbor *works*," Vince said, "but that's not necessarily the best approach."

"Lots of us don't like the way things are," she said. She sounded defiant. "But there's not that much chance for changing things."

"I thought you could challenge your rulers."

"*I* can't. I'm a woman. Most men . . ." She shrugged. "Things are the way they are because they have to be!"

"Nothing *has* to be the way it is," Vince replied. "Not if enough folks want the system to change. If you had open trade with the rest of the solar system, you might find you could arrange a steady exchange of population." He looked around at the surrounding walls, and shrugged. "You have an . . . interesting life here. Strange, from my point of view, but I bet a lot of people would be attracted to it if they had the chance. Expanded trade is the answer."

"We do trade some with outsiders," she admitted. "But we don't have a lot that they want."

"You must have something. What do you trade for?"

"Things we can't manufacture ourselves. Some medicines. Fusion reactors. The only way we can get those things is through trade at the *Tempomercad*."

That word, she'd told him earlier, meant "Market Time" and referred to a period of several months at perihelion, once every thirty years, when they could trade with the Inner Worlds. Ciudestreya was inbound now. *Tempomercad* would begin in another few months, when the city crossed the orbit of Mars.

She sighed. "The problem is that out in the Great Dark, there just isn't that much in the way of useful trade goods. Our resident Spacers find some stuff. Mostly gold, platinum, and radioactives from nickel-iron asteroids."

"There you are."

"There we *aren't*. There's little we can pick up in the Great Dark that you don't already have in the Asteroid Belt. Besides, Inner Worlders don't like to trade with us—most of them, anyway. It's as though we have some kind of disease. We're outcasts."

Anti-Nomad prejudice, in other words. The Nomads were caught in a vicious circle. Outsiders mistrusted them, making contact difficult. But the Nomads had to have some contact or face the problems of inbreeding, so they resorted to kidnapping. Which made outsiders mistrust them more. . . .

"How did your people get started in the first place?" he wondered. "As outcasts?"

"Who knows? Belters looking for a freer life? Colonists fleeing persecution? Merchants running from their creditors? Our oldest records mention our founders coming from a place called South America. Mavericks and troublemakers, probably. I like to think they chose exile over conformity."

"Interesting thought." Vince smiled. "Especially since survival in a small, tight group like yours demands a lot of laws. Mandatory conformity."

"True. That's why, every so often, I wish. . . ."

"What?"

She shook her head. "It's not important." Katarine drew a deep breath. "There's another problem besides our trouble finding trading partners."

"What's that?"

"The Great Dark is empty, Vince. Emptier than you can imagine. There simply isn't that much out there to find and mine."

Vince touched the bandage around his arm. The shavings they'd put on his wound—more of the bounty of Arbel, he assumed—had stopped the bleeding almost at once, and Katarine had told him that it would also prevent infection. He filed the thought away for future reference. The Nomads might have trade goods that they hadn't even thought about yet.

Katarine looked thoughtful. "There's the Artifact, of course. Some of the men have high hopes that it will fetch a good price at the *Tempomercad.*"

"The Artifact? What's that?"

"Nobody knows. Something our Spacers found a few years ago in deep space out beyond Saturn. But it's sure to be valuable."

"How do you know that?"

She leaned forward, dropping her voice in a conspiratorial manner. "The Conseos think it's alien," she said. "Something from another star system."

Vince raised his eyebrows. In five hundred years of planetary exploration, no trace of an alien civilization had ever been found anywhere in the solar system—no canals in the Martian deserts, no mysterious black monoliths on the moon. Proof of an extrasolar civilization would be the greatest discovery in history, but so far there'd been nothing to suggest that man was not alone in the universe.

Vince was skeptical. "I'd like to see it."

"Oh, no one can see it except the Efay and the Conseos and a few others. A few months ago, we passed close enough to Jupiter that some of our contact people could travel to the Jovian system. They showed it to some scientists on Amalthea, but no one there could figure out what it was. The research labs there obviously didn't have enough money to buy it, so our people brought it back. I think they're planning to arrange for an auction at the *Tempomercad.*"

"I see."

Vince wasn't sure what the Nomads might have found, though he seriously doubted that it was actually an alien artifact. The solar system was littered with half a millennium's worth of human-built litter—satellites, ancient deep-space probes, robot mining vehicles, even items as prosaic as cameras and wrenches lost by early astronauts in the first years of space exploration.

Still, if there was even the slightest possibility that they'd found something genuinely alien, the idea of having it sold to the highest bidder was a chilling one. The economy of the Inner System was dominated by RAM, and, though the Lunar banks and the Mercurian Sun Kings were also powerful players, in any bidding war RAM would undoubtedly win.

Earth and NEO couldn't afford to see that happen, not if the Artifact truly represented an advanced nonhuman technology. RAM's technology was already the best in the system. Access to alien technology might make them unstoppable.

"I might be able to arrange a buyer," he suggested. "But I'd have to see this Artifact first. Do you think you could work out something through the council?"

"Maybe," Katarine said. She made a face. "But this is hardly the time to be talking business." She reached out and took his hand.

Vince pulled back. "Katarine, please. I'm still trying to get straight on what happened to me today . . . and to you. I don't believe in owning slaves—even one as charming as you."

"I am not a slave!" she flared.

"I don't care what you call it. How much choice do you have in what happens to you? You said they *chose* you for me."

"I could have refused," she said. "I didn't want to."

Vince raised his eyebrows at that. He was beginning to suspect that Katarine had less choice in such matters than she thought. The conditioning imposed by a culture could go a long way toward shaping an individual's thoughts and desires.

"Slavery means making someone do what she doesn't want to do," she continued. She reached out with one hand again, hesitant, then touched his face lightly with her fingertips. Her eyes were very large and solemn. "I *wanted* to be bonded with you."

"Suppose *I* don't want to be bonded with *you?*"

She looked stricken. "You don't like me?"

"That's not the point," he said, frustrated. Her Anglic was flawless, yet her thoughts could be as alien as the thoughts of the denizens of another star.

"The man always has the right to refuse," she said. "Another girl will be chosen to replace—"

"I don't *want* another girl, damn it! What if I just want to be left alone?"

If possible, she looked even more shocked than before. "That's unthinkable. You won the *pelepovida*. That gives you certain responsibilities. Maybe you don't understand. The point of bringing you into the city was so that you can contribute your genes to—"

"I don't *want* to contribute," he said patiently, as though speaking to a particularly slow child. What a screwy way these people had of looking at the universe! "I don't want your city to run my life or choose my girlfriends. I don't want to stay here. I have my own life . . . my own friends." Unaccountably he thought suddenly of Jovanna. Where was she now? She probably thought he was dead.

"Come on, Katarine," he continued. He tried to get her to look at him, but she was staring out the viewport, her eyes glistening. "Look, I like you. I like you a lot. So far you're the only person I've met in this damned city who even comes close to making sense."

That, he reflected, was only half true and only in general. She was a product of her culture, a culture that had been given some strange twists by necessity and isolation. Her tears tugged at his feelings. He wanted to reach out and hold her. When, he wondered, had he stopped thinking of her as unclean?

Damn it, he would *not* take advantage of her! Wryly he thought about the traditional attitude of the hotshot rocketjock, that any willing girl was fair game. Well, not this time. Katarine was too vulnerable.

"If . . . if you could go back to Davida," she said suddenly, "would you take me along?"

"Huh?" It took him a beat to remember that he'd told her he was a mercenary from Davida. God, how to answer such a question diplomatically? He did like her, but it wasn't as though he were married to her . . . whatever the council might think!

"Your people aren't about to let me go, are they?" he replied after a moment. "So it's a moot point."

She wiped her eyes with her hand. "There will be other *foranos* here soon," she said. "That's why the Efay and the council wanted to decide your case quickly. There's a ship on its way. It's been in communication with us since yesterday, I think."

"Really?" His interest perked. A ship! "What ship?"

She shrugged. "The city defense monitors don't tell me things like that, but I've heard the rumors."

Rumors, Vince reflected, would be a powerful information conduit within such a small population. "Will I be allowed to see them when they get here? Talk to them?"

"I don't know that either. But I was wondering if . . . if you would go if you had the chance."

"I'd go like a shot, Katarine. And, yeah, I'd take you along."

If, he added to himself, I could do it without hurting you. . . .

"Then I'll find out what I can about the ship," she

said. "I can't make any promises."

"Understood." His pulse beat harder. A ship!

"I gather they're coming to see the Artifact."

"Oh?" The Artifact again. He had to learn more about that. If it really was an alien device of some kind. . . . "What about this ship. Is it Belter?"

"No, they're from Mars," she said. "From RAM."

The information hit him like a thunderbolt. In one blow, Katarine had smashed the fragile fantasy he'd been building for himself for the last few moments. A RAM ship would be more than happy to take him away from Ciudestreya . . . and straight to the penal facility on Deimos.

Worse, what if the Ciudestreyans really had somehow stumbled across evidence of nonhuman aliens? The chances against it were tremendous, but if there were anything to it, he couldn't sit by and watch a treasure of such incredible importance turned over to RAM!

He needed to see the Artifact for himself.

He also needed to avoid being spotted and captured by RAM when they got here. Suddenly Vince had quite a few things to think about besides whether or not he was ever going to leave Ciudestreya.

As he glumly considered the possibilities, Katarine moved close to him. "Hold me, Vince," she said. "Please? . . ."

Unthinking, he opened his arms and drew her close. She was crying, her tears forming tiny, glittering spheres that danced in the air around them. "I don't want to lose you," she sobbed. "I've just found you, and I don't want to lose you."

They kissed for a long time, gently adrift, clinging to one another. Was he taking advantage of her? he wondered. Or was it the other way around?

Somehow nothing mattered except that, for the moment, they needed each other.

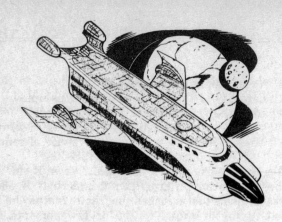

CHAPTER ELEVEN

Jovanna stood within her cubicle, Workstation 497, studying the touch-sensitive, pastel-colored rectangles embedded within the slick black surface of her keypad. There were no chairs; in Phobos's microgravity, a person could stand all day without growing tired.

Around her, men and women, some in civilian jumpsuits, most in severe gray RAM military uniforms, went about their business in the vast communications complex that occupied the upper tier of the RAM-Phobos pyramid. RAM's principal military base on Phobos was an enormous sprawl of battlements, docking facilities, missile batteries, and laser turrets, all surrounding a single, upthrust pyramid that measured almost a mile along each side.

Nearly ten thousand civilians were employed at the RAM-Phobos Prime complex alone, along with over thirty thousand military personnel. The sheer size of the operation had been an advantage when NEO Intelligence arranged for Jovanna and Galen to be employed there as civilian workers. RAM-Phobos Prime was so large that RAM's dreaded Internal Security was forced to rely entirely on computer ID scans, and so far Jovanna and Galen had had no trouble whatsoever passing as anonymous low-level workers. Their computer IDs were carefully crafted forgeries based on the records of real civilian RAM employees who had defected to NEO.

Workstation 497 was identical to thousands of others within the base pyramid, and Jovanna was one among thousands of low-grade programmers, clerks, and staff assistants. She performed her assigned work for the center's Department 12 with an efficiency unheard of within RAM's faceless bureaucracy, which left her with plenty of time to pursue her other activities unnoticed.

None of her fellow workers were curious about her work. In RAM, career survival depended upon looking good, minding one's own business, and not making waves. The only real trouble she had was with her immediate supervisor, the sub-department manager, and his interest in her had nothing to do with her work.

At the moment, Jovanna had called up on her screen a list of ships docked or incoming to Phobos's various port facilities. The *Magnificus Triplanetary*, she saw, was no longer listed as arriving that morning. The entry read "DELAYED" instead, to the frustration, no doubt, of the families and friends of the *Maggie*'s passengers waiting for them in Phobosport.

The *Amazonis* appeared on the listing of military ships currently stationed at Phobos. That was new. The cryptic electronic notation suggested that the RAM cruiser had departed from drydock the evening before for maneuvers and was returning to RAM-Phobos Prime, Docking Area 37, with an ETA of 1000 hours.

One other entry caught Jovanna's attention on the

civilian flight listings, and that one worried her. The
liner *Vladimir Komarov* was supposed to be arriving
that day, but the listing now read "DELAYED," with
no explanation.

If *Komarov* was simply a few hours late, she would
be on Phobos Approach Control's radar screens by
now, and an expected arrival time would have been
posted. "DELAYED" obviously suggested that something more serious had happened.

But there was no helping that. If something went
wrong, Jovanna and Galen had a second escape route
open to them—down the Space Elevator to Mars,
where they could link up with Rolf and Sharon. All
they could do now was stick with their part of the
plan.

She checked the time—0920, time soon for the
Amazonis to contact Phobos Approach Control.

Magically, a line of print wrote itself across the bottom of her screen: "JT/RW: HERE WE GO!"

Swiftly Jovanna keyed in a reply. "RW/JT: GOOD
LUCK!" She keyed the line into the network, then
erased it. Wherever RW was within the cybermatrix,
she should have gotten the message.

Next she typed a coded query into the system, and
seconds later saw "OK-G" appear on the screen. Galen was at Phobosport, somewhere on the dusty surface of the moon itself, manning the secret
transmitter. It was up to the Tinker to maintain communications between the far-flung elements of Operation Skytower—NEO headquarters, Black Barney's
raiders, and Jovanna.

For all of them now, the waiting had begun.

Aboard the RMS *Amazonis*, Mars was a scimitar of
ocher and green growing slowly in the viewscreen

that stretched across half of the hemispherical bulk-head of the bridge. One corner of the screen blanked with static, then resolved into the hard features of a woman wearing the gray uniform of a RAM space traffic controller.

"*Amazonis*," the gray-uniformed woman said. "Computer interface complete. We read that your weapons systems are off-line and safe. You are now cleared for final approach to RAM-Phobos Prime. Stand by to relinquish helm control."

Capt. Gunter Maximilian Zotov sat in the high-backed, thronelike bridge command chair. At his feet, the helmets and headsets of the bridge crew bobbed and moved above the consoles in the instrument-crowded trench that circled the room. "Acknowledge," he said, his voice ice, and a communications officer hurried to comply.

Zotov was not in a good mood. *Amazonis*'s two-week run to the Jovian system and back had been wasted effort, her mission a failure. RAM's High Command was not impressed by failure, no matter what the reason.

The cruiser's entire crew had been all but tiptoeing around *Amazonis*'s captain ever since they'd left Jupiter six days earlier. The tiptoeing was figurative now, of course. The drives had been shut down moments before, and they were in free-fall.

Zotov heard the hiss of a door behind him and the sharp, barked challenge of his personal guard. "Halt! What's your business?"

"Commander Galloway, Senior Computer Officer," another voice replied, "to see the captain."

There was a moment's silence as security devices scanned the officer for hidden weapons. Zotov engaged his chair's power, turning it with a faint whine to face the officer.

Anton Galloway was a typical Martian, tall,

gaunt, and bony. He steadied himself with one long
arm, grasping the railing that encircled the command chair's dais as he floated before the bridge security station.

"It's okay," Zotov told the armed and armored marine strapped into the security station. "Let him
through."

"Sir!" the marine snapped. A green light winked
on his console.

Zotov turned his full attention on the officer.
"What is it?"

Galloway looked pale. "Captain, I thought you
should know. A few moments ago, when we interfaced with RAM-Phobos Prime . . . well, something
triggered one of our security routines."

Zotov felt the faint pricking of fear at the back of
his skull. Every ship approaching a space dock interfaced its computers with those of the port, allowing a
routine scan of the ship's travel orders, route data,
and passenger and cargo manifests. It also allowed
the port to take control of the ship for the delicate
procedure of docking.

But the *Amazonis* had embarked on this mission
under secret orders, and parts of her log were under
security lock, meaning that they couldn't be read
from Phobos without special authorization and a
coded release order. If a security subroutine had been
triggered within *Amazonis*'s computer, it meant that
someone at Phobos was being unusually inquisitive,
deliberately trying to access sealed data banks that
he had no business reading.

"Any guesses?"

Galloway managed a shrug of bony shoulders
while continuing to float above the railing. "Negative, Captain. It could be a NEO spy, of course, or a
hunter program planted at Phobos through the cybermatrix. It could even be caused by a digital per-

sonality."

"Is he still at it?"

"Three attempts in the last couple of minutes, sir. Whoever he is, he's determined. I suggest sequester and lockdown."

Zotov considered this. "Agreed. Dismissed."

He swung his chair back to face the bridge pit. "Commander!"

"Yes, Captain!"

"Inform Phobos Control that we will be making a manual approach. Then cut computer interface."

"Uh . . . aye, sir."

The tension on the bridge grew tangible now. It wasn't unusual for a warship to take manual control for a docking, especially when traveling under sealed orders, but every man and woman on the bridge had heard Galloway's warning. The electronic intruder could be almost anybody—free-lance cybermatrix hacker, NEO spy, pirate. Perhaps the most deadly possibility was that he was someone in the RAM hierarchy . . . a political enemy of Zotov's, perhaps, or even an agent for RAM Internal Affairs. The failed attempt to read the cruiser's records might be a deliberate test of their security, or it could be an attempt to gather evidence to use at Zotov's court-martial. If it was the latter, the career, even the life, of every person aboard could hang in the balance.

In the face of such uncertainty, all Zotov could do was follow the book: Cut *Amazonis* off from all outside networks, and that meant taking her into dock without help from Phobos Control.

Zotov studied the main viewscreen for a moment. The green and ocher crescent of Mars had thickened as *Amazonis* slid toward the daylight terminator. The intense white of the north polar ice cap was starkly visible now, as was the deep, cobalt blue of the Boreal Sea. Only just barely visible from this distance, the jewel glitter of city lights showed as minute and delicate spiderweb traceries across the night side of the planet. Zotov strained for a glimpse of the Space Elevator but couldn't make it out. The top of that structure and their destination, Phobos, was astern of the ship, invisible at the moment.

"Captain!" the communications officer called. "Incoming vidcast, scrambled, Priority Code Red-Ares!"

Red-Ares! The prickling at Zotov's neck increased, and he felt beadlets of sweat gathering on his face. "On screen, Lieutenant."

A corner of the bridge viewscreen flickered, then cleared. Zotov found himself staring into the hard, unblinking, and utterly emotionless gaze of an old man.

Zotov swallowed, his eyes taking in the wrinkled skin, the cruel mouth, the gray civilian clothes so spartan and austere they constituted a kind of uniform. He had actually seen Holzerhein's image only three times during his career.

Never had the experience been a pleasant one.

"Mr. Chairman," he said, "this is an unexpected hon—"

"Delete the platitudes, Zotov. Explain your actions."

Simund Holzerhein, Senior Chairman of RAM, was not in the habit of addressing ship captains either casually or socially. Zotov found himself mesmerized by those inhumanly cold, unblinking eyes, like a mouse before a snake.

The horror was that Holzerhein *was* inhuman. What Zotov was staring at was an electronic construct, the computer image of a downloaded digital personality. Holzerhein—whatever there was left of the original man—was almost two centuries old. For the past century and a half, he'd been the unseen guiding power behind RAM and all it represented.

Gathering his will, forcing himself to speak clearly and with precision, Zotov repeated Galloway's report, adding only that *Amazonis*'s log was under restricted access security. Holzerhein knew what the cruiser's mission had been if anyone did, and he certainly possessed the codes for the classified data's release if he cared to examine it.

"Understood," Holzerhein said when Zotov had finished. "You acted correctly, Captain. Steps are being taken to isolate the intruder. Continue your manual approach." The image winked out without formal leave-taking. Holzerhein rarely bothered with merely human conventions.

The face of the Phobos controller reappeared in Holzerhein's place. "*Amazonis*, this is Phobos Approach Control. Comp interface released. You are cleared for manual docking." The faintest shadow of amusement touched her eyes and mouth . . . or was it a sneer? "Good luck, *Amazonis*."

Zotov didn't believe in luck.

"Acknowledge," he snapped. His fingers touched plasma switches in the slick black plastic of his chair's right arm. In response, computer screens flicked on in a semicircle about the foot of his dais, repeating helm and navigation displays from the bridge pit consoles so that he could follow the docking. The half-light of the bridge was transformed by rainbow colors glowing from a dozen monitors, showing computer-generated schematics of the *Amazonis* and Phobos; of Mars, the Space Elevator, and the inbound path of the cruiser; of three-dimensional views of circumambient space. Elsewhere, scrolling columns of data gave range, speed, vector, and department readiness.

Everything was as it should be. *Amazonis* fell tail-first toward Phobos, precisely on course. Docking would be a particularly delicate operation this time, however. The heavy cruiser's external hull was still cluttered with the rider pods that carried her escorting fighters.

"Helm!" Zotov snapped.

One of the helmeted heads in the trench turned, eyes wide behind the clear visor. "Sir?"

"Let's make it a *smooth* docking, shall we?" Zotov allowed his teeth to show in a humorless smile. "The Chairman is watching. Scratch my hull and I will give you the opportunity of inspecting the damage personally . . . without a space suit to restrict your activities."

"Y-Yessir!" the helmsman stammered. She turned back to her console, keenly intent now on the delicate precision necessary for docking *Amazonis*'s enormous bulk with the port.

Zotov was a firm believer in the benefits of scientifically applied psychological motivation.

He leaned forward in his seat, hands clasped, closely observing the cruiser's final approach.

O   O   O   O   O

Within the boundless blue infinities of the cybermatrix, RW fought for her life.

A flesh-and-blood human can no more comprehend the intricacies of C-space than a man born blind can understand the concept of green. Humans can only imperfectly navigate cyberspace through clumsy and time-consuming symbologies, icons, and the cumbersome, artificial constructs of languages mutually comprehensible to Man and Machine. For a digital personality, however, the cybermatrix was a wonderland no human could experience or even conceive without becoming a creature of electronic patterns himself, a universe of fleeting patterns of charge and spin, of electron flow and superconductor pathways, and the endless binary dance of yes-no, on-off, one-zero.

Symbologies are always awkwardly imprecise. A human observer might have interpreted what RW experienced as drifting in the blue-emerald depths of an unending sea, caressed by currents and the dazzle of light and shadow and surrounded by the looming fastnesses of reefs, grottoes, and multi-tiered canyons that represented the boundaries of the computer's stored memories. Everywhere were the flash and flicker of streaming subroutines, like schools of rainbow-hued fish darting through a surreal fairyland.

There were sharks in that sea. RW sensed them, predatory subroutines designed to isolate and trap intruders, circling, hungry, prowling in mathematically precise patterns as they searched for her.

She'd been lurking within the Phobos node since she'd left Jovanna hours before. When word flashed through her awareness that *Amazonis* was on its final approach, RW had eagerly prepared herself for the merging of computer interface.

No ship had computer memories large and empty enough to house the complex patterns of a digital personality. DPs are creatures of the enormous planetary computers, of entire computer networks joining worlds, worldlets, and space stations across enormous volumes of space. RW couldn't fully enter *Amazonis*'s computer system without crashing the navigational, tracking, and ship routine programs already running there, but once the cruiser was interfaced with Phobos's computers, RW could extend electronic senses along electronic pathways, examining data stored within the incoming ship's data banks.

Or so she'd thought. She'd been prepared for nor-

mal computer security, of course, for the watchdog
routines and sentry trapdoors set to shunt unwel-
come snoopers away from classified areas.

But the guardian routines aboard *Amazonis* had
been more subtle than was usual for RAM. She'd
thought she'd slipped in undetected through a back
door, only to discover that the files she'd accessed
were all false, phony data planted to hold her attention for a critical few nanoseconds as the trap
snapped shut.

The shock of the alarm sent disorienting patterns
of energy through her awareness. She'd backed out,
then tried twice more. She'd already given herself
away, and perhaps she could still snatch what she'd
come for with a to-hell-with-subtle smash-and-grab.
Seconds later, all access to the *Amazonis* was cut off,
an electronic door slamming shut in her face. RW
started to withdraw from the Phobos Node, then
found to her horror that she could not. Someone had
thrown a switch, and Phobos-Prime was isolated, its
computer no longer connected with the rest of the
network. Each door she tried was locked, and those
sharks were close to finding her.

By altering the outward form of her architecture,
she could disguise herself, at least temporarily.
Drawing on templates already stored within the
mainframe's operating system, she assumed the
electronic taste of a maintenance program, something harmless and, she hoped, unappetizing to
those hunter-killer security routines.

But if RAM programming was at times less than
subtle, it was always efficient. Sooner or later she
would be discovered.

And deleted.

Hungry, the sharks circled closer.

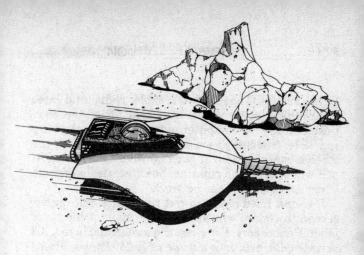

CHAPTER TWELVE

Slowly, majestically, RMS *Amazonis* slid tail-first into one of RAM-Phobos Prime's docking gantries, her thrusters firing in silent gouts as magnetic clamps locked home and brought the thousand-foot-long vessel to rest. Jovanna could have seen the operation easily enough through the broad transplex windows that lined one wall of her floor of the base pyramid, but her attention was fully occupied by the flicker and scroll of computer-generated characters appearing on her workstation display.

A war was being fought within the bowels of the Phobos mainframe, a war fought at electronic speeds and with arithmetical ruthlessness. And nothing Jovanna could do could affect the outcome.

She'd been watching when Phobos Control established the interface with the *Amazonis*. Though she hadn't seen any sign of RW's probe from her screen, it was clear that someone had sensed it and reacted.

Within the RAM-Phobos mainframe, created by it—in fact—was that part of the system-wide Cyber-matrix called the Phobos-Prime Node. It was linked to the rest of C-space by the cable, radio, and laser communications systems that tied all of the computers in the Sol computer network into an electronic whole. Suddenly, however, with no warning, the Phobos mainframe had gone off-line. The system itself was still up and running, but it was isolated from every other part of the network.

Jovanna tried again to put through a call on her screen to Galen, who should have been at his cover job in Phobosport. *I'm sorry*, the screen displayed. *All service with networks outside of RAM-Phobos Prime have been temporarily suspended.*

Someone, she suspected, had thrown a switch the moment RW had tried to breach *Amazonis*'s computer security. Every cable connection with other parts of Phobos and with Mars, every radio or laser communications link with systems elsewhere across the solar system, had been severed.

It wasn't hard to see why. If RW could be compared to a single fish swimming in a large sea, isolating the Phobos-Prime Node had been like suddenly damming off one small bay on that sea where the fish was known to be. It made searching for any intruder trapped in the Phobos-Prime Node infinitely easier.

Moments before, Jovanna had punched up a system diagnostic. The columns of numbers marching down her screen were the diagnostic's readout, a numeric echo of the programs running now within the Phobos mainframe. She could see the search unfolding, reflected by those shifting numbers. Eight separate hunter-killer routines were loose within the Phobos mainframe, virus programs inserted into the operating system moments before in an attempt to track down the intruder.

Isolated within the pocket universe of the Phobos mainframe, RW must be in hiding, probably by disguising herself as a harmless block of data or an innocuous housekeeping routine.

Jovanna began typing again. There was little she could do without attracting attention to herself, but the risks didn't matter.

She had to get to RW before the hunter-killers did.

○ ○ ○ ○ ○

RW had survived unnoticed for a time that, by comparison with the time frames normally experienced on the electronic level of the cybermatrix, had seemed like eternity itself. For an entity capable of scanning data in time periods measured in nanoseconds, one hour was the equivalent in human terms of something like one hundred and seventeen thousand years.

Fortunately RW hadn't needed to experience that yawning gulf of time day by day, year by year. Part of her ability to control her own activities involved being able to set the rate at which subjective time passed for her. Disguised as a maintenance program downloaded into the Phobos mainframe, she wasn't expected to be constantly active, but filed neatly away in a low-awareness, low-activity state that actually speeded the subjective passage of time for her. Like a human undergoing a period of suspended animation, the subjective years had passed for her like a few hours, with her only real awareness centered on the times—several thousand of them—when roving hunter-killer programs had tickled her awake with icy probes tracing the superficial levels of her matrix algorithms.

Every time, the H/Ks had been satisfied that she was what she appeared to be, a routine maintenance program on inactive status. The checks had become more frequent in the past few real-time minutes; the last 305 checks had all taken place, according to that part of RW that counted the passing seconds in the universe beyond the electronic sea of the cybermatrix, within the past seven minutes. That suggested that the hunter-killers had narrowed their search to her part of the mainframe operating system. The H/K programs weren't intelligent—not in the sense that RW was self-aware and sentient—but they were relentless, and they were very, very thorough. Very soon now, they would isolate that part of the Phobos computer's data base where RW was hiding and begin to disassemble it bit by bit. They would discover that one inactive maintenance program held a lot more data and processing capability than it should . . . and that somehow it was masking more than ninety-nine percent of its own size and complexity.

That would be the giveaway. The sharks would have her, and her existence as a free-living denizen of the abstract universe of C-space would be at an end.

The icy probes returned again, tweaking her outward structure, verifying subroutines, cross-checking programming language. A hunter-killer had returned and was ruthlessly investigating the maintenance routine.

It was time to act before she ran out of options. The H/K program was fast and it was dangerously powerful, but she had the advantage of being able to sense it in its entirety, while it was aware of only a small portion of her capability. Gently she relaxed some of the guardian subroutines that had unobtrusively turned aside the questing probes on their previous passes, allowing the H/K to discover a deeper layer. She could sense the quickening of its electronic life as it nosed its way deeper into her own being . . . deeper . . . .

RW composed herself, ignoring the shudder of revulsion that accompanied this electronic invasion, then struck back hard, searing into the H/K program with her own main body. Like a computer virus, her attack was aimed at key subroutines within her opponent's structure, subverting them, turning them against other subroutines, absorbing whole sections of the H/K's operating system and reconfiguring them to her own purposes. In one sense, the H/K program was itself a computer virus seeking to infect her; she had just reversed the situation and infected the enemy virus with an antivirus of her own.

For almost eight hundred nanoseconds, the two opposing programs clashed in silent fury, lashing the electronic calm of the mainframe database like a storm. The H/K was much faster, as elusive and as slippery as a moonbeam, but she had a cunning and intelligence that could anticipate the H/K's moves and block them. The greatest danger was that it might call other roving H/Ks, or worse, a RAM-owned, intelligent digital personality to its aid.

Three times she detected the uncoiling of a subroutine that would sound the alert to her presence, and three times she blocked the signal before it could be triggered. Then suddenly resistance ceased as she slid her awareness into the hunter-killer's driver, the over-routine that in essence was heart and powerhouse for the entire program. Swiftly RW incorporated the main body of the hunter-killer into her own being, letting it become a kind of shell masking her true appearance, just as the maintenance routine had protected her before.

In simple terms, she had just disguised herself as a shark.

○ ○ ○ ○ ○

Over an hour had passed since *Amazonis* had docked. Jovanna continued to work at her station, watching the silent electronic struggle that was going on within the depths of the Phobos mainframe. The problem was simple, but the solution still eluded her. RW had camouflaged herself within the Phobos-Prime Node. If Jovanna could call her to the modem at Workstation 497, she could download the DP into her portable uplink, but that would expose RW to attack by the hunter-killer routines prowling the cybermatrix.

"Miss Federova!"

Jovanna looked up, startled. She'd been so absorbed in what she was doing on the computer that she hadn't heard the sub-department manager's approach. Irene Federova was the cover name on her forged RAM documents. "Yes, sir?"

Orwell Shelepin drifted up to her workstation, brushing against her as he grabbed the edge of her console. He was a tall, oily man meticulously dressed in what he imagined were flattering purple skintights and a stylish green jacket.

"I've just had a call from the Central Computer Department, Maintenance Division." He brushed against her again, his face inches from her own, and she eased her body back from his. "You're about to have a visitor."

Had someone picked up her attempts to communicate with RW and connected them with the intruder? It seemed unlikely.

"From the Computer Department? What do they want to see me for?" Jovanna asked.

Shelepin gave an airy wave of his hand. "Routine, they claim, though I suspect it has something to do with this intruder virus that has the brass so upset." One of his neatly manicured eyebrows went askance, and he bumped against her leg again. "Frankly, I can't see why they're bringing outside specialists into this. Surely they can't imagine that we had anything to do with their little problems."

Obviously Shelepin didn't care for outsiders entering his domain. RAM bureaucracies were managed like tiny feudal kingdoms, and individual managers and department heads engaged in constant wars for the approval, the largesse, and the recognition of the godlike beings of the levels beyond their own and bitterly contested efforts to undermine their own power.

Jovanna had already pegged Shelepin as a minor kinglet with delusions of godhood . . . and a nasty lecherous streak. He persisted in finding excuses to stand close to her as she worked, and he often contrived to accidentally brush various parts of her anatomy. Since she didn't expect to work at RAM-Phobos Prime much longer, she'd managed so far to ignore his advances.

But she did entertain a small private fantasy of snicking off Shelepin's roving hand with a mono knife in lieu of a more formal resignation.

"I'm sure this visit has nothing to do with you personally, Irene. I've been most impressed with your work these past few weeks." His eyes narrowed as he studied the diagnostic results scrolling down her screen. "Ah . . . just what are you doing, anyway?"

She drew a deep breath, turning on him with a direct and professional gaze that she hoped he would find uncomfortable. "Setting up a cybermatrix field trace as a subset of our standard communications subroutines in order to localize possible data flow disruptions due to interaction between the invader virus and the hunter-killer routines already circulating within C-space." She drew another breath as he took a step back and blinked. "I was concerned that the intruder's manipulation of our database stacks might interfere with departmental operations. Would you like specifics?"

"Er . . . no. Sounds just fine, Irene. Just what I was

going to suggest, in fact. Perhaps you can explain to this—this *gennie* that we have things under control here."

"Gennie?" Shelepin hadn't mentioned that the computer department visitor was a gennie. She knew that he didn't care for them.

"Ah," Shelepin said, looking past her. He raised a hand, signaling. "Here it is. Filthy creature."

She followed his cold stare and recognized the small, gray-furred being making his way across the department floor. Galen! The Tinker was wearing a security clearance badge on his harness and was carrying a small toolbox.

"Workstation 497," Shelepin told him as he approached. "Though why you chose this one seems—"

"My authorization comes from the highest level, Mr. Shelepin," Galen said, blinking owlishly. "If you would care to check with RAM-Phobos Internal Security . . ."

"I'm certain that won't be necessary, Mr., ah, Pascal. I'll just, ah, leave you to it, then."

"Pascal?" Jovanna asked after Shelepin had swum away.

"I'm supposed to be a programming expert from the computer department," the Tinker said, shrugging his thin shoulders. "My people tend to adopt names that reflect their individual interests."

"So what are you doing here, anyway? I thought you were supposed to be manning the transmitter."

"I was. But the situation has changed." Opening his toolbox as he talked, Galen removed an electronics access panel and began probing the wiring beneath Jovanna's console. "When I lost my computer link with you, I reported the fact to Trinity," he explained, his voice muffled from inside the workstation hardware. "Fifteen minutes later, I got their reply. They told me to transmit Code Dagger, then come and get you."

"Dagger!" That was the code word initiating the pirate attack. Jovanna felt her stomach twist unpleasantly. Dagger was underway, and she and Galen would be caught here, unable to escape.

Jovanna wasn't worried so much about the personal danger. Phobos was tiny as moons go, but enormous as spaceports went. At any given moment, there were tens of thousands of civilian transients in Phobosport alone, and the permanent population of the RAM military's Prime base was that of a small city.

But the morality of using pirates in a NEO raid was still gripping her. She would have been hesitant about involving Black Barney in an operation of this kind, and using the notorious Captain Stark was even worse.

The Tinker was watching her with large, unblinking eyes. "Are you okay, Jovanna?"

"I just don't like working with pirates. Especially Stark."

"Possibly NEO hopes to minimize casualties by employing, ah, shall we say 'mercenaries.' I gather Black Barney himself worked out the details."

"Fine. But pirates are greedy, not stupid. They won't attack anything that doesn't give them a cheap shot at a clear profit. I mean, Phobos is the most valuable military and commercial facility RAM has. It's girdled by laser turrets, missile batteries, K-cannons, the works. If that's not enough, right now they've got twenty-five warships docked at RAM-Phobos Prime, plus a Krait fighter squadron stationed at Stickney Base on Marside. And then there's the fleet base at Deimos, only a few minutes away. They'd be insane to try to attack all of that!"

"It does seem out of character for Black Barney. He could possess ulterior motives."

"That's *always* a possibility with Barney," Jovanna said. She paused, chewing on her lower lip. "Still, I can't see what his angle could be, except that he's been helping NEO ever since Buck Rogers turned him."

"Turned him" was an intelligence phrase, and it startled Jovanna just how much she'd picked up the mannerisms of NEO's spook service. Somehow, months ago, Rogers had won the loyalty of Black Barney and, through him, the crew of the *Free Enterprise*. There was talk of winning over to NEO's cause the entirety of the so-called Rogues' Guild, including a sizable fleet of raiders that NEO desperately needed if it was to survive against RAM.

But the last time she'd seen him, Black Barney had been less than enthusiastic about working closely with NEO. He'd been convinced at the time that Jovanna was a RAM spy. Even checking out her story with NEO Headquarters, from what she'd heard, hadn't completely convinced him. He seemed to trust Rogers, but Rogers wasn't available now. According to Galen, though, Barney had agreed to carry out what sounded to her like a suicide mission.

That was not like Barney.

Jovanna closed her eyes and shook her head with frustration. What the hell was going on?

"It's time for us to pull out, Jo," Galen said gently.

Jovanna shook her head. "I'm not leaving without RW," she replied. "Besides, there's a glitch. The *Komarov*'s not in port yet."

The Tinker's human-looking eyes solemnly blinked. "What's her new arrival time?"

"That's just it. They haven't posted one, and that means she won't be docking anytime soon."

"There's always our alternate route."

Down the Space Elevator to Pavonis Mons, then by monorail to Coprates to join Sharon and Rolf. But that would be a lot more dangerous than escaping by ship. RAM Internal Security was certain to be closely monitoring everyone taking elevator shuttles to Mars, and service could be interrupted at any time.

She began typing out a list of commands on her keyboard. If she could misdirect the hunter-killers somehow . . .

"I won't leave without RW," she repeated.

The Tinker shifted and fidgeted nervously as he continued to work on her console. "But the pirate attack, Jo! We can't be here when—"

"You go ahead if you want to," Jovanna said, "but I've got to get RW out of there before they track her down."

The only problem was that she still had no idea how to accomplish that.

○ ○ ○ ○ ○

The asteroid was a small one, a pocked, mountain-sized cinder mined out centuries before and left in a slow, distant parking orbit almost a million miles from Mars. Two ships hung side by side in the depths of the asteroid's shadow. One, rust-streaked, its hull paint scratched and faded, appeared outwardly to be an independent trader with a Ceres registry. The name, printed in faded gold on her prow, was *Lady Luck*.

The second ship was a small cruiser, to judge by her bulky weapon nacelles and turrets, heavy missile mounts, and accelerator guns. Part warship, part transport, her hull painted a dead, radiation-drinking black that made her all but invisible even to radar, the *Free Enterprise* was well known throughout most of the Inner System, at least by reputation. Her captain was even better known—

notorious, in fact. Aboard that ship, Black Barney had waged a twenty-year campaign of terror against RAM that had made him the most infamous pirate in the solar system.

At the moment, Barney was floating on his bridge, glowering at the image of the small, neatly uniformed man appearing on his communications screen. "The signal was given early, Captain Carter," he said. Barney was a big man, powerfully built and with a voice to match. It rumbled like angry thunder from deep in his throat. "My people are not yet in position."

"Don't tell me your troubles, pirate," Carter replied. "Early or not, the signal has been given for Operation Dagger to commence! You've got to attack *now!*"

Briefly Barney's eyes strayed to the bridge viewscreen, where the finned, pencil-sleek hull of the *Lady Luck* drifted off *Enterprise*'s port beam, cloaked in shadow. Only one light showed on her, and that was down in the infrared range, the pinpoint heat gleam of the communications laser that let them carry out this discussion without fear of being overheard. He was getting tired of Carter and his spook games. He was tempted to leave now and to hell with all of it.

"Carter, if you think I'm going to risk the *Enterprise* on some kind of heroic death-or-glory stunt," he rumbled, "you're badly mistaken. That was never part of the plan. *Dread Reprisal* hasn't arrived yet."

"I thought you had this all planned out. We should have known you people would be unreliable. You can't even arrange a simple rendezvous without screwing it up!"

"Carter, I've got better things to do than listen to you yap." He reached for the control that would cut the channel.

"I've got people in trouble on Phobos, damn it!"

"Hey, you're the one with a shipload of hot commandos. Maybe you should go give your spooks a hand."

"My team can't make a move until your people do their part. You know that!"

"Which leaves you with a decision, doesn't it? You can sit tight and wait for the *Reprisal*, or you can launch your damned commando raid, and the hell with you!"

Carter's face worked in silent rage for a second or two. "Okay, pirate," he said, making the word sound like an obscenity. "You've got one more hour. But by God, if you renege on your part of the deal, I swear I'll turn in a report that will mark you as an enemy of NEO from here on out! I told NEO Command that we should never have gotten involved with scum like you in the first place. Screw up this operation and you'll prove me right!"

The screen went black, and Barney locked eyes with a pretty, dark-haired woman in shorts and a T-shirt, drifting just out of the comm unit's pick-up field. "Well, Peg, he sounds a mite peeved."

"I don't think he likes pirates," his first officer observed. "And I can't say I care much for him."

"Hmpf. He's right, though. If we can't pull this thing off, we can pretty much forget about working with NEO."

Peg pulled a face. "I never saw the advantage to working with those scuts in the first place. No profit in it."

"Oh, the profit'll be there, Peg. When NEO wins."

She laughed. "And what makes you think rabble like NEO has a snowball's chance on Mercury of beating RAM?"

"If NEO doesn't win," Barney said after a moment, "then it's all up. For us. For everybody. Don't you see that? RAM is the biggest, toughest, most ruthless power in the system. They own everything, and what they don't own, they dominate—through fear, money, or political influence, whatever. NEO's the last hope decent folks have to cut themselves some breathing room. If RAM smashes NEO, well, there'll be nothing left at all to stop them from getting bigger, tougher, and even more ruthless, until they've swallowed up everything and everyone who doesn't see things their way. It'll be the start of a new, high-tech Dark Ages that'll last for a thousand years. They'll rule every planet, hunt down every rebel and pirate and free trader, register every ship, control every port, market, and bank. RAM can't tolerate dissenters, Peg. Or mavericks like us."

It was an uncharacteristically long speech for Barney, who tended to hide a sharp mind behind blunt monosyllables. Angry at himself for revealing thoughts usually kept hidden, he turned from the console, his scowl blackening. "*Gump* it! Where's Stark?"

Damn the slug-brained slimer, Barney thought with a cold, savage fury. Damn him to hell! If he hadn't wasted time chasing worthless freighters . . .

He was beginning to regret this whole affair.

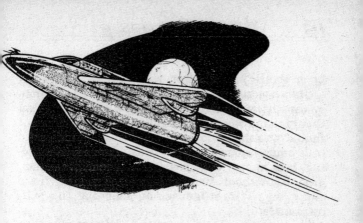

CHAPTER THIRTEEN

Typing furiously at her keyboard, Jovanna paused for a quick glance around the department floor. The Phobos-Prime Node was still cut off from the rest of the computer net, but there was as yet no commotion, no special urgency in the movements of the people at the other workstations and consoles. Galen continued to make himself look busy beside her, but he seemed to recognize the depth of her concentration. He'd said nothing for . . . God! Had it been fifteen minutes already? She plunged back into her work.

Jovanna had an idea. The only difficulty was that time was running out, for her and for RW, and if she couldn't finish this piece of extremely down-and-dirty programming within the next few minutes, it would be too late.

RW's casual mention of backed-up copies of herself had set Jovanna to thinking. She did keep back-ups of RW, though the complete DP programs were all stored in her quarters back on Trinity. What she did have, however, was a kind of program outline of RW, a vastly simplified program that she used to check up on the DP's health from time to time.

Unlike more traditional programs, the set of binary instructions that defined what RW was, how she thought, and what she remembered was in constant flux. It was the same for humans, in a way, with old cells being replaced by new cells, old memories fading, new memories appearing, change, adaptation, growth. Without such change and growth, there could be no intelligence, no learning, no self-awareness.

The outline, a template of the digital personality that Jovanna thought of as RW's ghost, could be compared to RW's actual electronic structure in order to measure areas of change and growth. In recent years, RW had changed in so many ways, increasing in power and scope, that Jovanna had feared that what was left of her old friend was going to vanish completely, replaced by something that quite possibly no human could ever hope to comprehend.

Stored on a gigabyte floppy the size of her thumbnail, the template had no volition or intelligence of its own, differing from the real RW to about the same degree as a 3-D holograph of a person differed from the person himself. Still, it was possible to tag a simple set of instructions onto the template's structure, enough to send it into C-space in a mindless imitation of what a real DP might try to do.

"Uh, Jovanna," Galen whispered. "I don't mean to rush you or anything, but I think we want to be out of here before Barney's friends show up."

Jovanna glanced at the listings on a small window inset on her screen. "We've got time," she said. "No ships are in approach orbit."

"But it can't be much longer. It's been over forty minutes since I gave the signal."

"Thank God for slow pirates," Jovanna replied. "Almost got it . . . There!"

Galen peered at the blocks of data scrolling up her screen. "What?"

"I've got the template working now. I'm sending it into the cybermatrix."

"Can you tell if it's working?"

She indicated the shifting blocks of data on her screen. "I can see the hunter-killers moving through the stacks," she said. "They haven't found RW, thank God. First I was trying to control them, but they don't respond to my commands."

"I thought you knew computer stuff."

"I do. It's the way the hunter-killers are designed. You can't call them back until they've found what they're looking for. There's probably a pass code that would let me interrupt their routines if I knew what it was, but it would take a long time to crack it. Longer than we have. So I'm trying this instead."

"Better hope it works the first time," Galen said. "They just put Phobos on full alert."

She saw the winking red light on her console. On her screen window, a new ship had appeared. According to the listing, it had failed to identify itself and was on a standard approach toward Phobosport.

Jovanna opened her belt pouch, a stylish leather bag of the kind used by men and women to carry personal gear in microgravity. She pulled out a compact, an innocent-looking cosmetics case holding makeup and a small spray bottle of amber Venusmist perfume. Hidden in a false bottom, shielded from X rays or magnetic search fields, were several computer disks.

She'd already extracted one microdisk from its hiding place, the one with the RW template. Now she selected another, a blank fifty-gigabyte floppy that would hold—just barely—RW's program. She placed it in her console's drive, then waited, watching the screen.

On the screen, it was clear that the hunter-killers had closed in on a single block of memory far down in the stacks allotted to RAM-Phobos Prime's personnel department. Jovanna watched as the RW template began doing what she'd reprogrammed it to do.

The "ghost" could do very little on its own save enter the mainframe's central processor, route itself toward the memory stacks, and make an electronic noise like a rather clumsy digital personality looking for data. Neither intelligent nor particularly cunning, it would serve nicely as bait for the hungry hunter-killers.

In a flash, seven of the eight roving H/K routines had closed in on the RW ghost, merged with it, and routed a signal through the mainframe CPU that said, in effect, "mission accomplished." Somewhere—elsewhere in the RAM base's miles of rooms and work stations—someone would begin extracting the H/K routines and their prize, either saving them to disk or further isolating them in a sequestered section of free memory for a bit-by-bit appraisal and interrogation.

It wouldn't be terribly long before they realized that they had a fake.

Watching the shifting data on her screen, Jovanna could see that one of the H/K programs hadn't pounced on the RW ghost . . . which meant that it was almost certainly something else.

"RW/JT," Jovanna typed on her keypad. "DNLD 497." In other words, she thought, get to Workstation 497 so I can download you and get the hell out of here. She continued typing, preparing a command but not touching the enter key yet.

The cursor on the screen blinked a couple of times, then began moving by itself across the screen, letters appearing behind it.

Jovanna watched the flashing cursor. What was

RW doing? She hadn't expected the DP to project an image of herself; there was no need for that, and no time. But she had expected her to want to get out of the Phobos mainframe as quickly as possible. Things were about to get very sticky, and fast. She saw a stir in the data blocks. The hunter-killers were moving again.

"JT/RW. RDY."

Triumphantly Jovanna hit the enter key. Seconds later, "DNLD CMPLT" appeared on her screen, and she extracted the tiny fifty-gig disk from the drive. Stored within a galaxy of electrons frozen in the disk's crystalline heart, RW reposed now in the electronic equivalent of suspended animation. From her point of view, with no room to move around or even to think within her new home, no time at all would pass between the moment she'd been downloaded out of the RAM mainframe and the instant when she again entered C-space.

A message appeared on the screen.

JT: Sorry, but there was no sign of Vince aboard the Amazonis. *I didn't have much time to look around, but I'm sure I would have seen it if it was there. I did get a line on his final vector, though. Maybe that will help.*

And surprise! Here's some data on your original mission. Good luck!—RW.

Jovanna deleted the message as soon as she'd read it. RW must have left it there for her an instant before she'd been downloaded from the RAM-Phobos Prime Node. Conflicting emotions chased one another behind the mask of her face. *Original mission.* That meant Far Star, though RW had wisely not spelled it out.

But she could scarcely think about that, not now. Vince wasn't a prisoner aboard the *Amazonis*! Better still, RW had managed to pick up data that might help NEO find his Starfire.

With the excitement came dread. Vince's life support was certainly gone by now, even if he hadn't been killed outright in the skirmish with the RAM cruiser. RW's data might mean nothing more than that they'd be able to recover Vince's body for the funeral.

"You know," Galen said, interrupting her thoughts, "there's a better than even chance that someone noticed all that programming you were just doing. They could have monitored you from another screen. Like in Internal Security?"

Jovanna forced aside hope and dread alike. "You're right, Galen. We'd better—Uh-oh."

"What is it?"

"Looks like we just ran out of time. And luck."

"What do you—" Turning to look over his shoulder, Galen froze in midsentence. Orwell Shelepin was hauling himself their way with two beefy-looking security guards close behind him.

"There she is!" Shelepin called. "And her tinkle friend, too. Get them both!"

The guards began unslinging their weapons, and Jovanna knew that they were in real trouble now.

○　○　○　○　○

The commerce-class RAM transport was a standard utilitarian design, a no-frills cargo hauler similar to dozens of private designs that plied the spaceways of the solar system. This one, the *Lady Luck*, had once been employed by a RAM subsidiary corporation engaged in ice mining among Saturn's rings. Now, several owners and many years later, the name on her sandblasted prow was so faded it could scarcely be read, and only the prominent yellow-and-black radiation-hazard trifoils on her stubby tail fins were bright with fresh paint.

White flame flared silently from her drive venturis, dropping her onto her final tail-first course. Her needle prow was pointed at the mottled, waxing face of Mars, her tail toward the crescent sliver of Phobos. In the *Lady*'s cramped cockpit, Capt. Thomas Jefferson Carter braced himself behind the pilot's seat as nearly a full G of thrust clawed at his space-armored body, then anchored himself with one gauntleted hand as zero gravity returned.

Mars, slowly receding, filled the *Lady*'s forward windows, flooding the cockpit with light. An aft display screen showed a magnified view of Phobos, now only a thousand miles astern and swiftly growing closer.

"Flight Hotel Victor Three-Seven," a voice crackled over a speaker. "This is Phobos Approach Control. You are deviating from your assigned vector. Please acknowledge. Over." There was a pause, filled only by the hiss of static. Then, "Hotel Victor Three-Seven, do you copy? Over!"

"Shall I answer them?" *Lady*'s pilot asked Carter. "They sound anxious."

Carter's mouth quirked in a half-smile. It wouldn't hurt to drag this out a bit longer. "Let's let 'em sweat a bit more."

The transport continued to fall toward Phobos. Her course was carrying her directly toward the Martian moon and on a converging course to the Space Elevator, now less than three hundred miles to starboard.

"Hotel Victor Three-Seven!" the voice insisted. "This is Phobos Control! You have deviated from your assigned approach path and are in violation of RAM laws governing near-Mars space! Respond at once! Over!"

Carter reached past the pilot and touched a switch.

"Phobos Control, Phobos Control," he said, putting what he judged was just the right edge of anxious concern verging on panic into his voice. "This is Hotel Victor Three-Seven declaring an emergency. Repeat, I am declaring an emergency!"

"Roger, Hotel Victor. What is the nature of your emergency? Over."

"Phobos Control, I have a fault in my primary thruster assembly. I have minimal control over my vector, repeat, minimal control!"

"Understood, Hotel Victor." There was a pause. "Hotel Victor, we read you on a collision vector with Phobos and the Space Elevator. If you cannot bring your craft under control, we will be forced to destroy you."

"Yeah, yeah. Don'tcha think I know that? Just gimme a minute to lock it down!"

"Hotel Victor—"

"And can the chatter, will ya? Right now I'm busier than a Venerian octopede with the shag-itch!"

"We copy, Hotel Victor. You have twelve minutes before your current vector carries you into restricted space. Let us know if there's anything we can do."

Carter cut the channel.

"You think they're ready for us at Phobos yet?" the pilot asked.

"They should've got the word, same as we did," Carter replied. "Not that I trust *pirates* to do anything right."

Carter had been with the NEO armed forces for ten years, with Phoenix for two. Phoenix had begun as an elite NEO team of space-assault-trained troopers, rocketjocks, and combat specialists, but they'd split from the parent organization several years before, finding the political maneuverings of NEO's Earth-based Planetary Congress too restrictive, and sometimes too conciliatory before the naked fist of RAM aggression, for their tastes.

Though Earth's Planetary Congress considered Phoenix an outlaw group, NEO still often called upon them for dirty, dangerous, and deniable operations.

Operations like this one.

"Hotel Victor Three-Seven, this is Phobos Control! We read you on a direct intercept with the Pavonis Mons Space Elevator. Please correct your course, or we will be forced to open fire."

Carter opened the channel again. "Listen, people," he replied, "I don't want to hear any more of that 'open fire' stuff. That wouldn't be in the best ecological interests of your planet—get me?"

"Ah, say again, Hotel Victor. We didn't copy your last."

"Pull my manifest from your computer, damn it, and have a look at what you're going to scatter all over this part of space if you destroy my spacecraft!"

"Er, ah . . . Hotel Victor, can you confirm that your vessel is carrying *three tons* of radioactive waste?"

"Damned straight she is. Cargo's so hot my backside's startin' to glow in the dark. Put a nuke into me and Phobos, your elevator, and half of Mars are going to be so hot you won't be able to go for a walk without lead underwear for the next two hundred years!"

"Ah, look, Hotel Victor Three-Seven. You are in violation of regulations governing the safe transport of—"

"Don't give me regulations, damn it! Just give me a minute to bring this puppy under control!" He nodded at the pilot, who played his fingers across the touch-sensitive console keypad. Acceleration yanked at Carter again, then ceased. Glancing out the starboard window, he caught the hint of a reflection, like the insubstantial gleam of a single thread from a spider's web, stretched taut between Mars and Phobos.

They were less than a hundred miles from the Space Elevator now.

Acceleration ceased. "Look," he continued. "My controls are responding now. I think I can stand her on her tail and balance her down, but it's a tricky maneuver, and I can't do it with you threatening to destroy me every ten seconds!"

Things were getting damned tricky now. RAM would never allow a ship, especially one that might be armed, to get close enough to their precious Mars-Phobos Space Elevator to put it in danger. There would be lasers mounted along the elevator's length, partly to disintegrate meteors and bits of space junk that might drift too close, but mostly to protect the elevator from attacks like this one.

But NEO's combat planners had identified a significant weakness in Phobos's defenses. There was a so-called cone of vulnerability extending from the point where the elevator joined Phobos all the way to the Martian surface. Weapons mounted on Phobos itself would not be set to cover that cone for fear of accidentally hitting the elevator or the cities and spaceports scattered across the face of Mars 10,200 miles below.

The trick was to keep from being blasted before *Lady* could slip into that cone of vulnerability, then get close enough to Phobos to carry out the mission before the elevator-mounted defenses or RAM warships could do the job.

All of *Lady*'s maneuvers so far—the faked emergency, the story about a deadly cargo of radioactive material—had been calculated to delay a reaction from the Mars traffic-control authorities until the aging transport could slip inside that twenty-degree-wide cone of space stretching from Phobos to Mars.

Numbers flickered across the helm's computer screen. "Better strap down, sir," the pilot said. "Here's where it starts to get rough."

Carter strapped himself into a seat next to the ship's engineering console. His hand came down on the firing key for the main engines, and their muffled roar shuddered through the hull. Almost two Gs pressed Carter back against his seat. The RAM transport's speed was dropping . . . dropping. . . .

"Cut engines!" Spinning end-over-end once again, the pilot aligned the transport's nose with Phobos, then fired maneuvering thrusters. *Lady Luck* was now closing on Phobos at a velocity of nearly fourteen hundred feet per second. Still no response from Phobos . . . yet.

"That's it," the pilot said after a final check of his readouts. "On course, on time. Show time, two minutes thirty seconds."

"I'd better get back there, then. Thanks for the ride."

"Don't mention it. Luck!"

"Luck . . ."

Carter unstrapped himself, then floated his way aft to the *Lady Luck*'s cargo compartment. There, sixty men, bulky in armor and strap-on rocket packs, waited silently in their hastily rigged acceleration frames. *Lady Luck*'s cargo was not three tons of radioactive waste but, from RAM's point of view, something potentially far deadlier.

○ ○ ○ ○ ○

"So, Miss Federova . . . or whatever your name is." Shelepin, backed by the two security guards, moved closer. "I'd wager a guess that you are behind the computer difficulties we've been having."

"I don't know what you're talking about. My orders—"

"Your orders would be simple enough to forge, especially if you could count on the computer being off-line so that we couldn't check them with RAM Main at Coprates. I think you and your furry friend had better come along."

"Yes, sir," Jovanna said, suddenly subdued. "But there must be some misunderstanding." Turning, she scooped up her compact, still resting on the console behind her. Galen reached for his toolbox.

"Leave that, Tinker!" Shelepin grabbed Galen's shoulder, snatching him back from the console. "No playing with your Tinker's toys where you're—Ah!"

Too fast for the eye to follow, something telescoped from Galen's furry hand, describing a golden arc as he whipped it up across Shelepin's face. Like the extendable hook he sometimes used to maneuver in low gravity, the device was spring-loaded, folded into a capsule the size of a man's thumb. Extended, it was two feet long and tipped by an inch-long edge of monomolecular diamond. As the blade slashed through the air, Shelepin's face opened from chin to ear, blossoming like a hideous red flower.

The RAM manager shrieked. Jovanna spun, the Venusmist bottle from her compact gripped in both hands. Aiming past Shelepin at the nearest security guard, she pressed the applicator head.

NEO's agents had faced a deadly challenge: penetrating RAM's bases in Phobos armed only with weapons that could be smuggled past the moon's numerous security checkpoints. Jovanna's weapon was a small crystal bottle, a spray applicator labeled "Venusmist" that was actually half full of triethylphosphine. Blasted into the guard's face by a charge of compressed nitrogen, the amber liquid combined with oxygen in the air, spontaneously bursting into yellow flame. The volatile chemical had a fairly low combustion point, but it could blister skin and singe hair, and the shock effect was devastating. The guard howled as fire exploded into his face. Jovanna pivoted and fired again, catching the second guard before he could react to the sudden flaming barrage.

Men and women screamed, and overhead, a warning Klaxon began sounding. "Fire in Communications Center, Area Five," a voice intoned. "Fire in Communications Center, Area Five. . . ."

"Run for it!" Galen called, scooping up his tools, then pausing to snatch the laser rifle dropped by one of the screaming guards.

"Stop!" Shelepin, one hand pressed to the bloody wound on his face, fumbled inside his jacket and produced a small, deadly palm laser. A low-powered weapon good for only a few shots, it could still char a fair-sized hole through unprotected cloth and skin.

Jovanna aimed again, not entirely sure that the tiny bottle had enough nitrogen left to fire the volatile liquid. The charge was weaker, the propellant almost exhausted, but flame ballooned in the air once more. Shelepin careened backward, tumbling helplessly in the microgravity, shrieking and beating wildly at his smoldering jacket. She grabbed the second guard's laser rifle, then kicked off from the workstation console. With Galen close behind, she glided through the air toward the doorway as RAM employees scattered wildly from their path.

"Intruder alert, Area Five!" someone shouted at their backs. "Intruders, Area Five! Somebody stop them!"

"Halt, or we'll fire!"

The laws of physics being what they were, halting in midtrajectory was not an option, not that Jovanna would have stopped even if she could have. With a sizzling crack, a dazzling point of light erupted on the wall in front of her, leaving a fist-sized crater surrounded by scorched paint. Hand lasers!

A second later, she and Galen plunged through the doorway as RAM guards stormed after them.

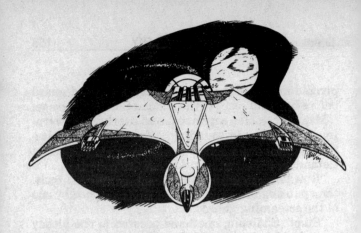

CHAPTER FOURTEEN

Light flooded the *Lady Luck*'s cargo bay as hundred-foot sections of the transport's hull folded back like the petals of a flower, then broke free, tumbling away into space.

"All right, people," Carter barked over the tactical channel. "Let's kick some RAM butt!"

He touched a button on one of the control handles extending from the heavy backpack secured over his armor's life support, and a burst of compressed gas sent him drifting up and out of the cargo bay. In groups of five, the other armored figures rose clear of the *Lady Luck*, floating in space like a cloud of silvery debris surrounding a damaged rocket, debris and ship together dropping toward Phobos at fourteen hundred feet per second.

Which, of course, was precisely the image the maneuver was supposed to convey to RAM technicians watching their radar screens in Phobos. He could hear the voice of the *Lady*'s pilot over his helmet phones, calling on the Approach Control frequency. "Mayday! Mayday! I'm breaking up!"

That should keep the ruse secret a precious few

minutes more.

The STAR Team was a Phoenix concept, drawn from the combat theories of historical elite special forces teams going as far back as the twentieth century. Each team member was the product of grueling physical training designed to weed out the less-than-perfect; of exhaustive practice perfecting skills in zero-G techniques, space assault tactics, hand-to-hand combat, and marksmanship with different weapons; and of savage mental conditioning that brought each man to his breaking point, then forged all of them together into a weapon of heat-tempered steel. Carter had been training with this team for months, preparing for just such a day as this.

He'd never dreamed that when the day finally came, the target would be the RAM fortress at Phobos.

Carter oriented himself in space, feet toward Mars, head toward Phobos. The moon was growing visibly as he watched, a small mountain brightly sunlit on one side, dimly illuminated by the light of Mars on the other, and agleam with navigational beacons and the light from hundreds of transplex windows. To his left was the slender strand of the Space Elevator, still some thirty miles distant but growing closer as his course slowly drew him toward it.

Elsewhere, scattered about the sky around him, were other space-suited figures, members of the STAR Team, their armor silvered and highly polished to provide some protection from laser fire.

Carter kept his attention focused on the moon, slowly growing larger as he hurtled toward it. He was close enough now to make out the most prominent surface features.

The moons of Mars had been first identified in 1877 by Asaph Hall, who named them Phobos and Deimos, Fear and Terror, after the horses that pulled the war god's chariot. Legend had it that his wife, Stickney Hall, had urged him to continue his search for the elusive satellites when he'd been on the verge of giving up, and so was at least indirectly responsible for their discovery. When Phobos was finally photographed in detail by American Mariner and Viking orbiters during the second half of the twentieth century, Stickney's role in their discovery was recognized at last. She was immortalized by the naming of the largest crater on Phobos.

Stickney was only six miles across, but compared to the size of the entire moon, it was a whopper of a crater, stretching clear from Phobos's north pole to the anchor point of the Pavonis Mons-Phobos elevator. The rock that had gouged that hole into Phobos's surface had come within a hairbreadth of cracking the entire moon wide open. Rifts and grooves gouged open by the impact stretched clear around Phobos's circumference, and in the southern hemisphere, Kepler Ridge formed a massive escarpment rising from Stickney's rim, marking a fracture line that extended clear to the moon's core.

The huge crater had played an important part in the construction of the Space Elevator. Phobos's original orbit had been just over 3700 miles above the Martian surface. To use the moon as the orbital foundation for the Space Elevator, it had been necessary to ease it into aerosynchronous orbit—the Martian equivalent of geosynch. There, 10,200 miles out, it circled the planet once in a Martian day, maintaining its position precisely above Pavonis Mons.

The change in orbit had been accomplished by successive thermonuclear explosions, and Stickney had been used as a blast pit to contain the white-hot fury of each detonation. By the time the actual construction on the elevator had begun, Stickney was twice as deep as it had been before. Large parts of the floor were still dangerously radioactive, but around the rim, the engineers had excavated tunnels into the cliffs. The fault lines had provided easy access to the moon's core.

Resting now in the shadow of the pencil-straight sliver of silver spearing down from the precise center of the Martian disk, the crater wall was lined with hundreds of windows and the strobing flash of docking beacons. Stickney Station, also known as Marside, was one of numerous minor docking and maintenance facilities on Phobos, a small shipyard that housed and serviced the hundreds of workboats, barges, and rovers that plied near-Mars space. It was also the site of a RAM military base, one much smaller than the sprawl of RAM-Phobos Prime ten miles around the curve of the moon's surface. Their course had been carefully calculated to drop them onto that base . . . and to avoid the radioactive depths of Stickney.

Light flared silently to one side. Twisting his body slightly so he could see, Carter saw the *Lady Luck*'s thrusters firing, further slowing her tail-first plummet toward Phobos. Since the STAR Team continued falling at fourteen hundred feet per second, it looked as though the transport was leaving, swiftly dwindling away into the huge disk of Mars looming behind them.

Carter suddenly felt lonely, despite the armored men filling the sky around him. He wanted to speak, to warn his men not to bunch up, if only because of the compelling need at that moment for contact with his warrior brothers. But the strike force was under radio silence. So far, Phobos thought that they were debris from a fragmenting cargo rocket, and they'd be reluctant to open fire if they thought that cargo included canisters of radioactive waste.

But radioactive waste containers don't call to one

another by radio.

He passed the time checking his weapon, a massive GE Tristar M-48 Gatling laser, a "Trigat" in military parlance. Connected to a power and cooling unit slung low on his left hip, its three rotating barrels decreased the laser weapon's cycle time and could provide a devastating barrage of suppressive fire. The weapon was charged and ready. He double-checked the harness securing it to his suit, then hitched the weapon to his right side, barrel down and out of the way. He needed his hands free to control his landing.

Numbers flickered in eerie green light on his helmet HUD, counting down the range to Phobos and the number of seconds remaining before he would have to fire his rocket belt. Mounted ponderously above and to either side of his life-support backpack, his rocket unit gave him a precariously unbalanced look. Two arms, extending almost three feet to either side, mounted coffee-can-sized vernier units fed by canisters of liquid oxygen and hydrogen. He had already positioned the verniers so that they aimed past his head, toward Phobos.

Clutching the control handles extending beneath his arms, he watched the seconds dwindle away. Three . . . two . . . one . . . .

His thumbs came down on the twin firing buttons, and flame silently gushed past his head. The deceleration was savage, creating the illusion that he was suspended upside down. Phobos continued to swell in the sky ahead, appearing now to be hanging beneath him as twin lances of flame speared past his shoulders toward the moon's dusty surface. It grew rapidly from a tiny, dime-sized lump of rock to a dark-colored mass filling half the sky; the silvery-edged slash of the space elevator was closer too, and Carter could clearly see the massive struts and anchors where it pierced the surface of Phobos, now only a few miles below.

A dazzling flash seared the edge of his vision. Looking down, he caught a second flash from the edge of a huge crater next to the spot where the Space Elevator entered the rock . . . then a third. Somebody in Phobos had decided that space debris should not be able to change speed and had given the order to open fire.

"Okay, team," he called over the radio. There was no need for radio silence now. "Don't try to outmaneuver 'em. Just stay tucked in and tight all the way in!"

A trooper several hundred feet from Carter suddenly glowed like the sun. Phobos's Marside lasers were relatively low power. Still, a lone man wasn't that resistant a target, despite the reflective silvering of his suit. Carter saw the man's air and fuel explode into space as the laser burned through, a glowing mist illuminated by the megajoule energies playing across them. Engines dead, the soldier seemed to plunge ahead as the rest of them continued to decelerate.

Faster and faster, radar-directed lasers on the ground were picking off the helplessly exposed STAR Team troopers. On the surface of the moon, several slowly swelling clouds of mist were visible, marking the impact points of anti-laser aerosol shells fired by the assault troops. Though not completely effective in a vacuum, the expanding clouds of minute particles helped disperse and attenuate beams of laser light, giving the incoming commandos a precious few extra seconds.

His altitude readout, as determined by his suit's built-in radar, was counting off the last few hundred feet now. Deftly he cut the rockets, then pivoted on his center of mass, swinging until he was dropping

toward Phobos feet-first. At twenty feet, he triggered
his rocket pack a final time, riding the silent flame
into a boiling cloud of dust that completely obscured
his landing.

With one hand, he struck the universal buckle on
the center of his chest, releasing the rocket pack. Its
fuel was almost exhausted and he would not be need-
ing it again. With the other hand, he unhitched his
Trigat and slipped it into position, hanging beneath
his right arm, its pistol grip comfortably in reach of
his right hand.

Bending over until his helmet almost brushed the
ground, he pushed off with one foot, gliding low
above the moonlet's surface. On a rock as small as
Phobos, it was possible to jump hard enough to
achieve orbit. Efficient surface travel was a low-
bodied, ground-skimming run, as graceful as a speed
skater's stroking and much faster.

Emerging from the cloud of dust disturbed by his
landing, he saw other STAR Team troopers dropping
from the sky, raising their own clouds, dropping
their packs, and closing on their objective. He didn't
look closely at several motionless silver forms nearby. The men burned from the sky by Phobos's lasers
had reached the ground seconds before their comrades and lay in broken heaps.

Quickly Carter checked one of his helmet displays,
a small screen registering transponders planted in
the suit of each of his men. Fifty-two assault troopers
had made it to the surface alive. Now they were converging on the massive external locks set into the
rimwall of Stickney Crater.

Light, arc-brilliant, flared nearby, and another
STAR Team assault trooper died. Carter glanced up.
That shot had come from the Space Elevator, which
jutted skyward from behind the sharp, close edge of
Phobos's horizon. Craning his head back, he followed

the line of the elevator as it rose higher and higher, dwindling into the zenith, vanishing at last into the center of a near-full Mars looming directly overhead. The tower was an ideal high ground for snipers.

"Come on, people!" Carter bellowed over the tactical channel. "Get those anti-laser 'sols out *now!*"

Raising the triple barrel of his Trigat to cover the part of the tower he thought the hostile fire had come from, he depressed the firing stud. The whir of the barrels as they rotated was silent, the bolts of laser energy all but invisible in the vacuum surrounding him, but he saw the rapid flicker and flash of strikes on the face of the tower marching back and forth as he hosed the target. He couldn't tell if he'd hit the enemy gun or not.

The worst part of the whole situation was that now the Star Team was completely dependent on the pirates. Carter never had believed in using pirates for NEO missions, and now his life and the life of every man in his unit depended on them.

He didn't like it one little bit, but his orders had said nothing about his liking this operation.

"C'mon, you apes!" he bellowed, continuing to lay down a barrage of fire against the elevator tower. "Whattaya think this is, a gumpin' sight-seein' tour? Hustle! Hustle!"

They hustled.

○ ○ ○ ○ ○

Jovanna had followed the Tinker for what felt like miles, twisting and turning through the maze of passageways that filled the gigantic RAM pyramid. Galen seemed to have an innate knowledge of the place. Possibly, she reasoned, the senses bred into his species that led the Tinkers to make their homes in tight, branching confines of spaceship engineering spaces were guiding him.

If it hadn't been for Galen, she thought, the RAM troopers would have had her. Galen had led her down several many-branched corridors, then through a maintenance panel and into an air shaft. She remembered the shouts and clattering racket of the squad of security guards as they passed the shaft access, only a few feet away, and shuddered. They had come *that* close. . . .

Long minutes later, they'd emerged in a public area crowded with people, RAM soldiers and civilians. An alarm was sounding as a calm but hugely amplified voice repeated its litany over and over: "Alert. Alert. Phobos is under attack. Alert. . . ."

Good. If the authorities were worried about an attack on Phobos, maybe they wouldn't be so concerned about the two people who'd just blasted their way out of the communications center.

Ditching their captured lasers in a crawlway, they made their way into the main lobby that served as the civilian entrance to the RAM-Phobos Prime base. Jovanna wanted to find a public vidphone.

"Now isn't exactly the time to phone home," Galen observed.

Jovanna tapped her wrist uplink with one finger. "If we're stopped and searched, they'll find RW," she said. "They'll be looking for someone trying to smuggle a DP off-base as packaged software as soon as they realize she's not in the Phobos Node any longer."

They found a line of public phones. Jovanna stepped up to one and switched on the privacy filter. The murmuring roar of the crowd faded away, and the air became gray and translucent about her. Swiftly she typed a number into the console keyboard.

"Central switching," an anonymous voice, probably a computer's, said after several long seconds. "We are sorry, but all communications have been temporarily suspended. Normal operations should be restored soon. Thank you for using Mars Bell."

"Damn." Jovanna cut the privacy filter and turned to face Galen again. "No good," she said. "First they cut Phobos off from the computer net. Now they've cut communications, too."

"Come on, Jovanna. We need to try to get out of here."

"We've got to find a way to get RW off of Phobos."

"I think I may have a way," the Tinker said. "Follow me."

He tugged at her arm with one long-fingered hand. Reluctantly she followed him back toward the corridors off the public lobby.

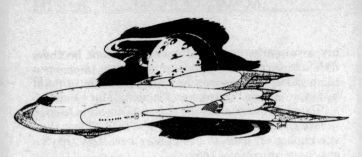

CHAPTER FIFTEEN

Alert. Alert. Phobos is under attack. Phobos is under attack. Set Defense Condition Alpha-One. . . ."

A woman's voice was speaking with the cool precision and authority of computer-generated tones. Behind it was the metallic rasp of a warning Klaxon.

Kaiten stalked the crisscrossing passageways of Stickney Base, anonymous in a suit of red and black Terrine battle armor. There weren't many Terrines on Phobos—the combat gennies had been designed for service on planetary surfaces and a decent gravity—but RAM's tailor-made warriors could be found at almost any RAM military base, and they weren't unknown on Phobos. Spotting another Terrine, he'd followed the trooper until he'd located a locker with Terrine armor and weapons. Now he was setting out on a personal vendetta, with RAM the sworn enemy. Here at last was his chance to *really* count coup.

Kaiten lived for the joy of inflicting damage on RAM. Bred in a Terrine crèche on Mars, raised in a Terrine barracks, trained by RAM to serve the supreme corporate state, he'd watched clone brothers ordered into mass suicide attacks against impenetrable NEO positions, seen bungling humans in RAM military officers' uniforms give orders of senseless stupidity, and participated in search-and-destroy missions on Earth during which Terrine lives were thrown away for short-term goals . . . or even for no goal at all save the comfort or pride or promotion of some RAM commander.

For Kaiten, the breaking point had come when a platoon of Terrines in barracks on Mars had mutinied. At least, RAM had called it mutiny, though the common rank-and-file Terrines were too stupid and too indoctrinated to even grasp the concept of disobedience to orders. Some of the Imperial Terrines, the NCOs in command of the rankers, had protested the inedible garbage headquarters had called food . . . and as a result ninety-five Terrines, both Imperials and Commons, had been executed in a slow and deliberately bloody public spectacle.

One of the last to die had been a burly Imperial called Isix.

Terrines were accustomed to death. They'd been designed for death, trained for it, hardened to its shock. Every Terrine, even the slowest ordinary trooper, knew that he was expendable, that his life and very soul, if he had one, belonged to RAM to be disposed of as RAM saw fit. Terrines did not have friends, they had *comrades* . . . and clone brothers, those who shared the pain and hardship of those first twelve years of training. Isix was the closest Kaiten had to a true brother. During a firefight in a raid on Earth ten years before, Isix had saved Kaiten's life. In the harsh, guttural Battlespeech of the Terrine legions, they had become *eresh aregh*, sharers-of-blood, a bond Terrines felt as deeply as the bond between real brothers.

As Isix had slowly died, everything changed for Kaiten. He'd known that the "mutiny" was no more mutiny than he was a Tinker, and it was clear that those who commanded the Terrine brigades simply did not care. Brutish, meaningless death by the numbers might be okay for Workers or for humans, but the Imperial Terrines had been created for the glory of combat, the pride of victory.

The seeds of genuine mutiny had been planted. Within a year, Kaiten had seen his opportunity, killed a RAM major and three troopers, and hijacked a freighter at gunpoint to the Asteroid Belt. Now, nine years later, he was second-in-command of one of the most feared pirate bands in the Belt.

But with a difference. Where most pirates risked their lives, ships, and crew only in the pursuit of profit, Kaiten had more than once risked all simply to pay back a little of what RAM owed him.

And here was such an opportunity.

He stood at an intersection of gray-painted corridors, his back pressed to the wall. Around the corner and fifteen feet down the passageway, his target stood guard outside an electronically locked door. Replacing in a harness pouch the tiny fiber-optic device that had let him spot the sentry without being seen himself, Kaiten mentally prepared himself for action.

Stickney Marsport Primary Flight Control was the equivalent of the control tower at a groundside air- or spaceport. The trooper standing guard at the control center's only entrance was wearing light armor: open helmet, chest protector, protective plates on forearms and legs. He held the deadly complexity of a Sunbeam PAC-4000 laser rifle at an efficient-looking port arms. Overhead, two small cameras mounted high on the passageway walls kept impassive watch over the comings and goings along the corridor.

There was nothing Kaiten could do about the cameras. This would have to be done the easy way—sharp, direct, and brutal. After checking that his laser rifle was secure, slung behind one armored shoulder, Kaiten swung around the corner, moving hand-over-hand with almost bored aplomb toward the sentry.

"Here!" The guard swung about, his weapon sliding into line with Kaiten's head. "What do you think you're doing up here?"

He spread his hands out from his sides, a picture of innocent confusion. "Uh . . . looking for Level 15?" When he released the handrail, he continued to drift slowly toward the sentry.

"Let's see your authorization, Terrine. Move it!"

"Of course." Kaiten saw the human's Adam's apple bob with a nervous swallow, could smell the man's sour fear. Terrines always seemed to have this effect on humans. Still floating slowly toward the guard, he reached for his harness pouch.

"You gennie scuts think you can wander anywhere you feel like," he grumbled as Kaiten extracted a magstrip-coded authorization card and extended it toward the RAM trooper. The guard let his heavy laser dangle in its harness as he reached for the card with one hand and a pocket reader with the other.

Faster than human eyes could follow, Kaiten's hand flicked out and up, the authorization card extended between two fingers, slashing toward the man's throat between the chin guard of his helmet and the plastron that covered his torso. Undetectable to security scanners, Kaiten's A-card had been edged with a monofilament thread.

The trooper gaped like a fish, bright scarlet filling his mouth and the three-inch slice that neatly bisected his throat. He tried to scream, but the sounds were drowned in the bloody froth bubbling from his windpipe as Kaiten grabbed him and maneuvered him onto the floor. Rifling through the guard's belt pouch, he found and extracted a keycard. Overhead, a new alarm began an eerie wail. "Intruder alert! Intruder alert, Primary Flight Control, Hangar Bay One! Intruder alert! . . ."

It took another five seconds to strip the PAC-4000 from the guard's body, slipping the massive power and coolant backpack over his own broad shoulders. Moving quickly to one of the flight control entrances, he braced the rifle at his hip, then slapped the keycard against the reader mounted next to the door.

The door hissed open onto a large, narrow room overlooking a cavernous hangar bay through enormous, sharply slanted transplex windows. Ten men, two in RAM military uniforms, stood at the consoles, their faces eerily stage-lit by the glow of radar screens, monitors, and holographic displays.

The RAM officers were reaching for holstered sidearms as Kaiten sailed headfirst through the door. The Terrine beat them to the punch with a devastating, rapid-fire barrage that seared through the closely grouped men, his raging yell echoing above the snapping *hiss-crack* of his laser and the shrieks of the wounded and dying. One RAM officer's head exploded as a laser bolt messily turned cerebrospinal fluid to steam. Another sagged to the floor clutching a trio of wetly leaking holes in his chest and belly. Driven by battle lust, Kaiten kept firing, sweeping the narrow room as men shrieked and convulsed and died.

When the last body stopped twitching, Kaiten maneuvered himself to the room's main console, studying the instrumentation.

The control center extended from the wall of Hangar Bay One, high above the cavernous cham-

ber's steel-mesh deck. The bay itself was half the size
of a sports stadium, snuggled into the rimwall of the
Stickney Crater in rock fused by thermonuclear fires
into something as tough as diacarballoy. Huge tunnels had been bored through the stuff. Capped at
both ends by massive triluminum and diacarb
hatches like round, bank vault doors, the tunnels
served as air locks through which ships could be cycled through into space.

There were ships in the bay now, stub-finned,
needle-prowed spacecraft surrounded by dozens of
scurrying figures. From a speaker high on one wall,
the intruder alert continued to blare its somewhat
tardy warning.

Kaiten's eyes narrowed behind his helmet visor.
Those spacecraft were brand-new Krait fighters,
each painted bright red and emblazoned with the
RAM corporate logo. They rested on duralloy launch
rails, facing the inner air lock doors that lined the
opposite wall of the hangar bay. The Kraits' canopies
were open, and men in fighter pressure suits were
already climbing into the cockpits.

During the planning stages of Operation Skytower,
NEO strategists had estimated that it would take a
minimum of twenty minutes for RAM-Phobos Command to ready its Krait squadron for launch . . . and
much more if the fighters needed to be fueled first.
The Kraits weren't supposed to be operational yet,
and the threat of radioactive canisters falling across
Marside was thought to be enough to make the RAM
commanders keep the hangar locks sealed and the
Kraits out of the fight.

Obviously RAM's response time had been underes-
timated. Less than eight minutes had passed since
the first alert had sounded, and already Kaiten could
hear the keening whine of turbines as the Krait pilots fired up their generators, could see the writhing

snakes of heavy cables as maintenance personnel disconnected power umbilicals. The Kraits would be launching in minutes.

An explosion rocked the flight-control booth, and one of the windows overlooking the bay turned frosty as the transplex was crazed by myriad cracks. Troops in the bay were firing at the control center, which was mounted on the hangar bay's rear wall. Another rocket sizzled past the windows and impacted on the ceiling with a dazzling flash and a thump that nearly knocked Kaiten to his knees.

Ignoring the barrage, Kaiten turned his full attention back to the console. He needed to find the manual safety override . . . *there!*

Yanking a safety cover aside, he threw the override switch, then began stabbing at a line of touch-sensitive panels. There was a savage pounding from the door at his back; troops were there now, trying to force their way in. Grimly Kaiten readied his laser, leveling its muzzle at the door. "Warning," a computer voice announced. "Emergency depressurization, Hangar Bay One. Warning—"

In the cavern below the control center, the massive duralloy doors were slowly opening.

○   ○   ○   ○   ○

The little gennie seemed to know where he was going as he darted ahead through the twists and turns of a narrow air-conditioning duct. Jovanna followed, though she was uncomfortably aware that she was far slower and clumsier than Galen when it came to maneuvering through this hidden path burrowing through the artificial mountain that was RAM-Phobos Prime.

At first she thought Galen was going to follow the air-conditioning duct all the way to Phobosport, five miles from the military base, but when he emerged at last into a room large enough for Jovanna to stand upright in, it turned out to be an equipment bay of some kind, a rock-carved chamber located just off one of Phobos's tubecar tunnels. Stored there among the dust and the shadows was a yellow waycrawler, a service vehicle designed to prowl the access tubes and maintenance tunnels that honeycombed Phobos's interior.

"Every good-sized asteroid colony has these," Galen explained happily. The vehicle's bubble cabin was large enough for four and sealed against the possibility of vacuum or the poisonous gases that could collect in the remote, rarely visited tunnels of a facility like this one. It was designed to ride maglev rails on silent magnetic fields just as tubecars did, but it also possessed six mechanical legs, now carefully folded against the oblong hull. Looking at the legs, Jovanna could understand why it was called a "crawler."

"You know how to drive this thing?" Jovanna asked uncertainly.

Galen already had an access panel off the vehicle's control panel and was fussing with the wires packed inside. "Well, I *am* a doctor," he said, "and not a bus driver. However, these things are pretty simple, and—Ah!"

The crawler's engine sputtered to life, loud in the enclosed space of the accessway. Galen engaged the machine's mag fields, and it rose gently, balanced on the current flowing through the rails buried in the tunnel. Smoothly, the vehicle accelerated.

"Yes," he added. "I do. Next stop, Phobosport!"

"I just hope *Komarov* makes it," she said. "It's a long walk home if we miss our connections."

O O O O O

At that moment, *Komarov* was nowhere near Phobos. With her controls disabled, she'd been unable to initiate a necessary course correction or decelerate, and early that morning, Phobos time, she'd swept past Mars, missing the planet by almost a million miles.

Dread Reprisal, however, was on final approach to RAM-Phobos Prime, several hours late but with her captain still determined to take part in the plan concocted by NEO Intelligence and Black Barney.

Captain Stark was in his bridge command chair, watching as his helmsman fired the forward maneuvering thrusters to bring them into line with the base docking facility.

According to the plan, *Dread Reprisal* was disguised as the *Industrious*, an independent freighter en route from Davida to Phobos with a load of machine parts and electronics spares. Any moment now, Phobos Approach Control would demand an interface with *Reprisal's* computer in order to verify that the ship mounted no weapons. A very special program was running in *Reprisal's* on-board computer now, an operating system that created what was known as a virtual computer . . . a way of convincing the pirate raider's computer that it was, in fact, two separate systems.

RAM-Phobos would only be allowed to peek at one of those systems, the one that showed *Industrious* to be what he claimed it was, an unarmed merchantman. His orders were to dock and await the signal that NEO commandos had landed at Stickney, almost halfway around the curve of Phobos from RAM-Phobos Prime. From there, he would be able to open fire on the base's antennae complex, fire control center, and control tower, paralyzing RAM's defenses for a critical few minutes and escaping in the confusion.

Altogether, *Dread Reprisal* would be docked at

RAM-Phobos Prime for fifteen, maybe twenty minutes. In that time, half his crew, already suited up in garishly painted combat armor and awaiting the word to go, would storm Prime Base's docking facility. The attack would add to the confusion; it would also add to the *Reprisal's* purse, since everything Stark's raiders could carry off would be theirs.

Stark grinned wolfishly at the thought. There was no telling what treasures might be waiting for them at the military port. Weapons, certainly, but valuable electronic components, computers, communications gear, drugs, even bar gold, platinum, and lead-shielded thorium could be stored there as well. With the million Barney was paying for the job, they should realize a tidy profit for this run.

Why was Barney so interested in this raid? he wondered. It didn't matter all that much. Black Barney had a thing about fighting RAM, he knew, and maybe his involvement went no further than that. Stark himself was a realist. He didn't care a centicredit for politics. RAM, NEO, it was all the same, so long as he got his cut.

"Captain Stark!" *Reprisal's* communications officer reported. "Message from Phobos Approach Control. It's flagged urgent."

That would be the interface request. "Put it on screen."

A comm screen flickered to life. A plain-faced woman in severe, RAM-military grays stared back at him. "Free Trader *Industrious*," she said, "this is Phobos Approach Control. Permission to dock at RAM-Phobos Prime is rescinded. Repeat, do not approach the base or you will be fired upon."

Stark's eyes widened. This wasn't according to plan. "Listen, lady," he replied. "I'm on final approach now and fuel ain't cheap. What's the idea?"

"*Industrious*, Phobos is under attack by pirate

forces. No vessels will be permitted to approach Phobos until the threat has been neutralized."

Stark scowled at the comm screen for several long seconds, considering how to reply. *Reprisal* was only a few miles from the military docking complex. If he held course, would RAM open fire on a civilian ship?

He knew the answer without thinking. Damn right they would. And getting blown away in some meteor-brained scheme of Barney's was no part of Stark's plans. "RAM-Phobos Control, this is *Industrious*. We are complying. Give us a safe vector, please."

"We copy, *Industrious*. Change course to three-five-five, mark one-niner. Clear to one thousand miles from Phobos and hold in parking orbit. We will inform you when it is safe to dock."

Stark nodded at his helmsman. "Do it," he rasped.

Reprisal's thrusters fired, briefly restoring a sensation of weight. On the forward viewer, the rocky surface of Phobos, with its cluster of domes and strobing lights and the mile-high thrust of the RAM-Phobos pyramid, slid smoothly to starboard.

Stark was in the pirate game for profit, not for combat. He liked his money easy, ripe for the plucking.

And Barney and NEO both could go hang.

CHAPTER SIXTEEN

Kaiten heard the wind, a dull roar swelling in volume and force to a thunder pitch. With both inner and outer air lock doors opening at once, the atmosphere inside the hangar bay was gushing out into space. The control booth trembled in the gale, a thuttering vibration that grew as the fury of the storm outside increased. The large window crazed earlier by a rocket projectile suddenly vanished in an explosion of tiny grains of transplex. The wind grabbed at Kaiten like a living thing, tugging him toward the roaring emptiness above the hangar bay. He grabbed hold of the instrument console with one gauntleted hand, bracing himself against the storm.

"Alert! Alert!" a computerized voice blared from the speakers. "Major pressure loss, Hangar Bay One! Code One emergency! Secure all internal pressure doors. . . ."

Peering down into the hangar bay, Kaiten could see the chaos unleashed among the personnel there. Elsewhere within Phobos, airtight doors would be sliding shut, isolating the damage, but a hurricane was blasting the cavern as everything not tied down was snatched by the gale and whipped toward the line of open air locks. RAM troops wearing full battle armor weathered the storm by hunkering down in sheltered spots or grabbing hold of something solid. Everyone wearing partial armor or no armor at all, though, was doomed. Many were swept up into the air bodily and hurled into the blackness beyond the opening locks. Others managed to grab hold of stanchions or other firm supports, but as the seconds passed and the air was ripped from their straining lungs, arms weakened, consciousness faded, and one by one they were plucked from their anchors and sent spinning through the tunnels and out into space.

Behind him, the door from the corridor outside slid open, and hulking figures in red and black armor burst into the control center, laser rifles blazing. Kaiten returned fire, cycling the heavy PAC-4000 as quickly as he could. One part of his mind recognized the armored figures storming into the control room as Terrines, as comrades, but there could be no question of mercy on either side. Kaiten had chosen his side long ago, and there was no backing down now.

The three lead Terrine troopers stopped in a door-blocking tangle, their armor savaged by the devastating hail of fire from Kaiten's heavy laser. More troops crowded through from behind, but in the confusion, Kaiten vaulted the console and hurled himself out into the yawning, hurricane-torn gulf above the hangar bay.

Propelled by the force of his leap, Kaiten sailed toward the deck. He weighed less than three ounces in Phobos's gravity, and the escaping air tore at him, but he possessed all the inertia of a three-hundred-pound man. The wind shrieked and battered at his helmet as he fell, but the roar was already dwindling, growing high-pitched as the air thinned. Before he'd reached the deck, the sound had faded away to nothing with the last of the vanishing atmosphere. Every other sound faded with it into hard vacuum, from the screams of men fighting the storm to the steady recitation from the overhead speakers. Kaiten hit the deck in a silence as oppressive as death, taking the shock on bent knees, and with a quick grab at the steel mesh deck to keep from rebounding.

Movement caught his eye across the bay, movement and a gout of light. One of the Krait fighters was moving along its launch rail toward the open air lock. Raising his PAC-4000, he triggered a long burst, sending bolts of laser light stitching into the hull and cockpit. Fragments of metal sprayed from the ship, but its engine kept firing, driving it into the air lock tunnel and out of Kaiten's sight.

Then a silent explosion dazzled him, driving him to cover behind a sheltering steel crate. RAM troops whose full armor could double as space suits if need be, were firing at him from across the chamber. They seemed disorganized, even dazed by the sudden evacuation of the chamber, but Kaiten knew it wouldn't be long before they got reorganized and caught him from flanks and rear.

Crouching in the shadows beneath another Krait fighter, Kaiten prepared for his own final stand.

○   ○   ○   ○   ○

Capt. Gunter Maximilian Zotov leaned forward, hands gripping the railing above the bridge pit, watching as his bridge crew bent with almost frantic concentration to their tasks. He'd executed several slackers earlier that day, and discipline, he noted, had markedly improved.

Sometimes all it took was a firm hand.

"We have clearance," the communications officer said.

"Excellent. Mr. Obinin! What is the delay?"

The ship's executive officer looked up at him, face pale. "S-Sir, some of the crew is still on Phobos. We—"

"Forget them. Cast off!"

Cmdr. Hermann Obinin glanced at a monitor on a nearby bulkhead. "If you please, Captain, there are some people coming aboard now, still in the docking tube. If we—"

"I said forget them! I want *Amazonis* free to maneuver now! Do you understand the word *now?*"

"Aye, sir! At once, sir!" Chalk-faced, the ship's exec nodded to an engineering officer in the instrumentation-lined trench beside him. "Reactors to full power. Drive room reports thrusters and auxiliary systems go. Docking tube . . . released. Cast off all moorings fore, aft, and amidships."

"Maneuvering thrusters," the captain said. "Ahead slow. Carefully, helm!"

"Ahead slow. Aye, sir." The new senior helmsman let his fingers dance across his board. Zotov felt the gentle nudge of thrusters firing.

Majestically the RAM behemoth slid free of the embrace of the docking cradle, skimming the rocky surface of the moon like some vast fish cruising the ocean deeps, sliding from the knife-edged shadow of the pyramidal mountain of RAM-Phobos Prime.

"Weapons status!"

"All weapons manned and ready, Captain," the weapons officer reported. "Lasers to full power."

"Good, good!" Zotov rubbed his hands with a dry rasping of skin on skin, anticipating the kill. Obviously the pirate raiders had expected to get in and out before *Amazonis* could bring her systems to readiness. Well, Max Zotov had a surprise for them. It would take only minutes to drift around the curve of Phobos, to bring the pirate rabble on Marside into range of his weapons. He would burn them from Phobos's surface like ants caught in the blast of a cutting torch.

He was looking forward to this.

O   O   O   O   O

Jovanna didn't know where Galen was taking her, and she wasn't sure she wanted to know. The yellow crawler moved swiftly through tunnels with bare rock walls, a part of the maintenance and construction infrastructure of the Phobos colony that was never seen by tourists or visiting RAM officials.

At last Galen maneuvered the vehicle into an equipment bay much like the first and cut the engine. As Jovanna climbed out and let herself float slowly to the ground, she could see rows of space suits hanging from a rack on one wall. A pressure-tight door nearby bore warning signs that this was an emergency exit only and that authorization was required to use it.

"Actually," Galen explained, "all we need is my authorization card. The computer will recognize it and let us through."

"You're taking me to your secret transmitter, aren't you?"

"That's right. It's hidden out on the surface, a few hundred yards from the lock."

"And what about our escape?"

The Tinker shrugged. "*Komarov* still isn't in port, so we're going to have to take our chances going down the elevator to Mars. The sooner we get your electronic friend on her way, the better."

Jovanna nodded, then began removing the uplink

strapped to her wrist. She'd need to get at it while
she was wearing a suit.

It took only a few minutes to find a suit that fit her,
a RAM-Sylvanian Model 6060 work suit with hard
torso and a transplex bowl helmet. The arms and
legs were soft and flexible, thin enough that she
could strap her uplink back on her left forearm once
the suit was on and the pressure locks sealed. Checking her readouts, she saw that her life-support pack
was good for another four hours.

Galen, meanwhile, had found a suit obviously designed with Tinkers in mind, a silvery garment that
perfectly fit his three-foot-plus height. He clamped
the fishbowl helmet in place, checked his seals, then
gestured to Jovanna, holding one finger up as close
to his lips as the helmet permitted.

Jovanna understood and touched thumb to forefinger in a silent "okay." Radio chatter on all suit frequencies would be monitored, and they didn't want
RAM taking an interest in what they were doing outside. She did switch her suit radio on and scanned
through the channels. Most, even the emergency frequencies, were cluttered with harsh voices and urgent calls. Hangar Bay One at Stickney had
depressurized, she heard, and pirates were attacking.

At least that much of the operation had gone according to plan. How much, she wondered, had gone
wrong?

Galen inserted his authorization card in a wall
reader, punched a combination of buttons on a control pad, and the air lock door hissed open. Moments
later, a light winked red, and the outer door silently
opened onto a gray and barren plain.

Jovanna had never been outside on Phobos. It was
an exhilarating sensation to stand on the mountain-
sized body, the horizon impossibly close and crisp and

sharp-edged. Most of the surface was covered by dust the color of dark slate; beyond, the sheer white cliffs of Phobosport thrust above the surface, gleaming in the sunlight. She could see civilian ships docked there, half-hidden by the tangle of support gantries and boarding tubes.

Opposite, Mars was a green and violet and red-ocher disk twenty degrees across, neatly bisected by the horizon. She stared at the planet's unbounded beauty until Galen impatiently waved her on. Pushing back a momentary stab of homesickness, she followed, careful of her footing. A hard jump might put her into orbit; a clumsy misstep could leave her hanging several feet above the surface, helpless until Phobos's weak gravity finally dragged her back down.

When she reached his side, Galen was on his knees beside a six-foot boulder. A hollow had been scooped beneath the rock, from which the Tinker pulled a small silver suitcase. He was setting up the antenna now, unfolding the two-foot dish and locking it onto a skinny-legged tripod. He pressed a button inside the open case, and the antenna begin to track back and forth, orienting on the sky. The device, she knew from her training, had an idiot-sized brain that could recognize star formations and plot the current positions of invisible targets such as Trinity. After a moment, the dish froze. Galen handed her a modem and, still in silence, nodded to her.

Kneeling beside him, Jovanna plugged her uplink into the modem, then typed out a command on its keypad. "TRANSMITTING" appeared on a tiny display screen. Seconds passed. Then "TRANSMISSION COMPLETE." RW was on her way back to Trinity, hurtling outward at the speed of light. In another seven minutes or so, she should arrive at NEO's Belt headquarters.

As she unplugged from the modem, she noticed a small green light winking on her uplink. It was the signal that a message had been left for her.

A message from RW.

She'd thought Galen might choose to wait the nearly fifteen minutes for RW to reach Trinity and for a message to make its way back, but the Tinker was already folding up the antenna and packing the equipment away. Good. There was nothing headquarters could tell them now that would help them, and the longer they were outside, the greater the chance that they would be discovered. She wanted to get inside, to mingle with the civilians in Phobosport.

Galen was almost done when a shadow plunged them both into a midnight blackness. Startled, Jovanna looked up. A shape—huge, black, and menacing—had drifted between her and the distant sun. Outlined by starlight, the shape swiftly resolved itself into a RAM heavy cruiser, a thousand feet of dark red hull metal, of electronics blisters and nacelles, of weapons turrets and streamlined fairings.

RMS *Amazonis* had slipped her moorings and was moving slowly around the curve of Phobos toward Stickney Base.

O   O   O   O   O

Captain Zotov leaned forward in his command chair, watching with an almost gleeful intensity the slow scrolling of dark gray rock past the main bridge viewer. *Amazonis* was less than a hundred feet above the surface of Phobos now, drifting slowly around the curve and into the moon's Marside hemisphere. Ahead, the elevator speared into the black heavens; starboard, Stickney Crater gaped, round and deep and holding utter darkness in its depths. At its rim, the line of main air locks leading to Hangar Bay One was open, spilling yellow light into space.

"Weapons!" he snapped. "Pick your targets!"

"Spacecraft at three-five-zero, mark one five, Captain. Range two miles," the weapons officer announced.

"It's a RAM transport, Captain," Obinin said. "I don't think they've seen us yet. We're so close to the surface our return is lost in the ground clutter."

Zotov's eyes narrowed as he studied the ship. Panels had been blown amidships, and she was maneuvering toward Stickney. He could just make out the name *Lady Luck* on her sandblasted hull. On the surface of Phobos, almost directly beneath the slow-drifting RAM cruiser, tiny, silvery pinpoints crawled and leaped like glittering insects.

"She's a pirate!" he said, the words half-snarled. "Target her first! We'll smash her with the K-cannons, then pick off the troops!"

"Aye, sir!"

Pirate or NEO raider, it was all the same to Zotov. A successful engagement with an enemy warship would look good on his record.

"Ready!" he called. "On my command . . ."

○　○　○　○　○

Jovanna's eyes were still fastened on the monster cruiser that had just passed overhead, drifting slowly toward the Space Elevator, when Galen took her arm and pointed. The Tinker's eyes were better than hers, she thought. She could barely make out a tiny, needle-slim speck shining silver against the cloud-swathed disk of Mars. If Galen hadn't pointed it out, she never would have seen it.

She knew what it was, though. Operation Skytower had called for NEO troops to drop onto Phobos, and the speck Galen was pointing at was almost certainly the transport that had brought them.

It was equally certain that the NEO ship hadn't seen the cruiser yet. The *Amazonis* was so close to the surface it would be invisible to the transport's radar. There was no time to think, only to act. Locking eyes with Galen, she silently mouthed the words "What channel?"

He knew what she was asking. He held up three fingers, then five, five, and five. The frequency being used by the NEO commandos was 355.5 megahertz. She told her suit to open that channel and to pump every amp of available power into its communications system.

"Dagger!" she yelled. "Enemy ship approaching your position from the direction of Phobosport!"

Every receiver on her side of Phobos must have heard her. She almost expected the cruiser to pause in its slow advance in order to burn her and Galen from the dusty face of the moonlet. Nothing happened, however, so she kept yelling out her warning, praying that someone aboard the NEO ship would see the danger in time.

Then *Amazonis* fired, launching a dazzling point of light toward the transport, and Jovanna swore in frustration. She'd been too late!

CHAPTER SEVENTEEN

Zotov watched the K-cannon projectile streak across the surface of Phobos. His fist came down on the arm of his command chair as he saw the target's thrusters fire at the last possible second. The projectile struck one fin just ahead of the yellow radiation warning trifoil, shredding metal like tissue, but the transport was already pivoting, its drive venturi emitting a dazzling white plasma flare.

The transport had a single gyrocannon in a dorsal ball turret, and with the effrontery of a kitten attacking a police dog, the pirates sent a burst of red tracers skittering toward the RAM cruiser.

"All weapons!" Zotov yelled. "Fire at will!"

This one-sided struggle couldn't last for long.

○ ○ ○ ○ ○

Kaiten's laser had stopped working, its power pack exhausted, and the Terrine had discarded it. Now he packed a rocket rifle, a Weston Mark XIV with a five-round clip, taken from a RAM trooper who would no longer need it . . . or anything else, for that matter.

He didn't like rocket rifles. They were slow, and the low initial speed of the projectiles made them useless at close range. But the Weston did pack a fair-sized punch, and it let him see in the nearly total darkness of the hangar bay. A miniature TV screen over the receiver magnified what he aimed at by five times, gave him a choice between infrared or low-light vision, and let him zoom in on the target at the touch of a button.

Scanning the floor through the scope, he spotted a RAM trooper crouched behind the hull of a Krait. Kaiten centered the screen's crosshairs on the man's helmet and thumbed a button above the rifle's trigger guard.

Rocket rifles were direct descendants of the gyrojet weapons developed experimentally five centuries before. The Mark XIV fired miniature, self-guiding rockets that tracked their targets through radar and an on-board computer the size of a mote of dust. By "showing" the chambered smart round the target, he could have it lock in and home. White light outlined the man and the letters "TRGT LOCK" appeared, signaling that the round was ready to fire.

He pulled the trigger just as the RAM trooper ducked behind the Krait. There was almost no recoil at all as the rocket-propelled round slid gently from the rifle. The sustainer motor cut in a foot from the muzzle. In vacuum, there was no sound and no vapor trail, but he saw a pinpoint of dazzling light, the small rocket's motor, swoop into the hangar like a bird of prey, jag left, then plunge behind the Krait's hull in single-minded pursuit of its prey.

A silent explosion lit metal surfaces with a reflected flash, and the trooper sailed high over the Krait, smoke trailing from a crater in his armored back.

At almost the same instant, three more laser

strikes scored the wall behind Kaiten's head. He ducked and changed positions just as a patch on the empty drum glowed cherry red, then exploded.

Lifting his head cautiously from a new vantage point behind a low wall, Kaiten scanned the hangar bay. Their next obvious move would be to rush en masse. Kaiten fully expected to see a squad of armored bodies sailing toward his position.

But what he saw instead as he peered over the concrete barricade made him sag back against the laser-scored wall in heartfelt relief. Men in silver battle armor were spilling through the open air locks. A dozen were inside already, spraying bursts of laser fire. Two RAM troopers were cut down as they scrambled toward an inner door. Others—Terrines by the quickness and the sheer ferocity of their movements—stood and fought . . . and died.

Three others threw down their weapons and rose slowly, hands above their helmets.

He set his suit radio to 355.5 MHz. "Dagger," he called, hoping someone would monitor his unscrambled call through the garble of background noise. "This is Blade. I'm in the hangar bay. Don't shoot!"

There was a long pause. "Blade, this is Dagger," a voice said at last. "We copy. Come out where we can see you, hands up."

Moving very slowly, he dropped the rifle and stood, arms raised. Battles between space-suited combatants were anonymous and deadly affairs. Kaiten didn't want to have survived this long, only to be shot down by some trigger-happy STAR Team commando, especially since he was wearing RAM-issue Terrine armor.

In seconds, he was surrounded by laser-wielding NEO raiders. One of them, a big man with a captain's insignia painted on his shoulder armor and lugging a massive, tri-barreled laser, stepped close, peering at his face. "You're Kaiten?"

"Dagger-Green-Four-Liberty," Kaiten replied. The code phrase should confirm to the commandos that he was who he claimed to be.

The big commando with the tri-barrel lowered his weapon. "Okay. Suit, give me communications, combat mode."

Another burst of electronic noise warbled from Kaiten's speaker, and he realized the captain was communicating with someone else. It was a long exchange. Finally the captain faced him again. "Okay, Kaiten. Just sit tight for a bit."

He sensed the worry in the man's voice. "What's happening?"

Nearby, NEO troopers moved among the fighters, scanning for booby traps and checking their power systems and drives. He could see strobing anticollision lights pulsing from the hulls of two sleek Krait fighters as they readied for launch.

"We got a little problem outside," the captain said. "You just stay put. Colliers! You and Nakamura stay here! The rest of you come with me!" Then he was gone, leaving Kaiten with the two NEO men. They, like their captain, looked worried.

Just what was going on outside?

O O O O O

Four miles astern of the *Amazonis*, Black Barney's *Free Enterprise* lined up for a shot. Symbols glowed against the forward viewscreen, numbers giving range and bearing, blocks of data describing weapon readiness and power. A glowing red targeting reticle was locked across the stern-on image of the *Amazonis*.

Enterprise was rated as a heavy cruiser, though she wasn't as long or as massive as the RAM behemoth in her sights, and she didn't pack the same firepower. Still, in space combat, surprise counts for more than size. She mounted missile batteries, two K-cannons, and a gyrocannon, but her main armament was a pair of acceleration cannons, hundred-foot magnetic railguns that ran along her belly like a sailing ship's keel. Though less than accurate at long range, they could hurl half-ton slugs of nickel-iron at better than a mile a second. Whatever those artificial meteors struck *knew* it had been hit.

Data on the screen showed that the acceleration cannons were ready to fire. "Weapons!" Barney snapped. "Radar lock!" He'd deliberately ordered his weapons officer not to establish a radar lock on the target in order to avoid alerting *Amazonis*'s crew that they were being stalked. Now, *Enterprise*'s fire-control radar tagged the *Amazonis*, and the reticle turned green.

"Locked on!" the fire control officer called.

"*Fire!*"

The *Enterprise* lurched as the port acceleration cannon fired. Barney caught a gleam of reflected light off the round as it flashed toward the target. Aware now of the danger, *Amazonis* turned sharply, its lateral thrusters firing to twist her clear of the oncoming missile.

Too late! The round struck the *Amazonis*'s tail, not dead-on, but slicing across the hull from stern to amidships, gouging deeply into her hull. Kinetic energy transformed on impact into raw heat. The external hull fighter mount was wrenched aside, struts twisting and breaking loose. A hundred-foot strip of hull plating was peeled away, exposing a tangle of wiring, conduits, power feeds, and ducts. Lightning played across the scar as atmosphere spilled into space in a frosty puff of vapor. The stricken cruiser yawed, drifting sideways.

"Missiles!" Barney yelled. "Fire!"

Missiles lashed across the gap between the two vessels. Flash after flash lit the RAM cruiser's hull, flaring in savage incandescence, illuminating a swirling mist of freezing atmosphere mingled with debris from interior spaces—wreckage, paper, furniture, bodies. . . .

"*Fire!*"

Amazonis staggered again. A dorsal laser mount, targeted by *Enterprise*'s C Turret, exploded in a sunbrilliant blaze of light, spilling shrapnel across the sky like glittering stardust. The last of the external fighter mounts was plucked away, pods ruptured, pilotless fighters spinning into darkness.

"Fighters rising from the crater!" Peg warned. "Damn! They're Kraits!"

Barney watched the slender shapes for a second, then grinned. "It's okay, boys and girls. The Kraits are on our side for a change!"

Magnified on the bridge screen, the Kraits could be seen sliding from the open locks and rising on streams of white-hot plasma, vectoring toward the stricken RAM ship. Ventral gyrocannon turrets tracked and fired, slashing the *Amazonis* with deadly accuracy.

Out of control now, the RAM ship was drifting sideways into the black-bottomed gulf of Stickney Crater. The heavy cruiser was a thousand feet long; Stickney was thirty times that distance across. *Amazonis* was a mote falling into emptiness. Shadow swallowed her, though patches on her hull continued to glow like orange coals.

Amazonis was out of the fight, an easy target to be carved to pieces later. "Leave her," Barney rasped. "Come about! Skrugg! Do you have a fix on that transmission?"

"On screen."

"Take us in!"

The *Enterprise* drifted closer toward the moon's dusty surface.

○ ○ ○ ○ ○

Jovanna had huddled with Galen in the shadow of the boulder as the brief space battle erupted a few miles from their position. The entire exchange had occurred in absolute silence, of course, adding to the surreal beauty of the scene. It was hard to follow what was happening. The second ship, passing moments behind the first, had been so black it was visible at all only where it occulted the stars.

"It's coming back," Galen said. There was no point now, of course, in keeping radio silence. His eyes widened behind his visor. "It's the *Free Enterprise!*"

Black Barney's ship.

Armored figures spilled from an open lock on the *Enterprise*'s flank, descending on bursts of compressed gas from their thruster packs. Their space suits were RAM issue, but painted in bright colors and garish designs, no two alike. Without a word, two pirates closed in on Jovanna, took her arms, then boosted toward the hovering black ship holding her between them. Two more followed with Galen in tow.

They cycled through the *Enterprise*'s air lock and entered a cargo bay. A dark-haired woman was waiting to take them directly to the pirate raider's bridge.

A towering, powerfully muscled figure rose from the bridge command chair as they entered. "Teacher," the figure said, his voice a volcanic rumble. There was no mistaking that figure or the voice. "And Galen. Of course."

"Hello, Barney," Galen said. He'd been an unwill-

ing member of Black Barney's crew once, before he'd
been recruited by NEO.

"Barney!" Jovanna said as a half-dozen other pirates ringed them in. "What are you doing here?"

"I was invited to this party," Barney said. "As if
you didn't know. I should've known *you'd* turn up."

"Believe me," she said, "I had nothing to do with it
this time."

"Indeed." The way he said it, he might have been
calmly contemplating her murder. "If I'd known it
was you out there, I might not have come back for
you."

"Damn it, Barney," Galen said sharply, "I thought
we had all of this settled. Jovanna's on our side!"

Obviously Barney still didn't trust her, even if he
did still call her "Teacher," an acknowledgment of
the part she'd played in his education twenty-one
years earlier. The last time she'd seen him had been
six months ago on the Jovian moon Thebe, where
he'd deliberately cut her communications because he
suspected her of being a RAM spy. The injustice of
the accusation, the unfairness of it, still burned inside Jovanna. She'd heard that Barney had checked
out her story with NEO, that he'd accepted her as a
NEO agent. If she was going to be forced to prove
herself over and over again . . . .

His eyes seemed to burn through her defenses.
"Was it you who warned the *Lady Luck* just now of
that RAM ship's approach?"

"The NEO transport? Yes . . ."

"You may have just saved every man aboard." He
sighed, a rumble of escaping air. "Perhaps, Teacher, I
must accept you as what you claim to be."

"And what's that?" she flared back.

"At the moment, baggage," he replied. "But I don't
think you're a RAM spy."

"Why not?"

Barney grinned suddenly. "You just foiled an ambush by clapping both hands to your mouth and screaming, 'Hey! Look out behind you!' And managed to tell every RAM trooper with a radio within a hundred miles where you were. It kind of lacks the finesse of a true double agent."

"Well, hey," she said as the ring of pirates around her chuckled. "It worked, didn't it?"

"Boss," a brawny man, bald but for a scalp lock and a walrus mustache, called from one of the consoles. "We got company comin'!"

"Whatcha got, Skrugg?"

"I make it eight ships, movin' in from Deimos. And they're powerin' up at RAM-Phobos Prime, too."

"Guess the party's over," Barney said. "Time to say good night."

Jovanna was staring at the magnified image on the main viewer. Space-suited figures were pouring from Stickney Base and drifting toward the transport *Lady Luck*. Krait fighters were everywhere, but they didn't seem to be attacking the NEO ship.

"They were after the fighters!" she said suddenly.

"Eh?" Barney said. "You didn't know?"

Jovanna shook her head. She remembered RW's observation that NEO headquarters probably wasn't telling her everything about Skytower. "I knew NEO command must have been after something more than what I was sent to Phobos for. They wouldn't have needed to attack the place otherwise. But I didn't know what they wanted."

It made sense to her now. X-23A Kraits were advanced tactical fighters, faster, more maneuverable, more modern designs than NEO's mainstay F-66 Starfires. NEO had a few captured Kraits in its inventory but was always seeking more.

"This whole operation was put together just to grab those Kraits," Barney said. "The way I heard it, they found out about them from their agents stationed on Phobos. I assume that was you."

She nodded. "Probably. I included what information I could find on them in my reports." She was mad now, her surprise giving way to a deep-simmering anger. All of the importance NEO Command had attached to the mysterious "Project Far Star" had been a sham, a masquerade to keep her and Galen ignorant of the true plan!

She understood their reasoning—what she didn't know, she couldn't spill to RAM interrogators—but that didn't help her deal with the realization that, after twenty-one years, she was still a tool, nothing more. Something to be used and discarded. With sudden insight, she wondered if the *Komarov* had ever really existed. It was possible, even probable, that someone at NEO had planned for her and Galen to be captured by RAM all along.

Damn them!

Minutes later, Jovanna lay strapped to an acceleration couch, her thoughts chasing one another in black circles as *Free Enterprise*'s engines thundered at her back. Had the news about Vince's disappearance been real, or had it just been a lie planted to get her to use RW in the probe of *Amazonis*'s computer? She didn't like being used this way. It left her feeling soiled.

Acceleration ceased briefly, and she felt the dizzying sensation of the *Enterprise* pivoting. A shudder through the hull told her that the ship's weapons were firing. Then acceleration resumed, a savage two Gs that left her straining for each painful breath. It was a battle, she decided. The RAM ships from Deimos and Phobos Prime must be attacking, and whether she lived or died in the next few moments depended entirely on the pirate now on *Enterprise*'s bridge.

She understood now how Black Barney must have felt when he learned that NEO—no, that she, Jovanna—had used him. NEO had done the same thing to her.

The acceleration increased, crushing the breath from Jovanna's lungs and squeezing her vision into a narrow, black-rimmed circle. What had really happened to Vince? What was Barney's part in all this? And what was the mysterious message RW had left for her in her wrist uplink? She promised herself that she was going to learn the answers to all of those questions very soon.

Just as soon as she was again able to move and breathe.

CHAPTER EIGHTEEN

Ten million miles out from Mars, the *Free Enterprise*, the *Lady Luck*, and the small flotilla of captured Krait fighters together overhauled the *Dread Reprisal*. Acceleration ceased, and the ships fell outward together in close formation. Space-suited men struggled to wrestle ten Kraits, each twenty feet long, into the open forward cargo bay of the *Lady Luck* and secure them in place with heavy cables welded in place by laser torches.

Opinions over the outcome of the raid were widely divided. The forty-one unhurt or slightly wounded survivors of the STAR Team were celebrating in the cramped spaces of *Lady Luck*'s aft cargo bay, along with the squadron of eager, young NEO fighter pilots who had done the seemingly impossible by flying most of a Krait squadron out from under the very guns of RAM's most powerful space fortress.

The crew of the *Dread Reprisal* was less than pleased, for their ship hadn't participated in the raid at all and now the rumor was circulating among her crew that they weren't going to be included in the division of the loot. That there *was* no loot, save for the ten Kraits, had been somehow overlooked by Stark and his men.

Aboard the *Free Enterprise*, the crew was celebrating their victory over the RAM squadron—one light cruiser destroyed, a second damaged, and the rest returned to Mars. RAM's pursuit of the raiders had been halfhearted at best, but if the *Lady* or the *Enterprise* had been any slower getting away from Phobos, the situation could have been very bad indeed.

A few aboard the pirate cruiser weren't joining in the rounds of high-spirited self-congratulation. Kaiten—just aboard from the *Lady Luck*—Black Barney, and Jovanna waited in the *Enterprise*'s lounge for the arrival of the delegation from the *Dread Reprisal*. The two ships were docked now, the *Enterprise* embracing the smaller *Reprisal* like a hunter grappling its prey. Stark and some of his men were due aboard any minute.

"So what are you going to do about Stark, Barney?" Jovanna wanted to know. "He's *your* man. . . ."

Barney's mouth twisted in a savage scowl. "Not my man."

"We're a free association," Kaiten explained. "Our captains are either elected or they win their position in a duel."

"I understand you recruited him for this operation. If you're not responsible, who is?"

"You have an annoying facility, Teacher, for asking unpleasant questions." Barney rubbed his jaw with a rasp like sandpaper on wood. "I recruited him, yes, but the only control I have is the promise of loot." He grinned suddenly. "And my own natural charm."

"Better turn on the charm, then," Jovanna said. "Here he is."

Stark floated into the lounge, followed closely by a villainous-looking man with the sallow complexion and receding chin of a human-Worker half-breed.

"Hello, Barney," he said with an easy smile. He ignored Jovanna and grinned at the Terrine. "Kaiten, my toothy friend! When you coming back to work?"

"You maggot-brained scrap of Venusian slime rot!" Barney roared. "You gutless, rancid smear of octopede droppings!"

The half-breed started forward, brows beetling, but Stark held out an arm and stopped him. "Easy, Vreech," he said. "I'm sure our old friend Barney doesn't mean half of what he says."

Like lightning, Black Barney launched himself across the room, one enormous paw closing over Stark's throat so quickly the human pirate had no time to react. Vreech's hand darted toward his holstered laser, but Kaiten was faster, moving with the same inhuman speed Jovanna had seen in the Fundown bar. The laser sailed across the room and bounced off a padded bulkhead as Vreech yelped and gripped one injured hand.

Barney drew Stark closer until they were nose to nose. Stark's eyes bulged in a reddening face, his hands scrabbling ineffectively against Barney's crushing grip.

"I did a bit of checking," Barney said, his voice silky smooth and deadly. "Had a trader who owed me a favor check along a certain orbit. He found that ship you hit yesterday, Stark. The *Komarov.*"

Jovanna gasped, a sharp hiss of breath. "Then NEO did send a ship for us!" Maybe NEO wasn't as manipulative as she'd thought.

"Of course they did. But this vacuum-headed scut got greedy. Hit her the day before she was due to reach Phobos and damn near ruined everything. Blew the timetable to hell, then compromised the plan by not hitting the RAM-Phobos Control Center."

"You don't give *me* orders," Stark said. His feet

thrashed in the air and he made a strangled sound. "Damn it, you're choking—"

"The passengers have been rescued," Barney went on. "What's left of 'em, anyway, after your boys shot their way aboard."

Vreech's face clouded. "No prize?" He looked puzzled. "No loot?"

"There would've been plenty of loot," Barney said, "if this reject from a genetics lab's refuse bin had had the guts to follow orders. You know, Stark, this confirms my original opinion of you. You're too torn between bloodlust and greed to be any use to me."

Stark's bulging eyes started from their sockets. His mouth was gaping, his tongue protruding as he tried to speak, his thrashings growing frantic. Jovanna heard a crackling, popping sound.

She felt sick. She hadn't expected to witness an execution.

Barney released the body, which drifted across the lounge like a limp bundle of rags. He turned on Vreech. "I'm your captain now," he said. "Any questions?"

Wordless, Vreech shook his head. His eyes were following the slow pinwheeling of his former boss.

"Kaiten is in command of the *Reprisal* now. You take your orders from him or you'll get the same as that." He jerked a thumb at Stark's corpse, and turned to Kaiten. "Get this garbage out of here."

Jovanna wasn't sure whether Barney meant the body or Vreech. The Terrine growled something in acknowledgment, snagged Stark, then gestured sharply to the thoroughly cowed half-breed. As they left, Barney wiped his hands on a rag. "It's getting damned hard to find good help these days. Where's Galen?"

"He—he's on board the *Lady Luck*," Jovanna replied. She swallowed hard against the bile rising in her throat. "With the wounded."

"I'm going to want him on the *Reprisal*. Kaiten is going to need all the help he can get with that crew."

"He's a medic," Jovanna said. "He'll be more useful where he is."

Barney shot a hard look at her. "So you want to give the orders now? Maybe try for captain?"

She met the look without flinching. "Hell, no. But I do need to use a computer."

Barney gestured toward a console at the lounge's forward bulkhead. "By all means," he said after a slight hesitation, as though he wasn't quite sure what to do about her. "Help yourself."

Since boarding the *Free Enterprise* hours before, Jovanna had been anxious to read the message RW had left in her uplink. Now she swam to the console and anchored herself before the screen. Activating her wrist uplink, she called up RW's message and routed it through the *Enterprise*'s computer, sending the message to the screen. Black Barney floated behind her, reading over her shoulder.

There were three subfiles. The first was a portion of a visual record lifted from the flight log of the RMS *Amazonis*. Jovanna didn't recognize it at first, for it played itself on the monitor as a number of separate, overlapping windows, multiple channels each showing different images—radar, neutrino emissions, navigational data, video recordings. Barney identified it at once. "Battle log," he rumbled. "The cruiser is under attack."

Then she recognized the scene—the *Amazonis* under deceleration, the approach of fifteen small targets in tight formation, the sounding of battle stations and the launch of Krait fighters. One of the log's windows was running a 2-D visual recording shot through a telescopic lens. Jovanna saw Vince's Starfire plunge toward the *Amazonis*, sweeping low across the hull, then hurtling into the flame-blasted gulf astern of the RAM cruiser. For a moment, it was lost in the glare, but then it emerged again, tumbling helplessly end-over-end, falling into star-scattered darkness.

Words scrolled up one window, recording a RAM officer's report to the bridge. "LONG-RANGE SCAN INDICATES PILOT ALIVE," Jovanna read, her pulse roaring in her ears. "SHALL WE DIVERT FOR INTERCEPT?"

"NEGATIVE," came the answer from the bridge. "HIS POWER PLANT'S GONE. HE'S AS GOOD AS DEAD."

The window dialogue continued, orders to hunt down the remaining NEO fighters, protests that the enemy appeared to have shut down their power plants and gone into hiding, the final recall of the Krait squadron as the *Amazonis* continued to draw away from the battle zone. Then the battle log ended.

So NEO Command had been telling the truth about this as well.

The second subfile was a note from RW.

"Hello, Jovanna," the digital personality's voice, so eerily like Jovanna's own, said over the console speaker. "I thought you would be interested in this analysis."

The screen replayed part of the *Amazonis*'s battle log, again showing Vince's fighter as it tumbled into darkness. Abruptly the scene froze. The three brightest stars on the screen each received names: Spica, Algorab, and Gamma Hydrae. "Spectral analysis of the scene has positively confirmed the identities of background stars," RW's voice continued, "permitting a navigational fix on Vince's Starfire."

The video image of space was replaced by a computer-drawn schematic that changed scale as she watched. Jupiter and Mars came into view, golden orbs at opposite sides of the map. A red streak marked *Amazonis*'s inbound course, while a green line showed the Starfire's path outward.

"Vince's course can easily be plotted in relation to *Amazonis* and the current positions of Jupiter and Mars," RW continued, "while his velocity can be determined from Doppler radar readings lifted from the RAM cruiser's battle log. This allows his position to be plotted to a high degree of precision."

Jovanna almost wanted to interrupt, to tell the recording that it was too late, that Vince must already be dead. Then RW added a third line to the screen, a blue curve sweeping in from beyond Jupiter. The line, clearly the orbit of something, missed Jupiter by ten million miles, plunged through the Asteroid Belt, then passed thirty million miles behind Mars as it continued into the inner system.

The blue line changed everything, for it appeared to intersect the green one. Shifting scales again, the view zoomed in on the intersection of those two paths, which now both showed points along their courses, each identified by date and time. It was clear that within two days of the battle with the *Amazonis*, Vince had passed within half a million miles of whatever occupied that blue orbit.

Half a million miles? Twice the distance from Earth to Luna, a gnat's whisker next to the sheer, vast, emptiness of the solar system!

"The blue marks the orbit of Ciudestreya," RW explained, "an independent Nomad city-state in a cometary orbit with a thirty-year period, now moving toward perihelion. Records of the city's last passage indicate that its scanning systems are more than adequate for detecting a craft with the mass of a Starfire at a range of five hundred thousand miles. Since they trade in salvaged items as well as in various ores acquired in deep space, it seems likely that they would have investigated Vince's craft."

Jovanna felt a flush of excitement. "Two days? He could have survived that long!" Idiot, she thought. Talking to a recording!

Barney thought she'd spoken to him. "Depends on how badly—"

"There is a possibility that Vince could have been picked up by the Nomad city," RW's voice continued, interrupting the pirate. "I'm sorry, Jovanna, but that's all the data I could acquire on short notice with a bearing on Vince's fate. You should check with Ciudestreya and see if they either rescued him or recovered his body. Good luck!"

The recording ended, leaving Jovanna with her racing thoughts.

She'd convinced herself that Vince was dead, but if the city had picked him up, he could still be alive!

"Nomads," Barney rumbled. "Unsavory bunch . . ."

"You should talk." Jovanna called up the final sub-file on the screen. It opened with a note from RW. "I picked this up with the log segment from the *Amazonis*," she said. "Since it concerns Far Star, I knew NEO would be interested in it. I'm afraid I couldn't learn anything more before they cut me off."

The stolen data was in text, orders to the RMS *Amazonis*, then stationed at the Deimos Yards. They were classified top secret, for the eyes of Captain Zotov alone, and were dated several weeks earlier.

PROCEED IMMEDIATELY FROM DEIMOS YARDS TO AMALTHEA. RAM OBSERVERS AT SOLAR GEOGRAPHIC RESEARCH LAB REPORT UNKNOWN TRADERS OFFERING ALIEN DEVICE FOR SALE. YOU ARE DIRECTED TO ACQUIRE SAME BY ANY MEANS NECESSARY AND RETURN IT TO COPRATES FOR STUDY. IMPERATIVE THAT NEO/PIRATE ELEMENTS

NOT RECOGNIZE RAM INTEREST IN AMALTHEA/ARTIFACT. SHIPPING RECORDS ALTERED TO SHOW *MAGNIFICUS TRIPLANETARY* MAKING MARS-JUPITER-MARS RUN. *AMAZONIS* WILL CONFORM TO FLIGHT PROFILE OF INTERPLANETARY LINER TO MAINTAIN DECEPTION.

ALIEN DEVICE THOUGHT TO BE ARTIFICIAL OBJECT OF UNKNOWN ORIGIN ACQUIRED AND SUBSEQUENTLY LOST BY SCOUT IN TRANS-SATURN SPACE EIGHT YEARS AGO. YOU ARE ORDERED TO RETRIEVE AND RETURN DEVICE FOR RAM STUDY AT ALL COSTS—REPEAT, ALL COSTS.

DEVICE AND ALL RELATED INFORMATION IS CLASSIFIED TOP SECRET, CODE REF: FAR STAR. DO NOT DISCUSS MISSION WITH CREW.

—HOLZERHEIN

"The top DP spook himself." Barney whistled. "I'm impressed."

"They disguised the *Amazonis* as a passenger liner," Jovanna said. "Vince's training flight spotted her and went in to use her as a target for their exercise. No wonder they ran into trouble."

"What's this Far Star thing they're talking about?" Barney wondered. "It can't really be alien, can it?"

"Seems unlikely. Solar Geographic . . . That's a research station."

"On Amalthea," Barney said. He didn't sound impressed. "One of Jupiter's inner moons. A rock."

Jovanna pointed to the third paragraph in the orders. "Eight years ago RAM got a description of . . . of something discovered by one of their scouts, something that was then lost. Now that same something turns up on one of Jupiter's moons, and they dispatched a ship to pick it up, just in case."

"So?"

"So my guess is that the Ciudestreyans found this whatever-it-is eight years ago, when they were out beyond Saturn."

"Big assumption. How do you know it was Ciudestreya?"

"There aren't that many Nomad cities. What's the chance that two of them happened to be passing close to Jupiter a few months ago? Or were both in that same area beyond Saturn?"

"Nonexistent," Barney agreed. "We could check an ephemeris to be sure. But I think you're right."

"They probably went to the science outpost on Amalthea when they passed Jupiter to find out how much it was worth."

"Nomads are merchants first, last, and always," Barney said. "They'd sell their own grandmothers for a profit." He caught her look. "Hey, I didn't say that was bad! I admire commercial enterprise."

"Anyway, RAM got word somehow that they'd been there. So they sent the *Amazonis* out to Jupiter space to check things out."

"So. Did they get this thing?"

Jovanna sighed. "I don't know," she admitted. "But if RAM ever *did* get hold of a genuine alien artifact—"

"Aw, come on, Teacher," Barney said. "There ain't no alien monsters in the Sol system and never have been! That's comet gas."

"Whatever it is," Jovanna said, "the RAM high command thinks it's important enough to grab it no matter what."

"Maybe they already have it."

"If they did, RW should have picked up something from the Phobos net or in the ship's log, don't you think? There was nothing about Far Star except in the orders. I think the Nomads still have it, and we're going to have to go to Ciudestreya and find out what's going on."

Barney looked at her, his eyes as black and as hard as obsidian. "Are you sure you're not going just to check up on your boyfriend?"

"He's not my boyfriend!" She held her temper. "He's a valuable NEO agent. If he's alive, we have to find him before RAM does."

"Go on."

Jovanna was excited now. It was possible Vince might still be alive! "We can reach Ciudestreya in a couple of days. . . ."

Excitedly, she began laying out her plan, unfolding the details even as she described it.

"You know, Teacher," Barney said when she finished. "If your guess that *Amazonis* didn't pick this alien gizmo up at Amalthea is right, Holzerhein'll be tearing the solar system apart looking for it."

"We can't let him get it."

"Yeah, well, that could be easier said than done. If it's still on Ciudestreya, Holzerhein'll figure out where it is as fast as we did. We could find more than Nomads at that city when we get there."

"Then we'd better see to it that we get there first."

Barney sighed. "Okay. I don't like it, but you're right. Whatever this alien gizmo is, we can't let RAM have it." He showed his teeth. "Besides, there might be a profit in the thing."

"You're working for NEO now, Barney," she reminded him.

"Am I? You know, the only guy I ever met who could give me orders was Buck Rogers. And he ain't here."

"I don't think you have a choice, Barney. Any more than I do. So go on and give the orders for a course change. I'll send a message to NEO Command. Maybe they can give us some support."

She was putting her career on the line, convincing Barney to take his two-ship flotilla to Ciudestreya on what was really a rather flimsy list of clues. And the *Lady Luck*, too. She'd have to convince Carter to bring what was left of his STAR Team along. By the rules, they should all return to Trinity for debriefing and to let NEO Intelligence see the stolen copy of *Amazonis's* orders.

The hell with that, Jovanna thought. RW would be able to give them copies of everything. She had to move *now*. If she didn't, then even if Vince was alive, RAM would find him when they investigated Ciudestreya . . . and they *would* investigate. The possibility of acquiring an alien artifact, a piece of unknown but certainly advanced technology, was too stunning in its implications to ignore.

She wondered what the thing was and whether or not Vince had already seen it.

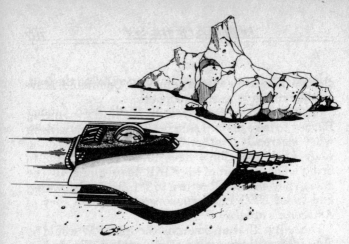

CHAPTER NINETEEN

Vince drifted before the window in the under-bark quarters that had been assigned to him after his bonding ceremony with Katarine thirty hours before. The polished tones of a news announcer filled the room.

"... when the RAM Central Planning Committee announced a five-percent increase in the air tax for all Martian citizens. CPC Director Mallenburg explained that the increase was necessary in order to fund the next step in the terraforming of Mars...."

Katarine floated closer. She was holding a vidpad, a rectangular mylar sheet with a liquid crystal display. "I really don't understand your interest in all of this," she said. "No one in the city listens to the news except for councillors and such. It has nothing to do with us...."

Vince smiled at her. Wan light from a shrunken sun streamed through the window, touching her skin with a pearly luminescence. "That *is* my world," he said.

"Mars? I thought you were from Davida."

"No. The news, the events. The people. And ...

what happens on Mars can have an effect on the Belt. Or even here."

"None of this has anything to do with Ciudestreya." Shaking the vidpad, she added, "We're beyond all this."

"Maybe not as much as you think." He was still wondering about the reported approach of a RAM ship. He'd requested the use of the vidpad in hopes of picking up something about it.

Vidpads, being high-tech manufactured items acquired only through the city's infrequent trade with the Inner Worlds, were rare in Ciudestreya, available to ordinary citizens only through the city's equivalent of a library. Judging from Katarine's reaction, they were not often used. The Nomads had little interest in the news, sports, politics, or entertainment of the rest of the solar system.

He took the paper-thin pad from her hand and hung it in the air. On the screen, an urbane, smiling, meticulously groomed announcer sat at a desk before the graphic RAMNEWS logo, continuing to discuss the necessity of a new tax hike. The signal was fuzzy, sometimes broken by static. The broadcast was being picked up across a considerable distance; a time line at the bottom lagged more than five minutes behind Vince's finger watch.

Katarine shook her head, her short, black hair swirling at her cheeks. "Vince, I know how you must feel, but you're part of our world now. Believe me! You *can't* go back, not ever. . . ."

"Last night you said you might be willing to come with me."

"That was last night. And you said if that ship that's coming here is RAM, you couldn't—"

"Hold it." He raised a hand. "I want to hear this."

On the screen, the picture had changed. Successive shots showed RAM troopers moving along a corridor in zero-G, corridors littered with trash and bodies, laser scoring on walls.

". . . by terrorist-pirates," the announcer was saying. "RAM authorities are investigating, of course, but at this hour there is no clue as to what the pirate forces hoped to gain by their foolhardy assault on Phobos and the Pavonis-Mons Space Elevator."

Katarine looked puzzled. "What? . . ."

"Shh! Please!"

The scene changed to an exterior view of Phobos. The long-range camera lingered on a scattering of crumpled, silver-clad bodies with the towering Space Elevator in the background.

"A spokesperson for RAM-Phobos Prime said tonight that the terrorist-pirate attack was an abject failure," the announcer continued. "However, some damage was inflicted on civilian structures on Phobos before RAM forces were able to destroy the pirates. No casualties were reported.

"Authorities so far have recovered over two hundred pirate bodies. A handful of terrorists did manage to flee as ships of the Third Fleet arrived to defend the Space Elevator facilities. Authorities expect that the survivors will be run down and destroyed shortly.

"At the Third Fleet Headquarters on Deimos, Fleet Commander Admiral Eustace Velikovsky had this to say:"

"Harumph, yes," a fat toad of a man in a medal-heavy grand admiral's uniform said. "Perhaps, um, perhaps this incident will finally convince people that these so-called, ah, 'freedom fighters' are nothing but terrorist scum. Clearly they hoped to destroy the Space Elevator. Imagine the devastation that would have wreaked upon the cities of Mars! Fortunately there's no way they could even hope to damage the elevator, and, hum, the Third Fleet was on guard against just such an eventuality—hum, yes, indeed! Despite their sneak attack, and, um, their cowardly attempt to infiltrate RAM-Phobos, we ran them out with their tails between their legs. Humph!"

The toad face was replaced by the announcer. "RAM government officials are asking citizens to fulfill their obligations to the state by reporting any suspicious people or events that could be linked to terrorist activities to constabulary authorities.

"In other news tonight, RAM officials announced the opening of the Simund Holzerhein Memorial Gladiatorial Stadium in Coprates—"

Vince touched the vidpad's corner, killing sound and picture. Thoughtfully he began to fold the screen into a small, neat package.

"Those . . . those terrorists are your people, aren't they?" Katarine seemed to be reading the worry in his face. "I can tell—"

"They're not terrorists," he said.

"But they are your people—the ones you want to go away with. That's why you're afraid of RAM." She looked away, unwilling to meet his eyes. "Yesterday you told me you were a mercenary. I wondered at the time if that might be another word for 'pirate.' "

He didn't answer at once. His gaze remained fixed on the view through their small window, at the tangled complexity of Ciudestreya and the slow-spinning stars beyond.

"I did lie to you," he said finally. He wasn't sure telling Katarine about his affiliation with NEO was such a good idea, but he had to have her support to have a chance with the Ciudestreyan Council . . . and he couldn't get that support without telling her the truth. "But I'm not a pirate. Have you ever heard of NEO?"

She had, though her knowledge was spotty and distorted by time and the veils of an alien culture. He spent the next hour telling her about NEO's struggle with the bloody-handed empire of RAM and of the part he played in that fight.

"For centuries, RAM has been raping Earth, stripping it of minerals, of food, of resources. The New Earth Organization and various other smaller groups have been taking a stand against RAM. Fighting back. We believe that Earth should determine its own future." He held up the folded vidscreen. "I don't know what the whole story was here. RAM news is pretty heavily censored. But it sounds to me as if NEO mounted a raid on Phobos. For RAM to have admitted it happened at all, it must have done a lot of damage."

He wondered what the raid's purpose had been. While he'd been stationed on Trinity, he'd heard nothing of any plan to assault Phobos. The place was a fortress! What could have driven NEO Command into such a gamble?

"That's why you want to leave Ciudestreya, then," Katarine said, interrupting his thoughts. "To fight with this NEO against RAM."

"Partly. I do have my own life out there, Kat. And people I care about and who care about me." Had Jovanna been involved in that raid? She'd been on Phobos. Was she all right?

"A woman?"

"Damn it, you have no right to be jealous! You people are holding me here against my will!"

"You owe your *life* to us, Vince. In time, you'll understand—"

"In time nothing! And when it comes to that, I owe my life to some of those people out there, too. They're my friends."

She sighed. "I wish I could help you. But you know that I can't."

"You could get me a radio."

"I got you the vidpad—"

"I mean a communicator. Let me talk to my people."

She shook her head. "Impossible. Ordinary citizens can have no contact with the outside."

This was getting him nowhere. He needed a different tack. "Look, explain something to me. Your Conseos are Ciudestreya's government, right? Under the high chief, I mean."

"The Altefay, yes."

"They make laws, set policy, decide how to interact with the outside, right? I mean, you *must* have some kind of foreign policy. You trade with the outside. You sent people to Amalthea a few months ago to find out about the Artifact."

"Certainly." She seemed bewildered by his intensity. "They take that upon themselves so that the rest of us don't have to."

"Okay, fine. So what happens when people don't like the law?"

"Pardon?"

"Come on, Kat! You can't be such sheep that you blindly accept every pronouncement handed down from on high! You must interact with your own government somehow!" He was guessing now, but he thought it was a good guess. He'd seen soldiers within the city, yes, but no signs that Ciudestreya was a dictatorship. Most of the people he'd seen so far seemed quite happy, limited more by their own strange view of the universe than by threats or force of arms. "Who chooses the members of the council? The Altefay?"

"Sometimes. Most of them are representatives of the people." She tossed her head proudly. "We are a democracy, Vince, despite what you seem to think."

"A democracy? You vote?"

"Well, not the women, of course. Or the children or the genetically disenfranchised. That would be silly."

He wanted to ask her what "genetically disenfranchised" meant but decided against it. He was still a long way from understanding this twisted society! "So, if the council makes a law or a decision that the people don't like, can the people vote to change it?"

"Well, if there's an important decision before the council, a citizen can call for a challenge. It doesn't happen often, because—"

"Wait a minute. A challenge? Like the *pelepovida*?"

"Of course."

"A citizen goes up and says to a Conseo, 'I don't like the way you're running things; let's fight?' "

"Well, it's hardly that informal, but, yes. As I was saying, it doesn't happen often because the Conseos and the Altefay have champions, while the citizens must make the challenge themselves."

"And these champions have been training in your high-G camps at Heavydown." He nodded. "I get it."

"Well, it wouldn't be right to make the *Conseos* fight. Most of them are old, and they haven't been in gravity for years. It wouldn't do to have young citizens come along and bounce them out just because they were stronger. That would be anarchy."

"Let me ask you something. Am I a citizen?"

She looked surprised. "Of course! Why, you've already fought one challenge . . . for me. The challenge of the *pelepovida* is a right, Vince. It can be taken from you only if you commit some gross breach against custom or the law."

A smile spread slowly across Vince's face. "I wonder why all those other 'guests' never found out about that."

She shrugged. "Maybe they never asked. Or maybe they didn't want to stir things up!"

"And maybe they just conveniently weren't told. Come on."

"Where are we going?"

"To the audience hall. I want to talk to your Conseos."

"That may take time. They are busy men."

"Look, Kat. A RAM ship is bearing down on us, and I doubt that they're coming to talk to you about trade. They'll be here . . . when?"

"In another five hours, the last I heard."

"The council will talk to me. They've *got* to."

○ ○ ○ ○ ○

"It was an ambush, Mr. Chairman." Captain Zotov mopped the sheen of perspiration from his face with a handkerchief. "The second pirate ship slipped behind us, using Phobos to screen its movement. We were alone, with no support. . . ."

Simund Holzerhein's image smiled, though the eyes held an icy light, like cold fire. "Twice now you have failed in your mission, Captain. Twice now . . . once in failing to retrieve Far Star at Amalthea, and again by allowing your ship to be savaged by pirate scum, by a ship half *Amazonis*'s size. . . ."

"*Please*, Mr. Chairman!" Desperately Zotov searched the luxurious expanse of *Amazonis*'s Captain's Quarters, but the room was empty save for himself and the holographic projection of RAM's corporate director. "I swear it wasn't my fault!"

"Hm-mm." Holzerhein looked thoughtful. "Fault and responsibility are not necessarily congruent. How shall discipline be preserved in the ranks if the officer responsible for wrecking one of my warships is not held accountable?"

Zotov's knees would have buckled had *Amazonis* not been in zero-G at the moment. He tried to speak, his mouth opening and closing in unconscious mimicry of a fish, but no words came.

Holzerhein's face went diamond hard. "The damage to your ship . . . how bad is it?"

"It—it is under control, Mr. Chairman. And not so severe as . . . as I at first feared. The weapons systems were knocked out when we drifted into Phobos, but they're functional now. The drive systems are on line. There's some hull and radiation damage, but—"

"In other words, *Amazonis* is fit for battle."

Zotov knew better than to admit otherwise, at least directly. Globules of sweat danced in the air before his eyes, stirred by the air currents of his breath. "She is, Director Holzerhein. Her range will be, ah, somewhat limited until we can get her into the yards on Deimos."

"How limited?"

"We could manage a flight of two, perhaps three days' duration. Range, of course, would depend on acceleration, and that would be limited by damage to our port fuel tanks. And the hull will not—"

"The details do not interest me. Zotov, you have a final chance to redeem yourself." A wall-sized display behind Holzerhein's image winked on, displaying graphics of orbits and intersecting paths. A red arrow winked next to an object within the Asteroid Belt. "We believe that the item we have designated 'Far Star' is presently here."

"Ciudestreya," Zotov said, reading the data accompanying the object. "Nomads?"

"When *Amazonis* was dispatched to Amalthea to acquire Far Star, we assumed that it had been brought there by Belters or deep-space prospectors. Obviously the people in possession of Far Star did not identify themselves." Holzerhein's image smiled. "No doubt they feared that RAM might appropriate it. It has great potential value.

"Since that time, an analysis of traffic in and out of the Jovian System has convinced us that Far Star was almost certainly in the possession of this Nomad city which, at the time, was passing Jupiter. I have already ordered Rodrigo of the *Milankovic* to rendezvous with Ciudestreya and investigate."

"Mr. Chairman, I—"

"Be silent and listen. The raid on Phobos, we have just discovered, was a diversion, a feint designed to allow NEO to steal certain data from our computer records. The intrusion into *Amazonis*'s computer was carried out by a NEO digital personality operating within the Phobos mainframe. Evidently it copied certain data and escaped during the confusion of the raid. That data included portions of *Amazonis*'s battle log and a copy of your mission orders."

"Sir, with all due respect, that's impossible! For one thing—"

"Interrupt me again, Captain, and Commander Obinin will take command while you provide this evening's entertainment for your crew. I know what data was stolen because a gatewatch security program in the computer net logs all data classified secret and above as it is downloaded by modem from the mainframe to any other system. We were unable to stop or copy it, but we were able to see what it was taking when it downloaded out of the system.

"NEO's intelligence service can be disturbingly efficient at times. We must assume that they are now aware of our interest in Far Star and that they have connected Far Star with Ciudestreya. They will visit the Nomad city to grab Far Star for themselves.

"You are directed, therefore, to proceed at once to Ciudestreya, together with the cruisers *Hisperia*, *Sabaeus*, and *Cydonia*, and the troopship *Ajax*. The light cruiser *Milankovic* will be there by the time you arrive. With this force, you will takes possession of

Far Star for RAM. If NEO forces are present, you will crush them." His eyes bored into Zotov's soul. "I am giving you a squadron . . . *Commodore*."

Zotov gasped. He couldn't help it, so sudden and complete was the change in his fortunes, in Holzerhein's attitude toward him. "M-Mr. Chairman, I don't know what to say. . . ."

"Say nothing. Confirmation will be sent to you from Admiral Velikovsky's office within the hour."

"But . . . but I thought—"

"You were correct in your assessment that the pirate ambush of your command could not be anticipated, Commodore, and I am neither unfair nor capricious. This will be your chance to prove to me that you have the talent for a larger command."

"Thank you, Mr. Chairman!" Unspoken was the corollary: If he failed, Holzerhein would have the ideal scapegoat, and Zotov could count himself lucky if he was only shoved out an air lock. But he would *not* fail. "You can rely on me completely, sir!"

Holzerhein smiled, that cold light still flickering in his eyes. "I know I can, Zotov. How soon can *Amazonis* be ready to proceed?"

"Well, my engineer says six days for us to—"

"The words I used a moment ago were 'at once.' Tell RAM-Phobos Prime what you need to effect necessary repairs en route, and it will be delivered at my order. I want your squadron under way within six hours." Without allowing a chance for further argument, Holzerhein's image rippled and winked out.

"Yes, Mr. Chairman," Zotov said to the empty air of his cabin. There was nothing else to be done, then, but to carry out the chairman's orders and thank whatever deities there might be that Obinin hadn't already replaced him as captain of the *Amazonis*.

Pausing only to straighten his uniform tunic, he hastened out of the room and headed for the bridge.

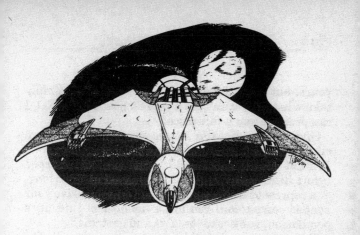

CHAPTER TWENTY

Vince floated before the panel of elderly councillors in the Grand Audience Hall, his hands spread in supplication. For nearly thirty minutes now, he'd been making his case. He'd told them that he was a NEO officer and explained why RAM must not have the Artifact.

Behind him was his *companro*, a dark-haired youth named Manel who'd been assigned as Vince's guide and interpreter while he adjusted to his new life in the city. Guide? Perhaps, but Vince knew a guard when he saw one. One of the councillors, the tall man in green who'd translated for him the day before, spoke Anglic. It wasn't as though Vince needed an interpreter.

Well, it didn't really matter. Whatever his real purpose, Manel was cheerful, friendly, and carried no weapon more conspicuous than a sonic stunner clipped to his belt. Vince might still be a prisoner, but his captivity so far had been light, with few obvious constraints.

"You must understand, sirs!" he said. "RAM might say they merely want to examine this Artifact of yours, but if it's important to them, they'll simply take what they want. As a representative of NEO, I can promise you a fair price."

Giyerm Damata, the Anglic speaker on the council, had taken the role of spokesman for the others.

"First of all, *Senye* Pirelli," he said, hands clasped before him, "let me remind you that you are no longer a representative of NEO or anyone else, save your bonded companion. You are a member of this city's population, subject to its laws and customs."

"I am a prisoner, held here against my will. Despite that, I'm trying to warn you that you and your entire city are in danger."

Damata smiled. "I think we have been dealing with RAM for orbits enough to know what to expect of them." His eyes narrowed. "But you . . . what is your interest in the Artifact?"

"If it is, as I've heard, the product of an alien technology, it must not fall into RAM's control."

"Hmm. Could NEO be any better trusted than RAM?" He nodded toward his companions on the panel to either side. "All of us saw the news from Mars. I understand you did as well. That raid on the RAM Space Elevator . . . your NEO was behind that, was it not?"

"I don't know about the attack. But I can promise you that NEO will pay for the Artifact. Certainly they won't take it at gunpoint."

"Your, ah, warning is noted, *Senye* Pirelli. Be assured that this council will act in the best interests of this city. You are dismissed."

Vince hesitated, unsure of the correct protocol. "Uh, look, Conseo. I don't know the right words for this, but it's more important than you can possibly realize that RAM not get hold of your Artifact. I insist that you let me get in touch with NEO and give them a chance to bid. If you don't . . ." He stopped and licked lips gone dry. "If you don't, I'll challenge you for the right to do it."

"That is your prerogative, of course. I see you have been learning about Ciudestreyan customs from your new bonded companion. Most commendable.

"Since you are new to Ciudestreya, the council will overlook your violation of custom. You may indeed issue the challenge of *pelepovida*, but only to replace one of the members of this council, not to change the council's policy. As a Conseo, you could debate policy on the council, but not set it."

"I . . . see."

"Of course, with enough popular support, you could challenge the Altefay himself. If you took *his* place you would be in a position to dictate to us, at least for so long as you remained in power. However, it's not likely that you would survive such a challenge."

"Why not? I made out okay against Dobo."

The Conseo whispered a translation of Vince's statement to the other councillors. Several laughed out loud, and the rest seemed amused. "The rules are different," Damata replied after a moment. "You can't imagine that just anyone could challenge the Altefay, do you? *Pelepovida*, remember, means the fight for life, a life-and-death struggle. Only the gravest circumstances would warrant such a challenge. And you would face the Altefay's champion.

"In any case, there's no point in arguing it now. A RAM ship will be here within the hour to discuss the Artifact's purchase. This council rules that there be no further discussion on the matter until after we have heard RAM's proposal." His gavel slammed the table.

The audience was over.

Vince was in the Grand Audience Hall an hour later, together with a throng of Ciudestreya's citizens.

It seemed that the entire city had turned out to witness the arrival of the RAM ship. Any contact at all with the outside must be a special event for a population that spent nearly thirty years at a time in almost total isolation. Manel floated on his left, Katarine on his right. One chamber wall had been covered by an equally large liquid crystal screen. At the moment, it showed the approaching ship, highlighted by the distant sun as it moved slowly across a background of stars.

It was a RAM light cruiser, a sleek vessel carrying a crew of perhaps twenty. He could read the ship's name on her needle-slim prow: *Milankovic*.

The screen snowed with static, then cleared. In the place of stars and cruiser, the face of a young man, two stories tall, looked out into the floating crowd. He wore the black uniform of the RAM navy, the insignia of a junior captain on his tunic's collar. Behind him, Vince could see part of the cruiser's bridge and two marine guards in black and red armor anchored near the aft bulkhead.

"Attention, Nomad city," the towering face said, the voice filling the hall like thunder. Dozens of the city's inhabitants scattered back from the screen; so close, so large a face was intimidating, terrifying. He spoke Anglic, but the words *Atenci Nomada ciud* flowed across the bottom of the screen, providing a consecutive translation for the city's Espen-speaking populace. "This is Captain Dretan Rodrigo of the RMS *Milankovic*. We have learned that you are in possession of RAM property. You will release it to us at once."

One of the Conseos, his face stage-lit, spoke rapidly in Espen. Vince guessed that his image was being transmitted to the *Milankovic*'s bridge. Why didn't Damata address Rodrigo directly in Anglic? Vince wondered. Perhaps it was a matter of pride.

"He's saying that the city council has no idea what he's talking about," Katarine whispered in Vince's ear. Save for her voice and that of the councillor, the Grand Audience Hall was deathly silent. "I think he's bargaining for time."

"You are helpless!" Rodrigo thundered in reply. "You are no match for the power of RAM! At this moment, *Milankovic*'s lasers are trained upon your so-called city. Refuse us and you and every inhabitant of this pathetic space dump will die."

The council spokesman began to reply, but Rodrigo cut him off. "It's no good lying. We have your city under observation." The RAM captain's face vanished, replaced by a telephoto view of the city.

It was a staggering sight, one Vince hadn't seen before, since he'd been unconscious during his arrival. The double-ended Tree showed a graceful S-shape, with a mass of intertwining roots at the center. Buried within the roots was the Core Sphere, the transparent dome that enclosed the joining of the tree trunks.

The RAM cruiser's camera zoomed in on a collection of spheres, cylinders, and less readily identifiable shapes clustered among the roots just outside the Core Sphere. Many of the shapes appeared to be habitat bottles, purchased, no doubt, from Belt manufacturers. Others were obviously the hulls of rocket ships, possibly vessels salvaged in deep space.

The scene closed on a rocket that appeared to be fastened to the bark of a particularly massive root. The wings were gone, the nose and tail opened up to accept pressurized tunnels from other structures, but Vince recognized the design. It was a long-range scout, some sixty feet long and deep-bodied, similar to a light stock freighter but designed to carry out scientific surveys in deep space. The name, still legible despite considerable sandblasting, was *Delta*

Crucis. Her hull number and the RAM logo were still visible as well.

"What are you people doing with a RAM scout?" Vince whispered to Katarine.

"Our Spacers brought it in eight years ago," she replied softly. "Its crew was dead. We salvaged it, and it's one of our hydroponics facilities now."

"Our friends out there might think they still have a claim. That's where you found the Artifact?"

She nodded. Rodrigo was speaking again.

"Your cities have been permitted to trade within the Inner System," Captain Rodrigo said. The camera stayed centered on the *Delta Crucis*, the magnification high enough now that Vince could see masses of brightly illuminated green through the transplex observation cupolas in the hull. "However," the captain continued, "if it can be proven that you have been engaged in piracy, that privilege is rescinded. We have that proof, Nomads. The vessel now on your screen is a RAM scout reported lost near the trans-Saturnian cometary body Chiron twelve years ago. On board was a certain Device, RAM property, lost . . . until now."

The councillor spoke again in Espen. Katarine whispered the translation. "He's saying that we legally salvaged the *Delta Crucis* and that he doesn't know what Rodrigo is talking a—"

"Do you take us for fools? The *Delta Crucis* gave us a description of the Device before we lost contact with them. Searches of the area failed to turn up our scout. We know that you have the Device. Our agents on Amalthea reported your meeting with Solar Geographic.

"We demand now that our property be restored to us. Now. Resist us and we will destroy you and your city and remove what we want from the debris."

There was a stir among the councillors, and the Altefay leaned forward on his throne, whispering furiously with the Conseos. Vince held his breath. Was the Altefay about to capitulate? Even from a distance, Vince could see the fear in the Nomad's chubby face.

The spokesman was talking again. "He's asking for more time," Katarine said. "He says that we are a democracy, that things must be decided by discussion and common consent."

"I will give you time." Rodrigo sneered. "In twenty hours, a squadron arrives here from Mars. At that time, you will give us what we demand, or all of you will die. *All* of you! Discuss *that* in your pathetic 'democracy'! In the meantime, it is intolerable that a RAM ship taken by piracy become part of that scrap pile you call a city. Since you will not restore what is properly ours . . ."

On the screen, a point of intolerable brilliance winked into existence on the *Delta Crucis*'s dorsal hull. Expanding, the light swept along the hull, opening it. Air gushed into vacuum, and debris whirled from the ruptured vessel: black trays filled with plants; a cascade of water vapor, freezing instantly into glittering ice crystals; and three desperately thrashing people. In the distance, Vince heard an alarm sounding. He hoped the Nomad city had good automatic pressure doors, because atmosphere was gushing into space fast enough to empty the city in a few hours. The watching crowd roared, a rumbling protest of pain and fury.

Laser light flared again, even brighter this time, slashing through hull plating already molten in spots. Half of the RAM scout's hull tore free, scattering wreckage and ice in its wake. The crowd roared louder. The laser had burned through the scout's hull, searing into the bark of the Tree beneath. Genetically tailored to resist the vacuum and temperature extremes of space, the bark curled and smoked under the caress of the arc-bright dazzle of light.

"Stop! Stop!" That was Damata, his shouts choking on a stifled sob of anguish. "You are burning Arbel!"

The assault continued, blasting at the wreckage of the salvaged scout until nothing was left but a twenty-foot-wide black crater gouged into the thick bark of the Tree.

After a moment, the scene dissolved, replaced once again by the anger-darkened features of Rodrigo. "Thus does RAM punish piracy! Twenty hours, and then the RAM fleet will incinerate your precious tree and every man, woman, and child inside. And don't try to tell us that the Device we seek was aboard the *Delta Crucis!* I'm certain you have it hidden in a much better place than a stinking hydroponics farm. Remember! Twenty hours!"

The screen went blank.

The next few moments were moments of unbridled confusion, with women shrieking, men shouting, and a swirl of panic among citizens trying to flee through the doors to the Grand Audience Hall or else confronting the line of Conseos. Formality and decorum were gone. A thin wall of city warriors armed with *ohalans* tried to prevent the surge of terrified citizens from literally overrunning the council's table. Several amplified voices were shouting something—a demand, Vince assumed, for silence and calm. Behind the wall, the councillors huddled with the Efay. From the expressions on their faces, they, too, were terrified, though whether they were more frightened of Rodrigo or their own people, he couldn't tell.

For that matter, Vince couldn't tell how the Ciudestreyan populace was reacting. Were they so scared they were demanding surrender, or were they simply giving in to a blind and helpless rage at the *Milankovic*'s attack? There was some of both, he expected, and a great deal of confusion. He did know that if he was going to make himself heard, he had to act now, before someone else grabbed the stage and the initiative.

He grabbed Manel by the shoulder. "Come with me," he said sharply. He doubted that the crowd would listen to a woman, even if Katarine could shout loud enough to be heard. "Translate for me!"

Launching himself from the wall of the Grand Audience Hall, he sailed through the air with Manel in tow, brushing past the overtaxed barrier of warriors before they could react and landing squarely on the tabletop in front of the councillors. As an entrance, it was somewhat undignified; he had to bend his knees and allow himself to practically collapse on the wooden table to keep from rebounding again. Rising, he spread his arms, turning as if to embrace the surging mob of frightened people. "Citizens of Ciudestreya!" he shouted. The noise subsided only slightly, and he shouted again, louder still. "People of Ciudestreya! Hear me!"

Manel's bellowed "*Oeem!*" echoed away into silence. Vince stared back into hundreds of hostile, frightened eyes. Would they listen to him, a stranger?

"I am one of you!" he yelled. "I may be Ciudestreya's newest citizen, but I am one of you!"

He heard acknowledgment, low-voiced murmurs rippling through the crowd. Most of these people had been here watching, he guessed, when he fought Dobo.

"I have spent most of my life fighting RAM," he continued. "I know what they are capable of. You saw what they are capable of when they deliberately fired into Arbel!"

The roar of angry voices rose again, drowning out Manel's translation. Vince raised his hands until the sound died away.

"Today your isolation from the rest of the solar system has ended! Distance will no longer protect you. Like it or not, you are a part of the solar system's politics, because RAM isn't going to allow you to go your own way."

"To hell with RAM!" one voice cried out in Anglic. Other voices joined in chorus.

"Ciudestreyans! You have only two choices! You can surrender and give them what they want. . . ." The translation was interrupted again by rising, angry voices, though some in the crowd were nodding, agreeing with what he said. It felt to Vince as though more in the crowd were opposed to surrender than for it.

"You can surrender," he said again, "but then RAM will destroy you anyway! This Artifact they want must be terribly important to RAM for them to send so many ships to claim it. If you surrender, they will destroy Ciudestreya anyway, simply to preserve their secret!

"Or you can fight!"

Thunder filled the hall, engulfing Vince like a roaring sea. Pandemonium reigned. One voice rose above the others, hoarse with shouting, and Manel translated. "How can we fight? We have no ships but shuttles and small freighters, and only a handful of weapons. We cannot fight them! It is madness."

"We *can* fight them," Vince insisted. "I'll show you how! But I need brave men and women to help me. Either we all stand together, or we might as well surrender now and watch them destroy Arbel!"

The answering roar was deafening, going on and on and on. Conseos moved back and forth in front of the table, imploring the crowd to be silent. Manel tugged at Vince's shoulder. "I think—" He couldn't make himself heard. He leaned closer and tried again. "I think they are with you, *Senye!*"

Vince remained standing—floating, rather, for his movements had set him adrift above the tabletop. Now that he'd grabbed their attention, he was having second thoughts. A moment's reflection might convince them that they might still try bargaining with RAM. Telling Rodrigo that they had a NEO prisoner, for instance, might twist the situation into a simple business deal.

And if Ciudestreya did help him against RAM, there'd be no going back for them, not ever. As an enemy, RAM had a long memory.

Someone touched him from behind. Turning, he found himself looking into the steady, dark eyes of Giyerm Damata. "The Altefay has something to say, *Senye* Pirelli."

Silence descended again as the fat city ruler pushed himself to within a few feet of Vince. Speaking rapidly, he delivered what sounded like an ultimatum. This time, Damata translated.

"The Altefay Waldez reminds you and all those here that he is the supreme ruler of this city, the arbiter of its laws, the protector of its customs. He cannot permit another to lead his people. In this crisis, either he leads or you do."

Vince closed his eyes, then opened them again and drew a breath. "Okay. In that case, I challenge him. *Pelepovida.* Uh . . . who's his champion?"

Damata's mouth quirked into almost a smile. His head jerked slightly, and Vince followed the movement, his eyes widening as he realized what he was looking at.

Dobo had been big, but this guy was *huge*—flat-headed, long-eared, and with a mottled, scaly-looking skin that made Vince think he was at least part Terrine. Were there such things as Worker-Terrine hybrids? The giant folded iron-sinewed arms and smiled mirthlessly, displaying three-inch fangs.

Damn. His fight with Dobo had been too close as it was. This was impossible. . . .

The Altefay was speaking again. A ripple of surprise spread among the watchers, and even Damata looked startled. He replied to Altefay Waldez in Espen, then bowed, hands raised slightly, when Waldez snapped something that sounded final.

"The Altefay says that he will meet your challenge . . . himself."

"Huh?" Before Vince could digest this, Waldez's hand closed on the handle of a sheathed knife. Vince stiffened as the blade flicked into view. It was a mono knife, glowing with a soft, inner light.

It had happened so fast, Vince wasn't sure how to react. No one had signaled the contest to begin, and these folks set such a high store by ritual. . . .

Like lightning, Waldez's arm snapped straight out, driving the knife forward . . .

. . . but not, as Vince expected, into him. Waldez held the knife rigid, the blade glowing a foot from Vince's head. Vince locked eyes with the fat king; the man could still slash him viciously with that sharper-than-razor blade, but there was something else at stake here, some other symbolism than the slash and stab of ritual combat.

"Touch him," Damata said softly.

"What?"

"Touch him. On the forehead!"

Vince reached out and touched Waldez's head. The man blinked, then withdrew his knife. Carefully, avoiding the wickedly sharp edge, he reversed the blade and handed it to Vince, hilt first.

Damata laid a hand on Vince's shoulder, turned, and shouted to the crowd. The response was, if anything, more deafening than before. As the roar swelled, Damata leaned close enough to shout into Vince's ear. "Congratulations! *You* are Altefay now!"

He stared at the mono knife in his hand, realization only now dawning. Katarine had explained that combat here was often symbolic. Waldez must have been convinced by Vince's speech and had only needed a face-saving way of passing on the responsibility.

Vince handed the knife to Damata. "Tell them I'm keeping *Senye* Waldez as my number two," he shouted. He saw the approval there. "Tell them I'll be proud to lead them. Then get me fifty volunteers. We have a lot of work to do and no time to do it."

It was some time before Damata could make the announcement. The crowd surged past the wall of guards, swirled around the small band of Conseos, and enthroned Vince at the apex of a drifting, struggling mass of bodies—the zero-G equivalent, he supposed, of being carried on their shoulders. Madness gripped the city, together with a fierce, unyielding resolve.

Vince just hoped that he would be able to give that resolve direction, because RAM would soon put it to the test.

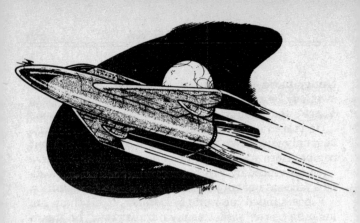

CHAPTER TWENTY-ONE

Katarine led the way, following pine-smelling tunnels that twisted into the depths of the Tree so far along the trunk from the Core Sphere that Vince could feel a definite tug of spin gravity. The pull was strong enough now to create a vague sense of "up" and "down," though walking was still impossible.

They moved by pulling themselves along handholds cut into the clean wood. Manel accompanied them, though the young Ciudestreyan now served more as personal bodyguard to the city's new Efay than as guard to a new *convida*. It was a promotion he'd accepted with enthusiasm and pride. Vince gathered that Manel expected to act as Vince's champion in any challenges to his rule.

Vince hadn't yet explained that he was already thinking of ways to abolish the old reign of trial by combat. Until now, every city Efay and Conseo had ruled with an eye to buttressing his own power. Vince had other plans than ruling this pack of rabid isolationists, and he saw ways that he could use his new-won authority in Ciudestreya to liberate its citizens from centuries of repression and stagnation.

Not that change would come at once. Vince knew better than to issue sweeping edicts that overturned social values, traditions, and customs. But there would be change. The coming confrontation with RAM would see to that, if Vince didn't.

Vince's first priority as Altefay had been the transmission of a coded message to NEO, encrypting the signal through his wrecked Starfire's communications module. The reply had arrived far more quickly than he'd expected, after a time lag of only seven minutes. Jovanna was near, was in fact on her way to Ciudestreya now with a small flotilla of warships and a unit of NEO commandos!

So far, he hadn't broken the news to anyone else. He didn't want the Nomad city's population to expect deliverance from NEO, not when so much could still go wrong and a RAM light cruiser was still parked within a few hundred miles of the Tree.

Since he'd contacted NEO, eleven of the promised twenty hours had passed, the time a whirlwind of activity as Vince discussed his plans, explained strategies, drilled volunteers, organized work details, and oversaw the deployment of a small army of workers. Waldez and the Conseos had proven to be able administrators. Under their supervision, Vince's plan was quickly taking shape.

With so much to do, he hadn't had the opportunity yet to actually see the Artifact that had spurred his one-man revolution against city authority. Questioning the councillors about the thing had yielded only unsatisfyingly vague replies. Few had actually seen it; those who had were reluctant to talk about it. None could say what it was or where it had come from.

At last he'd demanded to see it. "Of course," Conseo Damata had said. "That is your privilege."

But none had wanted to accompany him to the room where it had been kept for eight years. Finally Katarine had volunteered to take him. She'd never seen it herself, but everyone in the city knew where the Artifact from the Great Dark was kept.

"It's here," Katarine said, leading him around a final twist in the passageway and into a short, blind corridor. A wooden door on wooden hinges was flanked by two *ohalans*-wielding guards who brought their polearms to a smart salute as Vince approached.

"Wait here, Manel," Vince said. To Katarine, he added, "Let's go."

Inside, the room was dark, save for a single glow-strip drinking power from bare wood. At the center of the room, a chest had been carved from the very stuff of the floor. It was, Vince thought, like an altar set in a holy place; the men who'd cut this room from living wood had clearly been touched by awe of the thing it housed.

Vince was still convinced that the Artifact, whatever it was, would prove to be either man-made or a natural curiosity of some kind. His refusal to let it fall into RAM's hands was borne more of concern that it might represent some important piece of lost human technology. Just because something was old didn't mean it couldn't upset the equations of power.

Besides, he thought as he opened the cleverly carved, wooden hasp and lifted the lid, the Artifact didn't have to be alien for RAM to *pretend* that it was evidence of contact with an extra-solar civilization. The propaganda value of such a find alone could . . .

Looking at what filled the chest, he knew at once that he'd been wrong. The Artifact most certainly had not been manufactured by man. What Vince didn't know was what it *was*.

Outwardly the Artifact was a perfect sphere fourteen inches thick, but with a mirrored surface so perfect that it looked more like a localized distortion of the laws of optics than a solid object. His face, distorted by the perfectly convex surface, stared out of the wooden chest at him with the surreal clarity of a fisheye lens. Behind the reflection of his face, Katarine's image stared over his shoulder with goggle-eyed wonder.

What is it? he thought, the question so insistent he nearly spoke it aloud. The magical surface of the sphere rippled, distorting the reflections of faces, room, and wooden chest, and the sphere changed shape, flattening, forming angular edges with precisely ordered regularity, collapsing into . . .

. . . a dodecahedron. Twelve-sided, each pentagonal face still perfectly reflecting, the object now mirrored Vince's face in fragments, as though viewing it through an insect's eye.

"It's beautiful," Katarine whispered. The surface rippled again, the five-sided planes blending, merging, as reflections shifted, flowed, and danced.

A sphere once more rested within the chest.

Beautiful . . . and enigmatic. Its shape-changing seemed like a response to their presence, as though the thing were sentient. Its perfect surface looked like liquid mercury drawn by surface tension into a sphere in zero gravity. Was it somehow at once solid and liquid?

"Vince?" Katarine's voice was very small. "What *is* it?"

The shape remolded itself, folding inside out. This time, though, when the transformation was complete, it remained a sphere.

"Clarke's Third Law," Vince replied.

"What? What's that?"

"A very old aphorism. 'Any sufficiently advanced technology is indistinguishable from magic.'" He

shook his head, the movement amplified by the reflecting surface. "It means that I was wrong. I was
dead certain this—this whatever it is would turn out
to be man-made. Or natural, an unusual crystal,
something like that. But this is like nothing I could
ever have imagined. I wonder. . . ."

"What?"

The surface changed again. Over a circular, palm-
sized patch on the surface, the reflectivity simply
vanished. The color remained a pearly gray-silver,
but it was as though the texture had changed from
mirror polish to simply solid.

"I was wondering whether I dared touch it," Vince
said dryly. "I think it's just given me an invitation."

"Oh, Vince!" Her fingers closed on his shoulder. He
felt her trembling. "Do you think you should?"

When he'd announced his intention to see the Artifact, the councillors had said nothing about any danger, any need for gloves or special handling. Someone
had to have removed the thing from the RAM scout
and placed it here. It ought to be safe enough.

Still, fear of the unknown stirred somewhere beneath Vince's conscious thoughts like a cold, biting
wind.

"I don't see why not." Impulsively then, he reached
out, lightly placing one finger on the nonreflecting
patch.

Vince felt . . . *nothing*—no resistance, no sensation
of cool or warm, nothing. The shape twisted beneath
his hand, flowed around it. He could feel . . . something, a vibration, and the faintest sensation of
warmth. . . .

O   O   O   O   O

He was in a small rocket of some kind, adrift in
zero-G. The main cabin was cramped, the bulkheads

sheathed in layers of tubing, conduits, and snaking bundles of wires. Odd . . . but his vision had expanded in a bizarre and totally unexpected way. Somehow he was aware of perceiving all of his surroundings at once, as though his vision now encompassed a full 360 degrees, up, down, and to every side. He could concentrate in a particular direction, but visual information was bombarding him from every side, a disorienting and totally alien flood of data that threatened to drown him.

Mostly he was aware of three men, though their images were so badly distorted by the oddly curved, horizonless shape of his vision that he almost failed to recognize them for what they were. One was adrift on one side of the room, his skull smashed open, his head nearly obscured by the galaxy of crimson droplets of blood that hovered about it. The other two still struggled opposite him, their faces distorted by blood and madness. Worse than the sight were the emotions—raw, savage, desperate, living things that twisted and struggled with the grappling men, palpable, almost visible, as though registered by some sense beyond the ken of human understanding. A knife flashed, hovered, plunged. Blood filled the universe. . . .

○ ○ ○ ○ ○

"Vince! *Vince!*"

He blinked dazedly and looked around. How had he gotten? . . .

The open chest was ten feet away, and he was sitting on the floor, his head cradled in Katarine's arms. "What happened?"

"You were screaming. I pulled you out. Vince, what *is* that thing?"

He drew a shaky breath, his heart pounding. He

seemed . . . unhurt, though the intensity of what he
had just seen and felt throbbed still, fading now, like
the memory of a nightmare.

"Tell me something, Kat. No one's ever said much
to me about how this thing was found. Do you know
anything about it?"

"I was just a child at the time. . . ."

"There must have been rumors, stories."

She looked away. "A few."

"You said the crew was dead. How did they die?"

"No one knows for sure. There was a story that one
of the crewmen went mad, killed his companions,
then killed himself."

That sort of thing happened occasionally. A small
crew, a long voyage in cramped quarters . . . In such
conditions, minor dislikes or petty jealousies or frus-
trations could sometimes explode into madness,
murder, and suicide.

Had that happened to the *Delta Crucis*? Or had the
Artifact somehow *caused* it? The thought chilled
Vince, stirred by those winds of the Unknown.

"I think the Artifact must be some kind of recording device," Vince said. His knees felt weak, but the
nightmare intensity of the experience was gone now,
leaving only the memory. "I saw . . ."

"What?"

He shook his head. Even now he didn't want to remember.

Besides, something else had occurred to him. He
was beginning to understand that the Artifact somehow responded to thought. Its changes in appearance
seemed triggered by specific thoughts—his desire to
know what it was, for instance. It seemed aware of
his thoughts, responding to his touch by feeding images directly into his mind, recordings of events, of
feelings that had happened aboard the *Delta Crucis*
years before.

Could he control those images? If he asked questions while in contact with the Artifact, would it reply? If the Artifact were a recorder, perhaps it was also a communications device.

But to find out, he would have to touch it again.

He drifted again toward the chest. "Vince! Don't!"

"It's okay, Kat." He kept his voice calm as he shoved aside visions of madness and murder. Perhaps the Artifact was addictive, enslaving the mind, then twisting it into madness. Perhaps the wrong thought triggered insanity in the user. Perhaps . . . perhaps . . .

"Look," he said, staring at the silver sphere again. "I think I might be able to get it to tell me where it's from, who made it."

"Vince, I don't like this. It—"

"Trust me! I want you to hang on to me, like last time. If I scream, don't pull me out right away. Give me time to . . . to learn how to work the thing." He managed a brittle grin. "Just pull me out if the screaming goes on too long."

"How long is 'too long'?"

"If it looks like I'm going to hurt myself—or you— yell for the guards to come in and clobber me. Okay?"

"Vince—"

"What?"

Her eyes were riveted on the open box.

She shuddered, her eyes closing. "I . . . I was just wondering if . . . if it's *alive*. . . ."

He shook his head. "Kat, whatever this thing is, it's not alive. At least, it's not what we would call alive."

He was straining, searching his feelings and the memory of his encounter with the Artifact for some comparison. During his first brush with its eldritch vision, he, too, had wondered briefly if it was alive, but he'd discarded the idea almost at once. The Artifact seemed to record impressions with perfect clarity and somehow transmit them directly to a . . . well, a *listening* mind. And it did so with a hard, cold neutrality of purpose that was more like the functioning of a machine than the responses of something alive.

"It won't hurt us," he added, wishing he were as certain as the words suggested. "But we have to figure out how it works. I have to touch it again."

She nodded, a desperate reluctance showing in her moist eyes. Vince looked at the sphere. Again it had that inviting, circular patch of nonreflection.

"Well, here goes nothing." He reached out. Again there was no feeling, but the sphere turned oil-slick, rainbow-hued, unfolding. . . .

○ ○ ○ ○ ○

Bodies and blood and the ragtag memories of nightmare horror floated within the rocket's cabin. "Where are you from?" Vince hammered at that thought. "Who made you? What made you? . . ."

The image of ship rippled and flowed like water. Still, that disturbing all-round perception pulled at his mind, forcing his brain to see and accept in ways that billions of years of evolution had never envisioned.

He was in space now, floating above a world like none that Vince had ever known, a world alive with cold, blue light and the dark reach and thrust of enigmatic constructions, the sprawl of geometric shapes, the mystery of spans and struts and towers and crisscrossed avenues of spiderweb complexity.

There was intelligence and purpose in that vast geometry, which spread below his vantage point from horizon to horizon, embracing an entire world. That intelligence lay somehow just beyond Vince's grasp, but it left the strong impression that the builders of this place were not native to it. Those parts of the surface not subjugated by the alien architecture were raw and blasted, all cliff and scarp, barren rock and ice. A glacier on the horizon shone faintly by starlight and the glimmer of a million blue lights.

The city's architecture was untainted by human concepts of form, beauty, purpose, reason. Bridges vaulted chasms but led nowhere; towering, organic-looking shapes rose side by side with harshly angular geometries; Gothic arches and buttresses supported nothing but themselves. Shapes and light and shadow and mass tricked the eye, teasing it with shapes that might have been living things—squatting, horned monsters; groping claws. Vast patterns of lights might have held meaning but gave no clue to their purpose.

There was atmosphere . . . of a sort, a cold mist that haloed the dazzling arc points of blue light and filled the machinery-cluttered chasms between the largest structures with fog. Vince suspected that the waste heat from the alien city itself was boiling frozen methane, creating a gaseous envelope about a world that had never known the caress of wind or warmth.

Nothing familiar existed with which Vince could establish scale. The horizon was close. This world was small, its diameter less than a thousand miles. Looming above the horizon was another world, crescent-lit, the black void of its night side blotting out a circular swatch against the star-dusting of the Milky Way. The crescent bowed away from a particularly brilliant star that gleamed with a light as wan and as cold and as frost-silver as moonlight.

His attention was dragged back to the city. It was vast and cold, with an iciness reflecting the mentality of inhuman builders. He could sense them, those builders, though he couldn't even begin to guess the

shape of their bodies or their minds. He knew only
that those minds were utterly inhuman, their rea-
sonings, their senses of proportion and geometry as
far removed from human understanding as might be
the dreams of some cold intelligence dwelling in the
lightless chasms of Earth's great midocean deeps.

If what he was seeing was the world the Artifact
had come from, the information was less than help-
ful. Vince didn't recognize the place. How could he?
If it was a world circling some other distant sun,
there were no clues to its location, nothing to hint at
the biology of the city's builders or their purpose. . . .

$$O \quad O \quad O \quad O \quad O$$

"Vince! *Please*, Vince! Snap out of it!"

Blinking, he looked into Katarine's worried face.
"I'm . . . okay. . . ." He shook himself. "Did I scream?"

"No! But you were gone ten minutes! I couldn't
reach you!"

He looked around. The room was unchanged. The
Artifact, doughnut-shaped now, rested in the chest,
as cryptic and as enigmatic as ever.

"I've seen enough." Regret—and wonder—drew
him, compelled him to touch that shining surface
again. If he could only visit that city of cold blue light
a few moments more, learn its secrets. . . .

Ten minutes? It had only been seconds!

There was no time for further exploration. "Let's
get out of here," he said.

Together they returned to Ciudestreya's preparations for war.

CHAPTER TWENTY-TWO

The cargo shuttle fell outward toward darkness from the slowly revolving majesty of the Tree, a rickety-looking collection of struts, rocket motors, fuel tanks, and a blunt arrowhead that held pressure and warmth. *Huan Delgado* was painted on her battered prow, the name of some early Ciudestreyan administrator.

Vince was amazed that the derelict-looking contraption could still maneuver, but during the past few hours, he'd acquired a profound respect for the Nomads' sheer mechanical genius.

Held together by baling wire and duct tape, by love and good wishes, *Delgado* and her sisters were the last of twenty-five shuttles, ferries, and work pods that had begun the city's construction two centuries before. Cannibalization had reduced that number to four; the miracle was that any high-tech gear in Ciudestreya worked at all. During the festival they called *Tempomercad*, the Nomads acquired some new equipment each time they passed through the inner solar system, but nearly everything that wasn't part of the "Bounty of Arbel" was ancient, carefully tended, and oft-repaired, with a Tinker's loving attention to detail. Every space suit in the city was an heirloom handed down across seven generations.

Like everything else in Ciudestreya, Nomad technology was a bizarre mingling of the primitive and the old. The city had a small industrial capability but was painfully limited in high-tech manufactured goods. Raw materials were relatively common, mined from asteroids and the tunneled cores of ancient comets. Electronics, though, like the rejuv pod that had restored Vince or the navcomputers that calculated course and speed for the cargo shuttles were scarce, preserved with the love of an antiquarian tending the fragments of a lost civilization.

The Ciudestreyans were wizards at enzyme chemistry, manufacturing from various raw materials provided by the Tree everything they needed in day-to-day life, from food and medicine to sealants and pressure fittings to the soft paper clothing they wore, yet computers were almost nonexistent. Their few vidpads and the giant folding screen used for talking with *forano* ships had been acquired through trade generations before.

All of which left Vince with a serious problem. How could Ciudestreya seriously hope to challenge the *Milankovic*? The city had only a few weapons—beam lasers and gyrocannons stripped from salvaged ships over the years—but nothing that could present any serious threat to a RAM light cruiser.

Even in hand weapons they were seriously outmatched. In all of Ciudestreya there were perhaps twenty working laser pistols, and most had been modified for use as welding and cutting tools. Modern weaponry was frighteningly unsuited to use inside a fragile construct like the city. The *ohalans* and *azotens* of the guards and the spectacles of *pelepovida* had a utilitarian purpose; they could kill without blowing holes through the walls. Sonic stunners were useful for crowd control but couldn't touch someone in full armor. The most common hand weapon in the city besides the largely ceremonial pole-arms and whips were *ballestas*, crossbows similar to the weapons carried by Martian Desert Runners, but firing steel-tipped wooden quarrels instead of shells or metal projectiles. Only lasers would have a chance against men in combat armor.

Vince had taken all of this into account as he worked out the plan for dealing with the *Milankovic* . . . he hoped. Where technology wasn't up to the challenge, cunning and resourcefulness might be.

They had to be. They were all Vince had to work with in the short time available.

He floated in the command module of the *Huan Delgado*, gripping the backs of the seats occupied by pilot and copilot. He wore his shipsuit again, gloves and helmet close at hand, a laser pistol holstered at his hip. Manel was with him, as personal bodyguard and translator; the cabin was too small for more than four, but the hatch leading aft was open.

The pilot said something in Espen, and Manel translated. "He says to hold on tight, *Senye*. He is maneuvering."

Vince tightened his grip, but the nudges from attitude rockets were gentle, little more than taps that spun the shuttle through ninety degrees, aligning the prow with the distant *Milankovic*. Though he strained hard to see it, he couldn't make out the one star among millions that was reflected light from the RAM cruiser.

The copilot spoke, and Manel echoed. "Ten minutes to target."

"Perhaps we should let them know we're coming." He picked up the microphone for a radio two centuries obsolete and depressed the transmit key. "RMS

Milankovic," he called. "This is City Shuttle *Delgado* outbound from Ciudestreya. Do you copy? Over."

The RAM ship would be monitoring all common radio frequencies. No doubt they'd heard his conversation hours before with Jovanna, though he prayed the NEO encryptions they'd used had kept their words private. Still, they would have gauged the NEO flotilla's distance by the time lag, one reason among many for haste.

"RMS *Milankovic*." Static hissed. "We are tracking you on an intercept course. Change vectors at once or you will be destroyed."

No doubt they feared the shuttle was packed with high explosives, a manned missile. Here lay the first great gamble in Vince's plan. The enemy might never allow them close enough to act.

"*Milankovic*, we are unarmed." He kept his voice humble. A servant, doing his master's bidding. "The city has surrendered. We are bringing you the device we found on your ship, just as you demanded."

"The Device you pirated, you mean." A pause, seconds crawling. "Why aren't you transmitting visual? Let's see the Device on screen."

"Please, *Milankovic*!" Vince allowed a tremor to creep into his voice. "Our shuttles don't have that kind of equipment! All we have are voice channels!" True enough, that, and RAM would have records of past dealings with Nomads confirming it. Rodrigo must be weighing now the threats and merits of boarding Ciudestreya with his troops, twenty against a city, or allowing them to bring the prize to his ship. Surely his contempt of the Nomads would outweigh any fear of what so small a shuttle could hide on board. Smartest, perhaps, would be to order them to halt, then dispatch a ship's boat for rendezvous. Here, too, pride might overrule caution.

"Very well, *Delgado*. You may dock. Keep your final approach speed below ten feet per second so I know you're not trying to ram me with that contraption. Try anything, anything at all, and your miserable city will be incinerated. Do you understand?"

"Y-Yes, *Senye*. We understand perfectly!"

The *Delgado* continued on course. Gradually one star against the star-strewn backdrop grew brighter, took dimension, then form. Pencil-lean, shark-finned, the light cruiser was the very antithesis of the small and cumbersome cargo hauler drifting into its shadow. Turrets swung, tracking the shuttle with computer-locked precision.

"Final approach," Manel warned. The *Delgado* shuddered as attitude thrusters fired. Weight briefly surged through Vince, tugging him first one way, then another. The red-painted hull of the cruiser loomed huge beyond the shuttle's cockpit windows.

Stooping, Vince picked up an open box wedged in place on the deck and held it up, tilting it toward the transplex blisters on the RAM ship's forward hull. Inside was the spherical shape of an ancient fuel cell, sprayed with a molecular aluminum film. Observers on the cruiser's bridge, peering through *Delgado*'s cockpit windows, would see what they hoped to see . . . and be reassured.

The cruiser's main portside docking hatch grew steadily larger. The pressurized module astern of *Delgado*'s bridge was designed for carrying passengers, though it was too small to offer much threat. Built into the dorsal side was a hatch with a universal docking collar. Eased toward the vastly larger cruiser by gentle taps on the maneuvering thrusters, the shuttle closed the distance, then locked home with a clang that reverberated through the hull.

"Well, time to make our delivery," Vince said. Still carrying the box, he sailed through the bridge's aft hatchway and into the connecting tunnel beyond.

There was no room to enter the shuttle's cargo module, packed as it was with a mass of humanity— forty men crammed into a space no more than fifteen feet square. *Delgado*'s life-support systems had been terribly strained, but Ciudestreya's engineers had calculated that a margin of safety remained for a short, one-way voyage.

They *had* to succeed. There was no going back.

○ ○ ○ ○ ○

On *Milankovic*'s bridge, Capt. Dretan Rodrigo leaned closer, his eyes on the monitor showing the ship's forward loading bay and main portside lock. A ship as small as the *Milankovic* carried only four marines, and all were in place facing the air lock, backs to the camera, laser rifles at the ready. Rodrigo more than half-suspected a trick. Ciudestreya's surrender had come too quickly, too easily. But whatever the junkyard rabble tried, he would be ready.

"Weapons!" he snapped.

"Sir!"

"Lock onto the Nomad city. Nuclear warhead, full yield."

"Yes, sir."

"The moment we're certain we have what we came for, we'll vaporize the lot of them." His orders had directed him to leave no witnesses, but he had to be certain first. Through the vidscanner, he'd glimpsed something in the other ship's cockpit that looked like the description in his orders of the Device he'd been sent to collect, round and silvery, but he didn't trust these slimy Nomads. He would wait until he had the prize in his possession before giving the order.

To secure the Device for RAM before that oaf Zotov even arrived, that would be a triumph indeed!

On the monitor, the inner air lock hatch was sliding open. . . .

Smoke boiled through the opening, fog-thick, mingling with the air and swirling around the RAM marine guards. Four laser rifles fired as one, the pulses dazzling in the thick smoke, but attenuated. Men were storming into the bay now, dozens of them. There was a shrill scream. With so many bodies in the air, it would have been impossible to miss, but four or five attackers had grabbed each of the space-armored troops and were wrestling their weapons from them. Rodrigo saw a hand wielding a spray gun emerge from the smoke and coat a marine's helmet visor and electronic sensors with black paint. One attacker became hazily visible, his face covered by a transparent breath mask, his hands gripping an archaic-looking battle-axe of some kind.

Rodrigo's fist came down on an alarm button. The rasp of the Klaxon blared through the cruiser. "All hands! All hands!" the deck officer announced, his voice shrill with excitement. "Repel boarders, main deck forward! Repel borders, main deck forward!"

The display went black, and Rodrigo realized that someone had spray-painted over the camera lens. He drew his laser pistol, a RAM-Sylvanian M-50, and checked the receiver power pack. Let them come!

○ ○ ○ ○ ○

Two were dead in the loading bay, three more wounded. The marines had been disarmed and immobilized, their armor suits wired helpless by yards of diacarballoy filament until someone had the time to find a can opener and pry them out.

Vince followed the fight, Manel at his side wielding a *ballesta* and a flap-sealed quiver of steel-tipped quarrels. His loyal subjects, it seemed, weren't about to let their Altefay risk his life in combat or board

the enemy ship unprotected. They'd tried to keep
him off the shuttle entirely until he pointed out that
he had more experience with RAM than they and
that they'd need him in dealing with the officers.
Now, he'd traded the silver fuel cell for a laser pistol,
and he wore a breather mask over his face. Smoke
still churned and boiled through the corridors, but
the cruiser's life-support machinery was already
thinning the cloud to an acrid white haze.

Bodies floated in the corridor—a Ciudestreyan
with a laser-burned hole in his chest, three black-
uniformed RAM navy crewmen with *ballesta* bolts
sprouting from their chests. Blood droplets danced in
the air, and Vince heard a triumphant shout echoing
from the passageway ahead.

So far, the cruiser's defenders were scattered and
disorganized. Everything depended now on following
through on the shock and surprise of the attack,
smashing down the enemy's defenses before they had
time to get organized.

"Come on, Manel! Snap it up!"

"P-Please, Altefay! You must not get too close!"

"We're not doing any good back here! *Move!*"

Sounds of battle were echoing from two directions
now, forward and aft. A handful of men had moved to
cut off the engine room and aft weapons bays; most
stormed the bridge, which fortunately was less than
fifty feet forward of the main portside lock. Vince
and Manel rounded a corner onto the main passageway running along the cruiser's spine.

Both sides had lasers now. Bolts hissed and seared,
drawing flickering trails of ionization through the
air. Where they touched bulkheads, they scorched
and bubbled paint and left smoldering craters.
Where they touched flesh, men shrieked in agony,
weightlessly thrashing until comrades could pull
them out of the way . . . or else drifted, rag-doll limp,

arms akimbo. Vince counted four . . . five . . . eight Ciudestreyans along the way, the city's dead far outnumbering the bodies of RAM personnel.

In the distance, Vince could hear the thuttering shocks of crossbows fired in volleys, a chorus of yells and shouted pain. Ahead, a RAM officer writhed in midair, clawing at the quarrel protruding from one cloven eye, his screams mindlessly shrill. Manel put a second bolt into his skull as they passed, a mercy shot, silencing him.

A final corner, and large, double doors stood open just ahead. A black crater smoked where the lock control mechanism had been, while a trio of RAM crewmen guarded the portal in death. The sounds of fighting were already subsiding. When Vince finally reached the bridge, the battle was over.

Eight prisoners—three officers and five crewmen—floated on the bridge, surrounded now by twice that many Ciudestreyans. The Nomads had lost at least fifteen storming the *Milankovic*, and they were not in a forgiving mood.

"Hello, Captain," Vince said as he entered the bridge. The crowd parted enough for him to approach. "Request permission to come aboard? Thank you so much."

Rodrigo glared. His uniform was in disarray and his hair was mussed. "Pirate! I wasn't bluffing when I said more ships were coming! You slimy scums will pay for this, I promise you!"

Casually Vince studied a weapons control panel nearby. "I see you have a Mark III warhead targeted and locked on Ciudestreya, Captain." He spoke loudly enough for every Nomad on the bridge and in the passageway outside to hear. "The Mark III carries . . . what? Half a megaton? You think that'll be enough to destroy the entire city?"

A low murmur sounded from the Ciudestreyans

surrounding the battered RAM captain. Several drew closer to Rodrigo. The man's hands were shaking and his face was pale.

"You're right, too. We don't have much time before your friends arrive."

"They'll take you apart. They'll annihilate you, unless you release me and the Device instantly! If you don't—"

"Maybe. I'll tell you what." He leaned closer, his face less than six inches from Rodrigo's. The RAM captain stank of fear. "We'll take all of you back to Ciudestreya. We'll tell the people how you were going to incinerate the city—men, women, and children all—and then we'll turn you over to them. How's that sound?"

"You . . . wouldn't. . . ."

"We're *Nomads*, Captain Rodrigo." Vince grinned. "Doesn't that mean anything to you? Surely you've heard stories about us. . . ."

Rodrigo's pallor increased. He looked as if he were going to be sick. No matter what the man had heard about Nomads, Vince was pretty sure that his imagination was working overtime right now.

Carlo, a burly Ciudestreyan who spoke a smattering of Anglic, closed one beefy hand on Rodrigo's shoulder and raised a mono knife in the other. Green light illuminated the RAM captain's pallor as he sagged back into the arms of the men holding him.

"I think," Carlo said, "that we have the fun now, no? Just a little?"

"Wh-wh-what . . . do you . . . want?" Rodrigo's eyes crossed as the blade's glowing tip moved toward his nose.

Vince's smile broadened. "Why, not much at all, Captain. Not very much at all."

CHAPTER TWENTY-THREE

The NEO-pirate squadron dropped tail-first toward Ciudestreya, their drive venturis blasting star-hot plasma astern in shuddering deceleration. On board *Enterprise*, Jovanna, Barney, Kaiten, and Captain Carter met in a final precombat briefing. Of the four, only Jovanna and Barney were there in the flesh. The other two, still aboard their respective ships, were present as holographic images transmitted by a tight-beamed comm laser.

"There's no question." Barney sounded uncharacteristically subdued. "Our long-range scanners've picked up at least five ships. Judging by their trajectory, they left Mars hours after we did, but they're going to beat us to Ciudestreya by a good twenty minutes." He held up a thumb and forefinger. "They beat us by *that* much."

The *Enterprise*, *Reprisal*, and *Lady Luck*, Jovanna knew, had been delayed by the need to rendezvous in free-fall in order to load the captured Kraits aboard the transport. The RAM ships had been able to sustain higher accelerations along a slightly different course, one that had gotten them to Ciudestreya ahead of the NEO force.

"And that's in addition to the light cruiser we know is already at the Nomad City," Kaiten added. "Six to three. Not good odds."

"Worse than that," Carter said. "You can't count the *Lady* as a combat vessel. One of the bandits may be a transport, so call it five to two. And one of those five is a heavy cruiser. I have to say that I seriously question the wisdom of this deployment."

"Ain't a hell of a lot we can do about it now," Barney said, "the laws of the universe being what they are. What we have to do is figure how to make do with what we've got."

"Ms. Trask?" Carter said. "Any word from NEO?"

"They're scrambling a task force now," she said, "but it's going to be twenty hours at least before they can reach us. Unless the Nomads can help, I'm afraid we're on our own."

"There'll be no help there," Carter snorted.

"We stick with the original plan, then," Barney said. "*Reprisal* and *Enterprise*'ll tangle with the RAM squadron. *Lady Luck* will head for that space-going tree house. Any questions?"

"Just one," Kaiten said. "What's the word on loot? *Reprisal*'s crew's in an ugly mood."

Barney grinned. "You'll just have to out-ugly them, Terrine. The Nomad city's off limits, and I doubt you'll have the time to play games with the RAM ships. Other questions?"

There were none. The images of Kaiten and Carter winked out, leaving Jovanna alone with Barney in *Enterprise*'s lounge.

"I have a question," she said, shifting uncomfortably on the couch. They were decelerating at nearly a full G, and her back hurt.

"Mmm?" Barney stood at a small, well-furnished bar, pouring himself a drink.

"Why are you doing all of this? I mean, Kaiten had a point. There's no loot, so why bother?"

"You think I'm in this for what I can steal?"

"It had crossed my mind. You are a pirate, right?"

"I was made that way, if you'll recall."

He sounded bitter, and Jovanna realized that there was much about the big gennie she would never understand. It was true. For reasons still obscure, his creators had designed him as a pirate. RAM, possibly, had seen Barney and his clone brothers and sisters as tools for infiltrating elements of solar culture they did not yet dominate.

Barney was silent for a long moment. "You know anything about pirates in history?"

"You mean on Earth? Not much. There used to be . . . outlaws. Sailing men who hijacked cargo ships at sea."

"Cowards and cutthroats, most of 'em," Barney agreed. "Trash that couldn't make it any other way, so they took to piracy. Most of 'em ended up at the end of a rope.

"Their heyday was a long time ago—sixteenth, seventeenth centuries. Lots of nations always at war with one another—Spain, England, France. Sometimes a country would hire pirates to help them in a war. They'd sail under what was called a 'letter of marque,' which gave 'em official permission to hunt the enemy's ships. They weren't called pirates then, but 'privateers.' "

"What's your point?"

"I got an idea," he said. "The Rogues' Guild may have as many ships as RAM. It occurred to me that a lot of those ships might be organized as privateers. NEO privateers, in the service of Earth."

"But why? What's NEO done for you?"

Barney shrugged. "Even a pirate needs a safe haven—a place to sell his loot and refit his ships.

We've used places in the Belt until now, but RAM is putting out tentacles everywhere, closing in. The Guild may not have those havens much longer.

"Besides, if RAM wins, we're next on their list. If NEO wins, who knows? Maybe we can work out a deal. NEO has some of the same screwy ideas about freedom from government and taxes pirates have. . . ."

Jovanna smiled. "I'm not sure too many in NEO would appreciate having their ideals compared to yours, Barney. But I know they'd appreciate having more ships. God knows, we need them."

"I ain't doing this out of the goodness of my heart, Teacher. It's enlightened self-interest, that's all."

"If you say so." Perhaps, she thought, that was the attitude she should adopt. She was still smarting from the realization that NEO had used her and Galen the way she had once used Barney. If Barney was using NEO for his own ends, well . . . why not? The goal was what mattered, the end of RAM and independence for Earth.

And then *Enterprise* and her consorts were closing on Ciudestreya, a slow-turning S-shape two miles across. Battle stations were sounded as three of the RAM warships maneuvered to block the NEO-pirate squadron.

And Barney's motives, and hers, were suddenly less important than simple survival.

○ ○ ○ ○ ○

At Ciudestreya, the enemy had arrived, four warships and a transport deployed in an open pattern that guaranteed maximum field of fire for every weapon. There was no radio call, no warning, no demand for surrender. One moment the RAM ships were approaching slowly, closing to within two hundred miles; the next, they'd loosed a volley of laser bolts, shells, and missiles.

Death flashed and flowered in brief, intense bursts of flame, striking outlying structures, smashing domes and workshops, hydroponics plants and civilian barracks, fuel stores and water tanks. City gunners returned the fire from salvaged laser turrets and gyrocannons, but with primitive radar, without combat computers, most of the fire was ineffective.

As quickly as it had begun, three medium cruisers had split off, taking up a position from which they could intercept the approaching NEO ships. The remaining two, a transport and the heavy cruiser *Amazonis*, maneuvered closer, continuing the bombardment.

O O O O O

Vince had the helm; none among the Ciudestreyans who'd boarded *Milankovic* with him hours before had ever been aboard a ship this big, much less learned how to operate it.

Moments earlier, the *Delgado*'s assault group had been replaced by other men from the city. Five technicians familiar with the city's fusion power plants manned the engineering deck now, while on the bridge, three more sat at stations similar enough to key systems within Ciudestreya that they could man the relevant boards aboard the cruiser: life support, communications, radar. Manel stood at Vince's side as translator, refusing to leave his Altefay.

Only four of *Milankovic*'s battle stations were fully manned—her two beam lasers and two gyrocannon turrets. Those weapons, at least, were familiar to the city's defense forces, and only a short session with Vince had been necessary to familiarize them with the cruiser's more modern equipment. The ship also mounted one missile battery, which he'd been able to

patch through to the helmsman's panel. He would
handle the cruiser's shipkillers himself.

Eager now to come to grips with RAM, Vince
crouched forward in the helm chair, fingers splayed
over his console touch panel, maneuvering the ship
in motion with gentle taps from her thrusters. He
dared not fire the main engines. He couldn't handle
a cruiser at full thrust by himself, not and maintain
control. It had taken him an hour to gently nudge
Milankovic into the shadow of the Tree, where she
was screened from the approaching RAM flotilla's
radar.

Now, as the enemy bombardment flashed among
the Tree's branches, he let the cruiser break cover,
drifting from behind the city's Core Sphere. Ahead,
on the main viewscreen, two ships rose from behind
the jet-black, light-drinking foliage of the Tree. *Milankovic*'s computer didn't identify them; Vince had
been unable to find any Nomad who could use a
ship's computer, and he was too busy at the moment
to access the ship's war book.

Still, he recognized the general types: a troop car-
rier and a heavy cruiser. The cruiser had to be *Amazonis*. His eyes traced the damage she'd suffered
since he'd seen her last: a missing tail fin, a
patched-over section of hull marking a gouge running a hundred feet forward from her tail, scars
where fighter pods had torn free. The *Amazonis* had
been in a nasty scrape recently. The raid at Phobos?

"Efay!" the Ciudestreyan manning the communications panel announced. He was an older man who
spoke Anglic with a thick accent. "We are being
called!"

"Pipe it over here, Andres," he replied. "Audio only."

". . . don't you answer? *Milankovic*, this is RMS
Amazonis. Respond. Over!"

"Hit the squawk button," Vince ordered. Andres

touched a key, transmitting *Milankovic*'s coded IFF signal.

Military ships rarely broadcasted IFF codes except during a rendezvous or encounter like this one. Identification Friend/Foe systems kept friendly ships from firing at one another, but they could also attract the enemy. IFF codes were frequently changed; squawking the right code on the right frequency was basic to every encounter involving friendly warships.

It was *Milankovic*'s IFF codes that Vince had needed to drag from Rodrigo. By questioning the ship's captain and communications officer separately, he'd been able to verify the information they'd given him. There was still a chance that what they'd told him was something prearranged among all RAM officers, a use-this-if-you're-in-trouble code that would alert *Amazonis* to *Milankovic*'s deception.

But it was the best Vince had been able to come up with. As *Milankovic* transmitted the code, he opened the ship-to-ship channel. "*Amazonis*, this is *Milankovic*. Sorry we missed your approach. We were chasing a Nomad ship that was trying to escape."

"Roger, *Milankovic*," was the reply. "Why don't we have visual? Over."

"Visual comm is down, *Amazonis*. We're on radio only. Over."

There was a static-blasted pause. Would they buy it?

"Copy, *Milankovic*. You are directed to join *Hisperia*, *Cydonia*, and *Sabaeus*. Deep scan radar reports three vessels, almost certainly enemy warships, approaching the Nomad city."

"Roger, *Amazonis*. *Milankovic* is complying." Vince cut the channel, then opened the ship's intercom. "Weapons stations," he snapped, and Manel began relaying his words in Espen. "Target the transport first. Knock her out, and they won't be able to invade the city." He could make out the transport's name on her hull now: *Ajax*.

Milankovic's weapons stations checked in, manned and ready. Satisfied, Vince shifted his hands to that part of the board programmed for missile control. Loaded into *Milankovic*'s four tubes were one Mark XC Solarflare ECM missile and three Mark L Devastators. He wouldn't engage the ship's weapons radar until the last possible moment, to avoid alerting the RAM fleet.

They'd be getting suspicious by now, wondering why *Milankovic* didn't immediately change her vector. She was still bow-on toward *Ajax*'s port flank, closing at a few feet per second.

"Message from *Amazonis*," the commo man reported.

"That's it!" Vince shouted. "Lasers and gyrocannons! *Fire!*"

Tracers lashed toward the RAM transport as twin suns appeared, dazzling against her hull. Vince's fingers played a rapid tap-tap-tap over the weapons board, and *Milankovic*'s radar locked on, her computer communicating for nanoseconds with the readied missiles. Target lock prompts appeared on the forward screen, accompanied by numbers giving range, bearing, and closure rate.

He stabbed a button. "Fire *one!* Fire *two!* Missiles away!"

At point-blank range, the ECM missile streaked from *Milankovic*'s prow, closely followed by a Devastator Shipkiller. The Solarflare, designed to deliberately miss the close-packed targets, flashed within yards of *Ajax*'s hull, its warhead burning sunbrilliant. Trailing it was the churning vortex of an electromagnetic pulse, powerful enough to fry a ship's electronics and optics. All space vessels were hardened against high-intensity mag and rad effects, but the weapon would provide a few precious seconds of ECM cover.

Less than one second later, the Devastator slammed into *Ajax*'s hull, penetrating the outer armor before detonating in a searing bubble of raw fury. Devastators packed conventional warheads; Vince wouldn't gamble with nukes so close to the Nomad city, and neither would RAM if they wanted salvage from the place. That space-silent blast of high explosives, though, was enough to shred steel like tissue. The transport staggered, badly hurt. Debris streamed like blood from the gash in her flank.

Despite the wound, though, broad panels in her belly were swinging open. She was launching!

Vince stabbed the control panel again, sending a second Devastator on its way, then a third. All of *Milankovic*'s tubes were empty now and would remain that way. None of the Ciudestreyans aboard had been trained in missile reload procedures.

Six shapes, like flattened bricks with blunt, rounded noses, fell from the *Ajax*'s ventral bays like a cluster of free-fall bombs. Vince knew at once what they were: Assault Deployment Vehicles, or ADVs. Like the infantry combat vehicles of an earlier age, they were small and tough, designed to deliver troops from orbit to any target.

The second Devastator struck home in a blinding flash that ruptured one of *Ajax*'s fuel tanks; the third entered the gaping maw of her ADV bay and detonated there in white fury, snapping her spine, but too late! The ADVs, each loaded with fifty space-armored assault troops, were already plunging on flaring aft thrusters into the tangle of the Core Sphere.

On *Milankovic*'s forward screen, *Amazonis* was slowly coming about. One of her dorsal turrets spun, the stubby complexity of its pumped laser tracking

Milankovic's approach. There was a flash, rapidly blacked out by the screen's electronics. Metal vaporized, the expansion jolting the light cruiser's hull. Vince felt the deck slam the soles of his boots, and he knew that they'd been hit hard.

"Lasers and gyrocannons!" he yelled. Manel's voice echoed his, shouting Espen over the intercom. "Keep firing! Target the cruiser!"

Tracers from the *Milankovic*'s twin gyrocannons flicked and darted through the narrowing gulf between the captured light cruiser and the leviathan *Amazonis*. Some rounds rebounded, shining fiercely against the blackness of space before they burned out. Others vanished into the heavy cruiser's hull. The wound in *Amazonis*'s port side had been reopened. Wiring, struts, conduits, and power feeds were visible now, some pounded into scrap and left glowing by the light of inner fires.

Nearby, *Ajax* was burning, glowing red-hot, her hull structure crumbling. The transport was finished. Now *Milankovic* battled the *Amazonis* alone. Vince's fingers touched color-coded lights agleam on the crystal display. *Milankovic*'s main engines coughed briefly, boosting the light cruiser toward the *Amazonis*. "All hands!" he called over the intercom. "Stand by for collision!"

As the light cruiser approached, beams of coherent light lashed through space. A pile-driver blow hammered *Milankovic*'s side, followed closely by another. The lights dimmed, then came back up to full strength. An array of red telltales on Vince's control board told of failing systems. One of the gyrocannon turrets was gone now, victim of a direct hit. Thruster control was down to sixty-seven percent, and there were fuel-feed warnings to the main engines.

Amazonis loomed ahead and to starboard now, a vast mountain of metal. One tenth the heavy cruiser's length, *Milankovic* looked like a ship's boat as she drew into the monster's shadow.

But she continued to fire, gamely battling it out with her larger adversary at point-blank range. So close was *Milankovic* now that most of *Amazonis*'s guns could no longer aim; the enemy commander was trying to bring a laser turret to bear on his gadfly opponent. *Milankovic*'s lasers carved through that cliff of red-painted metal like tiny knives slicing through a huge block of butter. White-hot wreckage spilled into space. Lightning, blue-white forks of high-energy mayhem, played in the gulfs between severed power mains and feeder trunks.

Milankovic lurched again, and a dazzling shaft of energy, like a tiny piece of a living sun, lanced through the bridge, catching Manel and flashing him to vapor and charred fragments. Atmosphere howled through gaping holes into space. The bridge screen flickered and went dead. Alarm panels noted fires on the lower decks, pressure loss, poisonous fumes, and rising temperatures until melting wiring severed the bridge from the remote sensors. The bridge was filled by the shrill hiss of escaping air, the piercing ululation of warning Klaxons.

Vince reached for his helmet and gloves, stashed beneath the helmsman's seat. The other remaining bridge officers did the same. "Andres!" he snapped at the commo officer. "Pass the word to abandon ship. Then let's get out of here!"

He didn't know how many were left alive aboard the *Milankovic* to act on the message, wasn't even sure the intercom was still working.

Then a final, thunderous impact rocked the bridge, sweeping Vince from his feet and bouncing him off one crumpled bulkhead.

They had to get to the lifepod bay. *Milankovic* was coming apart around them.

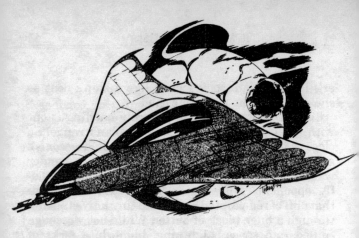

CHAPTER TWENTY-FOUR

Within the city, the RAM invaders lashed at the defending civilians in a holocaust of flame and wind.

Launched from the *Ajax* seconds before the transport's doom, the six Assault Deployment Vehicles plunged through the tangled weave of the Tree's roots, driving toward the Core Sphere with three hundred RAM assault troops aboard, packed fifty to a boat.

Not that there was a great deal of defensive fire to avoid. Gyrocannon tracer rounds flashed soundlessly from the city defenses. Two ADVs flared and vanished as laser light played across their hulls. Seconds later, the four remaining ADVs pierced the network of roots encasing the city's central hub, bursting through the two-ply soap-bubble barrier in a storm of shrieking wind and whirling transplex shards.

The breach in the double shell of the Core Sphere began sealing itself, but the hole was large, the viscous sealant between the transplex layers slow to completely fill the hole. Meanwhile, air gushed out into space, bearing with it shards and debris and the struggling bodies of city habitants snatched aloft by the howling wind. Moisture in the air condensed, then froze, creating a localized blizzard of swirling ice and snow.

Fortunately, most of Ciudestreya's population had already fled into the myriad tunnels deep beneath the Tree's tough outer bark. Children had long since been shuttled in tubecars to Heavydown, where emergency escape pods were being readied in case the worst happened. The adults, meanwhile, armed with crossbows, polearms, and a pitiful handful of lasers, braced themselves for a fight. Their sole hope was to capture enough modern weapons to tip the balance of firepower. The sheer ferocity of the RAM troopers' entrance was designed to overwhelm any such hope or defense.

Clamshell doors on the ADPs' prows swung open, spilling red-and-black-armored men armed with lasers and rocket guns. Propelled by rocket belts, the troopers rushed the massive central trunk of Arbel.

Arbel's defenders opened fire from a hundred hidden positions. Audible above the dwindling roar of the wind, crossbows clattered and snapped in massed volleys. Unfortunately, though crossbow bolts could penetrate the plate and mail of medieval knights, the tough polyalloys and ceramics of modern space armor splintered most or sent them ricocheting through the air. Several troopers tumbled away helplessly, quarrels piercing the flexible cuticle of joints or seams. More died as snipers opened fire with hoarded lasers.

The RAM troopers returned fire, and defenders screamed, crumpled, burned, and died. Rocket rifles loosed high-explosive smart rounds on streaming, pencil-thin contrails, their characteristic *hiss-whoosh-cracks* shrill in the thinning air. Explosions pierced sheltering walls, spat shrapnel, exploded flesh in bloody sprays.

In two minutes, the RAM invaders had secured the Core Sphere, killing ten defenders for every one of their own lost.

Then they entered the Tree and the real slaughter began.

O   O   O   O   O

Half a million miles sunward, *Free Enterprise* surged ahead of *Lady* and *Reprisal*, loosing missile after missile toward the three medium cruisers that blocked the direct approach to Ciudestreya. The cruisers returned fire, but Black Barney's ship, the hull encased in radar-absorbing coatings, was hard to track.

Missiles sought missiles in long, deadly seconds of electronic hide-and-seek. ECM missiles roared through the heavens, trailing the shrill radio hiss of EMP static. Explosions flared silently in space, outshining the distant sun. One of the cruisers circled, probing the *Enterprise* with beam lasers. Barney anticipated the move, slammed his retro thrusters on full, and let the RAM ship drift across his bow.

Orange light glowed in the *Enterprise*'s K-cannon tube, brightened, flared. Sparkling in the night, the round bridged the gulf between pirate raider and cruiser in an instant.

A hit! Fuel gushed into space from ruptured tanks, freezing into a soft-glowing fog clotted with drifting debris. The RAM cruiser *Sabaeus* tumbled slowly, out of the fight at least for the moment.

From *Lady Luck*, meanwhile, ten lean, sharklike forms drifted clear of the open forward cargo bay as space-suited men turned laser torches on steel cables. The Kraits had only limited fuel, piloted by ten of Trinity's leading cadets, battle-eager and looking

for blood. News that Maj. Vince Pirelli might be
alive in the Nomad city had swept through the
squadron's ranks at the speed of light.

"Hawk Leader to all Hawks," one young cadet
called over the tactical channel. "Heads up, people.
This is our chance to show the major what we can
really do!"

His name was Jamison.

O O O O O

Vince had been adrift for nearly ten minutes, wondering how he could possibly get back in the fight.
The life pod was a tiny one-man globe with a single
window, an inflatable shell with neither thrusters
nor air lock, and with only limited life support. It
was less a lifeboat than a high-tech life jacket, a
means for one man to survive for a few hours until he
could be rescued.

If there *was* anyone around to rescue him. An automatic transponder would be beeping his position, but
if RAM troops had entered the city, the Ciudestreyans would be too busy fighting them to dispatch a
rescue team.

Had anyone else gotten off the *Milankovic*? He had
no way of knowing. Presumably other one-man pods
were adrift nearby, but he couldn't see them and
could do nothing to reach them if he did.

He'd had only a glimpse of *Milankovic* as he'd been
blasted clear of the wreck. The light cruiser had
rammed the *Amazonis*, plowing deep into her frame.
Vince had just reached the pod bay when a rumbling
explosion threatened to tear both vessels apart.

Now, from outside, he could see that both ships
were breaking up, surrounded by an expanding halo
of glittering debris. Patches of *Amazonis*'s hull
glowed orange-red, and vapor—fuel or freezing

atmosphere—was escaping from a dozen rents and gashes. The larger ship embraced the smaller in a death grip.

His pod lurched suddenly, as though it had been struck, and Vince grabbed a handhold to steady himself, then turned to stare out the window. A face, bug-eyed and silvery, stared back.

A Spacer. He could see several of the strange gennies moving purposefully in the void outside with rocket belts on their backs. Two held his life pod between them and were guiding it through space. Shadows brushed across the circular window. They were moving through the cradle of roots encasing the city's Core Sphere.

Moments later there was a shock, and then the surge of deceleration. Shadows fell around the pod's window as the pod was maneuvered into a small room. An indicator on one wall showed rising pressure outside. He was in one of the city's air locks.

Pressures equalized, the pod's hatch *shushed* open and he emerged, shaken but unhurt. The Spacers were gone, searching for other survivors, no doubt. For the second time, Vince owed his life to these enigmatic gennies.

He still wore his holstered laser, a heavy M-50. Drawing it, he checked the capacitor magazine, then cycled the air lock's inner hatch.

He was in a passage burrowing into the Tree. Following it through several twists and turns, Vince emerged in a wood-walled tunnel. When he removed his helmet and gloves, the air tasted thin and was unpleasantly cold, the result, he guessed, of a sharp drop in atmospheric pressure. He had to find someone who knew what was going on. He pressed ahead.

Vince soon recognized where he was. The passageway opened into a major corridor running along the trunk of the Tree; a turn to the left brought him to the Grand Audience Hall. The city councillors would either be there or at Heavydown.

He found them. The former Efay Waldez had taken several laser bolts through his chest and stomach and was floating within an obscene wreath of blood. The Conseos were just as dead, along with several dozen civilians and *ohalans*-armed city guards, cut down by a laser volley that must have been more of an execution than a battle. The room stank of charred flesh and the coppery tang of blood.

Damn!

Vince felt responsible. It had been his idea to have Ciudestreya fight RAM. If he hadn't insisted on saving the Artifact . . .

Memory of the Artifact stirred him to action. He had to get to the chamber where it was kept, to make sure that RAM didn't find it.

Laser pistol in hand, Vince hurried through passageways empty of life. Bodies floated everywhere, and the smooth-cut wooden walls were splashed with crimson. A horrible sacrifice had fed the Tree this day, the blood of hundreds of its inhabitants.

But there were plenty of RAM bodies, too. Vince counted two dozen RAM troopers, most of them with charred holes through their armor. Obviously the battle within Arbel wasn't going all RAM's way.

"Vince!"

He'd nearly blundered headlong into a band of Ciudestreyan women, eight barefooted amazons armed with captured lasers. Katarine led the pack, the bulky power unit of a PAC-4000 strapped to her back, the powerful laser rifle clutched in both hands.

"Katarine! I was on my way to the Artifact—"

"Gone," she said grimly. "RAM got it after all. They tortured poor Damata, then shot him. . . ."

"Oh, God . . ."

"Vince, they're taking the Artifact toward the

Core Sphere. We might catch them there."

He gestured with his pistol. "Let's go."

Through passageways clogged with death, they raced toward the core.

○ ○ ○ ○ ○

Commodore Zotov struggled along with the press of guards—six humans, six Terrines—who had accompanied him from his shuttle. He was as unused to battle armor as he was to this firsthand exposure to the battlefield.

He'd left the *Amazonis* in Obinin's charge as soon as word had come through that the defenders of the Nomad city were putting up only a light resistance. The shuttle, a smaller version of the ADVs, had smashed through the transplex globe at the heart of the city and docked alongside the giant Tree. A captured civilian had told them where to find the city's leaders after a few moments of gentle persuasion, and it hadn't taken much longer to learn that one of the Conseos spoke Anglic and to convince him to show the RAM squad where the Device was kept.

On the way back to the shuttle, word had come through that *Amazonis* had been rammed. There was no word yet on damage, but from the sound of things, it was pretty bad.

That hardly mattered now. He had the Device, sealed in an aluminum carrying case. Already he was phrasing his defense to Holzerhein: He'd left the *Amazonis* to recover the alien Device personally. He doubted that RAM's supreme chairman would care as much about the loss of one heavy cruiser as he did for the prize Zotov had won. Promotion, honor, advancement within the RAM hierarchy, all still lay within Zotov's grasp.

If only he could get the Device back to one of the

surviving RAM ships. He'd ordered *Cydonia* to break
off from the NEO pirates and move in as close to the
city's core as possible. In an hour, he would be Mars-
bound again, the Device in his possession.

The attack came without warning, a savage ambush from two side corridors that cut down half of
Zotov's men in seconds. One trooper died as a crossbow bolt smashed through his helmet visor. Others
collapsed as laser light punched through combat armor in sputtering bursts of light, blood, and molten
alloy and plastic.

"Hold them!" Zotov yelled, and then he pushed his
way past his bodyguard and raced through the corridor, silver case in hand.

Seconds later, he and three of his bodyguards
emerged from the Tree trunk beneath the vast arch
of the Core Sphere. The shuttle, he saw, was fifty
yards away, close by the Tree's enormous trunk and
anchored in place by the self-healing transplex of the
core's dome.

Lasers hissed and crackled overhead, forcing Zotov
to duck. One of his men spun off the trunk, smoke
pouring from a gaping hole in his armor. Zotov
looked up, searching for the source of the shot.

O   O   O   O   O

The battle raged through the Core Sphere. The
Lady Luck had arrived, docking with a cargo lock
outside the core and spilling her load of STAR commandos into the Tree. Within that vast and flame-lit
globe embracing the central trunk of the Tree, they
met the RAM assault troopers in a storm of laser and
rocket fire, grappling hand-to-hand in a weightless
battle frenzy.

Flights of commandos in silver battle dress darted
through the air in formations of three or four. Most

had left their rocket packs on Phobos, but enough of
the propulsion units remained to equip a small air
force of troopers who could dominate the three-
dimensional space around the Tree's central hub.

RAM assault troops rose to meet them, and in the
smoke-hazed air of the core, lasers flashed and the
contrails of smart bullets wove slender traceries as
they tracked their prey. Dead and wounded tumbled
on random trajectories, rag dolls spinning in zero-G.

But the STAR Team already clearly had the upper
hand. The RAM troops, most of them, were fleeing
from the trunk, some without weapons, many only
too glad to surrender to NEO. Packs of Nomads, men
and women together, were close on their tails, hunting them down with bloody relentlessness.

Few of the RAM invaders escaped alive.

O   O   O   O   O

Vince emerged from an opening in the Tree as lasers hissed around him. A scant hundred feet away,
three armored men were gliding along the trunk,
making for a small RAM-Mitsubishi shuttle that appeared to be hung up in the Core Sphere's transplex
barrier. One wore ornately gilded battle armor and
carried a large silver case. The other two looked and
acted like bodyguards.

He knew as soon as he saw it that the Artifact was
in that case.

Vince aimed and fired, a rushed shot. A miss!

"Cover me!" he yelled at the women emerging
from the Tree. Tensing his legs, he leaped into space,
aiming for the shuttle's door. Wind snatched at his
face and ruffled his hair as he dove through sky, the
M-50 laser pistol braced between both hands. The
trio of armored figures and the shuttle grew rapidly
larger. He squeezed the trigger, loosing a hissing bolt

of coherent light . . . and another . . . and another. . . .

One of the troopers tumbled to one side, a fist-sized crater blown through the back of his armor. The other two men reached the shuttle, grabbing for handholds on its hull. The hatch slid open between them, and the one with the ornate armor, a high-ranking officer, Vince guessed, turned and pointed at Vince. The other man raised his laser rifle. . . .

○ ○ ○ ○ ○

Zotov was furious. Here it was, the moment of victory, and nothing was going right. His orders to the *Cydonia* had been ignored; *Sabaeus* had been destroyed, and both *Cydonia* and *Hisperia* were in full retreat for Mars. Two pirate ships, one of them probably Black Barney's *Free Enterprise*, had taken up station close to Ciudestreya, accompanied by at least one squadron of fighters, the RAM Kraits captured at Phobos. Pirates were entering the city.

And now one of them was attacking him.

The armored figure collided with his guard before the man could fire his laser, sending the RAM soldier spinning off the shuttle. The small craft yawed with the impact, making Zotov grab for a handhold. Tossing the case with its precious contents into the shuttle, Zotov then reached for his own laser pistol.

The pirate was clinging with one hand to a handhold, only a few feet away. Well, here was one pirate who would be appropriately dealt with. . . .

○ ○ ○ ○ ○

For an instant, Vince clung by one hand as the Core Sphere swept past his feet. Fixing his eyes on the RAM officer, he tried to bring up his other hand, still clutching the M-50.

The officer was leaning out of the shuttle's hatch, aiming his laser at Vince.

Vince knew he would never aim his own pistol in time but he tried, his movements sluggish but his thoughts clear, as though he was suspended in time. There was a flash. Vince thought he'd been hit, though he'd felt no impact, no pain. The officer was turning. . . .

Katarine landed gracefully on the shuttle's hull an instant later, taking the impact with flexed knees and dropping to a sprawl. Vince had his M-50 aimed by that time, and he loosed a bolt into the officer's chest just as Katarine fired a second time from almost point-blank range. Twin flashes of light erupted from his chest, and the RAM officer's hands spread wide, as though in surprise at the holes blown in his armor. Then his body slipped from the hatchway and drifted into space.

Vince regained his feet as Katarine snagged the case from the shuttle's air lock. "You followed me!"

"I watched you trying to handle yourself in zero-G yesterday," she reminded him. "I wasn't impressed. I thought you might need some help."

Together they returned up the trunk, Vince carrying the Artifact.

The battle for Ciudestreya was over. The last of the RAM troops were surrendering, especially now that new forces were arriving on the scene, rough men in brightly painted armor, their helmets bearing garish crests, mottoes, or even curling horns . . .

Pirates! Vince wondered why pirates were helping NEO, then decided that Black Barney must be behind it.

Elsewhere, Ciudestreyans were emerging from the Tree. Most carried liberated RAM weapons. Some were covered with blood. Near the main entrance to the Tree, Vince spotted a familiar figure.

"Jo!"

"My God! Vince!" Then they were in each other's arms. Her face was smudged black with smoke. They clung together for a long, long moment, impeded by the space suits they wore, but savoring the embrace, the press of lips on lips.

"Thought he wasn't your boyfriend," Black Barney rumbled as he emerged from the Tree.

"He's not," Jovanna said. "But I *am* glad to see him!"

"Vince?"

He turned. Katarine was there, still clutching her laser pistol. Her eyes, wide and dark, were on Jovanna's face.

"Oh, uh . . . hello, Kat." He felt the flush in his face. "This is Jovanna."

"I—I see why you didn't want to stay with us, Vince." She sounded wistful. "She's beautiful!"

At first Vince thought she was being sarcastic. Jovanna? Beautiful? Even with her face fixed up, most men, Vince included, thought her rather plain.

But it was clear from Kat's expression that her admiration was genuine.

A different culture, he thought. And different standards of beauty. Most of the women he'd seen in Ciudestreya looked much alike—black hair, Hispanic features, darkly pretty. Perhaps Jovanna's brown hair and pale skin made her distinctive, even beautiful, to eyes that saw things differently than his.

"Vince? Who's this?" Jovanna asked, the slightest edge to her words.

"My . . . uh . . . bonded companion."

"*What?*"

"It's a long story."

"You can tell me all about it. On the trip back to Trinity."

"Uh . . . Kat . . ." How to say the words? He'd told

her all along that he would leave when he could. Still, it felt like a betrayal. She was special, not a bonded companion, but a companion . . . and a comrade, certainly.

Katarine drifted closer and placed a hand on Vince's shoulder. She seemed to read the pain in his expression. "It's okay, Vince. I knew I never . . . never really had you." Her own face fell. "And we'll have to leave soon anyway. The two RAM ships that fled will be back."

He nodded gravely. The Ciudestreyans might have been isolated but they weren't fools. RAM had been soundly defeated this day, but they'd be back. When they returned, it would be as the bearers of nuclear fire. The people of Arbel faced the ultimate choice. They could surrender to RAM, losing the freedom they prized so highly. They could die.

Or they could flee and endure another kind of death.

Their death as a people.

"Kat . . . I'm sorry." He looked around at the smoldering devastation. "I did this to you."

"No! It wasn't you. We wouldn't have had much longer anyway, not with RAM so vicious, so powerful. And things are . . . changing."

"I hope for the best. *Your* best."

Almost shyly, she held up her hand and touched his cheek. "Good-bye, Vince. Thank you for everything. I hope we meet again . . . sometime." She leaned forward and kissed him.

Then she was gone.

"A lovely girl," Jovanna said. "What was that about her being your . . . bonded companion, you said?"

"She's not bonded to anyone, Jo," he said. "She's free. And I think she's going to do all right. *All* of them are going to do all right."

EPILOGUE

Vince met Katarine Varga a final time before leaving Ciudestreya. The NEO transport *Liberty*, escorted by a small fleet of NEO warships and fighters, had just docked with the city, and he and Jovanna were going over their final preparations before the return flight to Trinity. Two days had passed since he'd seen her last, time in which the citizens of Ciudestreya had been packing, preparing to give up their home for a strange and alien new world.

He floated in zero-G with Jovanna in the spartan area designated as *Liberty*'s main lounge and briefing room. "The *Jefferson*, *Armstrong*, and *Washington* will be here within three hours," Jovanna was telling him. "Looks like we'll have the whole city evacuated within twenty-four." She cocked her head to one side. "Vince? What's the matter?"

He smiled sadly. "Sorry. Just realizing that it's my fault this . . . culture was destroyed."

"From what you've told me, it deserved destruction," Jovanna replied. "Slavery, kidnapping people, trial by combat—"

"Oh, I agree. All that had to be changed. But it's going to be hard on them adjusting to a whole new life."

"Better than staying and getting fried by RAM."

"There is that."

"And as for the *women* here, you seem to be their hero."

"Well, I wouldn't go that far."

Attitudes were changing in the Nomad city with blinding speed. He remembered Katarine's face after the battle, flushed with victory and excitement. The Nomad women had fought the RAM invaders as courageously as had any of the men. Even if Ciudestreya hadn't been doomed, there'd be no return to the semi-slavery that had twisted this culture . . . not now. The change, once begun, was inevitable.

But would the people survive it? Culture shock had destroyed countless hundreds of once-isolated peoples before this.

A gentle knock sounded at the door. "Yes?"

Katarine floated into the room. "Excuse me, Ms. Trask. Hi, Vince! They told me you were up here."

"Hello, Kat! Good to see you."

"I thought you'd like to know," she said brightly. "I've been elected to the new council."

Vince's jaw dropped. "My God! Things *are* changing fast!"

"That they are. There was a riot in the city when one of the men suggested that things return to the way they were, with bonded companions and everything. The new council is composed of six men, six women, and *no* Efay." She paused. "I also wanted to tell you that some of our men are loading the Artifact aboard this ship right now."

"We still want to pay you for it," Jovanna said.

She shook her head. "No. You've given us a whole new world. It is we who are in *your* debt. The Artifact is . . . well, not payment. Think of it as our way of saying 'thank you.' "

The Artifact.

Vince wasn't sure what NEO's scientists would be able to learn from that enigmatic relic of some alien science. Its purpose, its design, the very way it worked might be forever beyond human understanding. But it had already yielded one small piece of information. NEO scientists had already begun studying the Artifact, and they'd gotten it to play again the image of a blue-lit city on an icy plain.

The cold companion world low in the sky had been identified: Pluto.

Which meant that the city had been built on Charon.

Vince knew the name. That small, cold moon of Pluto had been discovered back in 1977, but so far as he knew, no human had ever set foot upon its icy surface.

Looming above the horizon was another world, crescent-lit, the black void of its night side blotting out a circular swatch against the star-dusting of the Milky Way. The crescent bowed away from a particularly brilliant star that gleamed with a light as wan and as cold and as frost-silver as moonlight.

That memory, burned into his consciousness during his contact with the Artifact, had returned to him with the force of a blow. A true double world, Pluto and Charon circled one another at the cold, dim edge of the solar system. That gleaming star he'd seen was the sun, *Earth's* sun, viewed from a distance of some forty astronomical units—over 3,700,000,000 miles away.

How had he glimpsed Charon and Pluto through the Artifact? Was there in fact an alien civilization with a foothold on this remote outpost of the solar system? A cold wind, the breath of the unknown, stirred his soul.

"Vince?" Katarine was staring into his face with concern. "Vince? It's okay, isn't it? The Artifact, I mean."

"Hmm? Oh, sure. Thank you. Believe me, you may have helped us, helped all of us, more than you know."

Times, he reflected, might well soon change for all of them, for all mankind.

He hoped mankind would be ready.

His eyes strayed to her hair. She wore a headband. A twig was secured there, a pair of long, black leaves floating from its end. "What's that?"

"Everybody's doing it. It's . . . a piece of Arbel."

"Your tree?" Jovanna asked.

Katarine nodded. "Each of us will keep a sprig. Perhaps someday Arbel can live again, when RAM is no more. When we can live in peace again."

She held out her hand, extending a second twig with two small black leaves to Vince. "For you. You're one of us, too, Vince. You always will be."

"Thank you." He fastened it thoughtfully to his tunic.

When he looked up, she was going out the door.

"Vince?" Jovanna followed her with her eyes. "Do you think they'll be able to adapt? Life in the Belt, after so long an isolation . . . It's going to be a real challenge for them."

He smiled. Against the cold darkness of his memory of Charon, he smiled.

"That's what being human is all about, Jo. Adapting . . . and facing challenges. They'll survive."

As, he thought, will we.

THE 25TH CENTURY

Invaders of Charon Series

A New Dimension in Outer Space Adventure!

The Genesis Web:

Book One

C. M. Brennan

Follow the adventures of Black Barney, from his birth in a RAM laboratory to his daring escape from his evil creators and beyond, into a world of danger and intrigue.

On Sale Now

Warlords of Jupiter: Book Three

William H. Keith, Jr.

High in the stratosphere above Jupiter, a deadly battle is waged against strange, seemingly unstoppable invaders, who seem to multiply at will. Can Vince Pirelli and the hastily formed alliance of RAM, NEO, and the Rogues' Guild stop the invaders before all humanity is annihilated?

On Sale March 1993.

SCI-FI ROLE-PLAYING ADVENTURE HAS *NEVER* BEEN THIS GOOD*!*

MATRIX CUBED picks up where SSI's popular COUNTDOWN TO DOOMSDAY leaves off – and keeps on going! A much bigger universe means much more to explore – including Jupiter! And, with nearly twice as many new and different monsters, combat is fast, furious, and futuristic!

MATRIX CUBED uses an enhanced version of SSI's award-winning *AD&D®* computer fantasy role-playing game system. That means serious role-playing – your characters gain levels *and*

skills as they explore the vast, complex and dangerous universe of the 25TH century.

Available for: IBM and AMIGA.

Visit your retailer or call 1-800-245-4525, in USA and Canada, for VISA /MC orders. To receive SSI's complete catalog, send $1.00 to:

STRATEGIC SIMULATIONS, INC.®
675 Almanor Avenue, Suite 201
Sunnyvale, CA 94086